A special thank you to There For You Editing (https://www.thereforyouediting.com) for editing and Ideality Consulting LLC (latrisa@idea-lity.com) for proofreading.

D1565026

Eric's Inferno

Prologue

Eric

You fucking dumbass! I berated myself while lying under the pile of rubble that had once been the second-floor roof of the factory building we'd entered.

"Harvard! Can you hear us?"

"Harvard, call out!"

I heard the anxious voices of the guys of my squad but couldn't respond. They sounded so far away, and I was struggling to breathe. I attempted to push what I believed to be slabs of concrete off of me, but they barely budged and it made the pain in my abdomen so much worse.

Fuck! I yelled out in my head when another wave of white-hot pain radiated through my stomach, up my chest, and down my legs. I did my best not to tense up, knowing that'd only make the pain worse. Instead, I did the dumbest thing I could do—I reached up with my one free arm and removed my helmet and facemask. Tossing the cracked facemask down, I flipped my dented helmet upside down to see the picture I taped inside it months ago. In spite of the waves of agony emanating through my body, my lips spread into a smile causing even more pain. But I didn't care. I needed to rest my eyes on her.

Angela.

My Angel.

The woman I kissed just a few hours ago, before rushing out the door to make it to the firehouse on time for my shift. I reached up to my mouth and bit down on my glove, pulling my hand free from it, so that I could better grab the picture. Plucking it from my helmet, I held the image closer to my face, only able to see clearly out of one eye. But I didn't need to see to remember her beautiful face. Pecan brown skin, and shortly cropped dark brown curly hair with streaks of purple throughout. Big, doe-like tawny eyes that sparkled when she smiled, just as she was in this picture. A smile that spread across her face when she noticed me holding up my phone as she danced behind the bar serving drinks. That smile was just for me, and I captured it to carry with me always.

This was the woman who held my heart.

The woman I was supposed to marry in a few short months.

The woman I had lied to.

On our fourth date, I told her I would always be safe working at Rescue Four. Told her we were the best of the best, and if anything were to happen to me, those guys were coming in after me. I meant it when I said it. What I hadn't told her was that there were no guarantees. Even the best of the best couldn't prevent roofs from collapsing, or fires from surging. We tried. God knows we did everything in our power to try. But in the end, we weren't the ones running the show.

I pulled the image to my chest as the sounds of the guys seemed to be drifting away. Either they were moving farther away, or I was falling into unconsciousness. Likely, it was the latter. My head felt woozy, but I kept the image of my smiling Angel close to my heart. I let out a moan when I thought about the Fire Department Chief showing up on Angela's doorstep telling her that I died. No, they wouldn't go to her doorstep. It was Tuesday, and at this time of day, she'd be at the bar, prepping to open.

Maybe they'd send the captain or Sean. I knew Sean would want to be the one to tell his sister the news.

And my parents. I wondered who would tell them. After seven years, they were just starting to come around to accepting my career, and here I was dying because of it. I hurt for them, too. But I didn't have any regrets...no, that was a lie. I had one regret: I told Angela I wouldn't get her pregnant until we were officially married. That was the dumbest shit I ever did. Now, she wouldn't even have a child to remember me by. Just an engagement ring and six months of memories.

"I'm sorry, Angel," I barely whispered right before my eyes closed one last time.

Chapter One

Eric

Stepping out of my red Ford Escape into the parking lot of my firehouse, I looked up and did the same thing I did every time I parked in the lot for my shift. My eyes scanned over the brick fire station and I read the lettering that spelled out "Rescue Four" on top of the building in big, gold letters. A usual warm, tingling feeling expanded in my chest. The sense of achievement I've felt for the last seven years flooded my body. More than half a decade on the job and this feeling never went away.

Instead of moving toward the door, I turned and went in the opposite direction, to the *Starbucks* across the street. My second ritual of my morning shifts was heading to get coffee. I made my way to the street, checking for cars, and thanks to my long legs, within a few steps I was completely across. I held the door open for a female patron who was just coming out. Even with the two full cup holders in her hands, she eyed me up and down. Her pink-tinted lips spread into a seductive smile. I returned her stare with a smile of my own. After seven years, it still amused me how women responded to a man in uniform. Plus, I'm not too bad on the eyes, if I do say so myself.

"Thank you," she stated airily.

"No thanks needed." I winked and entered the door after she passed, pausing to get a view of her backside. When I finally stepped across the threshold, I could see her continue to eye me through the window. I took one last glance before heading to the counter to give my order.

"Oh, thank you, Mr. Fireman, sir," I heard a mock girly voice in my right ear behind me.

My lips turned downward. "Fuck off, Don."

"Ladies do love a man in uniform," he laughed.

I turned to face him to do our usual handshake. Don stood just a hair short of my six-foot-two height. He, like me, was coming in to start a twelve-hour shift. We were on the schedule from nine a.m. to nine p.m. that day.

"You would know," I responded to his earlier comment. "You're the consummate playboy."

"Consummate? Here you go using all those fancy words, Harvard."

Harvard. That was my nickname around the fire station. In the beginning, it irritated the hell out of me. But the more I let the guys know it bothered me, the more they used it. Finally, I let it drop, and now, seven years in, I accepted it.

"If you say so. What're you drinking? Coffee's on me this morning."

"Just a regular brew. You know I don't like all that fancy shit. The only reason I'm here is 'cause Rookie Two's making the coffee this morning, and I swear if I have to drink his slop again, I might light him on fire myself," Don grunted.

"Easy, Don. It's your job to investigate fires, not set 'em." I ordered our Venti-sized cups of regular coffee.

"Would you like those iced?" the barista asked.

"No thanks." I could just imagine the type of ragging Don and I would get walking into the firehouse with iced coffee. No thank you.

After a few minutes of Don and I talking about sports, our drinks were ready. We each grabbed them and headed out the door to start our day. Once we got to the parking lot, we stopped.

He clapped me on the back. "It never gets old, does it?"

"Not for a second."

We stood for another heartbeat, and then Don followed me to the door into our fire station, more like our second home.

"Harvard!" one of the younger guys called. "We thought you forgot about us," he teased.

Looking up at the clock on the wall, I noted it was five after nine. Even if is was five minutes early, I was considered late. I overslept this morning thanks to a late night with a female companion, causing me to run behind my usual eight forty-five arrival.

"Harvard here was making googly eyes at a pretty little thing in *Starbucks*," Don interjected, tousling my hair.

"Fuck you, Don." I smacked his hand away. "If it weren't for your iced coffee, I would've been on time," I teased right back.

That started a round of laughter from the four or five guys who stood around.

"Donnie drinks iced coffee now? Do you need us to put the toilet seat down so you can sit while you piss, too?" Corey yelled out, setting off another round of belly laughs.

"Corey, the next time you call me Donnie, you're gonna be walking away with a black eye," Don threatened. He hated the name Donnie, and everyone knew it. Unlike me, though, he never got used to it and threatened anyone who dared call him that. The younger guys wouldn't dare, but Corey, Don, and I came up together. All three of us went through training at the fire academy together. I joined Rescue Four right out of the academy. Don was assigned to another firehouse and joined Rescue Four five years ago, while Corey came a year after that.

"Pssh, imagine that!" Corey returned, sounding unfazed.

"All right, let's get this over with," I began, grabbing the clipboard to make sure everyone who was leaving was signed out, while Don, Corey, and I signed in for our shifts. Ordinarily, this was supposed to be the job of the lieutenant, but Rescue Four had only one lieutenant for close to two years now, and he wasn't on this shift. We didn't even have a captain. That left me the unofficial lieutenant due to my seniority.

Once the overnight shift left, Don, Corey, myself, and a few other men filed into the kitchen.

"Ack! This taste like something my dog threw up!" Tommie's face was twisted up in disgust as he poured the contents of the coffee pot down the sink drain.

Don looked at me. "Thanks for the coffee," he said, holding up the Starbucks cup.

"Somebody needs to teach that fucking rookie how to make a damn pot of coffee."

"Who wants grub?" Corey called out.

An array of "me's" and "fuck yes's" echoed around the room. Corey began pulling out packages of eggs, bacon, and bread out of the fridge. For the morning shift, we kept a well-stocked fridge. One of our traditions was cooking breakfast at the station, if time permitted, of course.

Within thirty minutes, we were all sitting around the table, full plates in front of us. One of the rookies talked about hearing about a firefighter being injured the other night in a fire. Don looked at me. I gave him a nod and he slapped the rookie upside the back of his head.

"What the fuck?" the rookie yelled.

"We *never* talk about an injured firefighter around the table," Corey commented, not even lifting his gaze from his plate.

"It's bad luck," I finished, shoveling another forkful of food into my mouth. Firefighters, much like baseball players, were a superstitious lot. You can talk about a lot of shit at this kitchen table—such as rescues and sexual exploits, or some of the guys talked about their kids and wives—but there were two things we never discussed: the death of a fellow firefighter and the injury of one. Not at the table.

I glanced up from the table at the rookie who was now rubbing the back of his head, miffed. *He'll learn.* We all did.

"You know Carter's supposed to come back soon?" I paused, peering at Don, whose voice had taken on a serious tone. He was staring directly at me.

"You spoke with him?"

"No, heard it through the grapevine. Corey, you?"

Corey looked between Don and I, and shrugged. "Nah."

I remained silent, opting to place my breakfast dishes in the sink.

"Hey, Rookie," I called. "For that fuck up at the table, you're on dish duty this shift. Pete, Jacob, and Vince, you three are scrubbing down the truck today. The rest of us are cleaning the equipment. Capisce?"

"Last time I checked you were Korean, not Italian," Don's smart ass remarked.

"My mother's a professor of linguistics. I learned a word or two in other languages."

"No wonder they call you Harvard," I heard the rookie at the sink mumble.

"*You* can call me sir. Capisce?" I said to him, crowding his space.

"Capisce."

Only then did I back off.

"Don't worry, Rookie. One day it'll be your turn to pay it forward," Don reassured the rookie, smacking him with the dish towel.

I chuckled as I left the kitchen and moved to the equipment room where all our gear was stored. Rookies always got the shittiest jobs and the most hazing in the fire station. It was part of their birthing process. We all went through it. If you came out the other side, you could consider yourself a real firefighter, but only if you made it through the fire.

****

"Come on! Fucking move!" Corey yelled out the window as he tugged on the lever that sounded the truck's horn. His dark skin was already glistening with sweat. I felt the sweat running down my back, but I was more focused on maneuvering this truck down a one-way street to make it to our destination. We were on our third call of the day, and the yells through the walkie-talkie were saying a firefighter was trapped on a roof.

"We better get there before Rescue Two!" Corey shouted from the passenger seat.

"Let's go!" I yelled, pressing on the horn at a car moving too slowly in front of us. I rounded the corner onto the street where the burning building stood.

"Fuck!" Corey and I yelled at the same time when we saw the fire truck for Rescue Two already on the scene. Parking a little ways down the road, in front of a fire hydrant, I threw open the door, and the five of us piled out of the truck, grabbing helmets and gear as we went.

"Where do you need us?" I asked the Captain of Rescue Two.

"We need an additional line run into the ground floor. I got a man on the roof."

Peering up at the roof of the four-story building, I saw the red brim of a fireman's helmet.

"Corey, you and the rookie run a line into the ground level. Kill anything that looks hot. You got me?"

"Copy!" Corey returned. "Let's go, Rookie!" I watched Corey run around to the back of the truck to grab the hose.

"Anyone else inside?" I asked the captain.

He shook his head. "We pulled out three before the second floor caved in. Our guy had to go up to the roof."

"Ladder's not high enough," one of the Rescue Two squad called out.

"Shit!" the captain yelled. "He—"

"I'm on it," I returned before he could finish the question. I ran back to the truck, yelling to Don that I needed to move closer to pull up our ladder. Carefully but quickly I inched the truck as close to the building as possible, and then pressed the button to send up the ladder that rested on top of the truck. I heard the tell-tale beeps alerting me that the ladder had released. Exiting the truck, I climbed up on top to hold the ladder still for the man to get down, but within seconds I heard shrieks coming from overhead. Above me were two pairs of skinny limbs waving, and I realized the firefighter had two children with him. One of which was hanging dangerously close to the edge of the roof. I called for Don to watch my back. I didn't turn around to see if he came to assist. I knew he'd be in position just like I knew the back of my hand. I ran up the ladder as fast as my body allowed. Less than a minute later, the only thing that kept me suspended in the air against the brick building was the ladder.

"Help me!" a young girl, probably about ten years old, shrieked as I reached her.

"I got you," I soothed, using one of my arms to grab her from the edge of the roof and the grip of the other firefighter. "I need you to hold onto my ladder. We're going to go down as quickly as possible, okay?"

"My brother!" she yelled.

Glancing over, I saw the little boy was cradled in the other firefighter's arms.

"Your brother's coming down right behind us. We're all getting out of here." I held onto her with one hand. "Keep your eyes up for me, okay?"

She was trembling with fear, and my biggest concern was that she'd see how far off the ground we were and would slip or lose her balance.

"That's it, nice and easy. You're doing great," I consoled as we made our way down the ladder. I glanced up to make sure the firefighter and the little boy were following. When I saw they were, I returned my attention to the girl.

"We're almost there," I stated until I felt my foot hit the top of the truck. When I stood on the truck, I picked the girl up and handed her off to Don, who then passed her over to the paramedic. Seconds later, I was passed her younger brother, who although frightened and crying, didn't appear harmed.

"'Medic says they're going to be okay," Don came over a while later to tell me.

The three story home held three apartments. We were able to enter the building once the flames were out and it had been cleared. From the looks of it, faulty wiring caused the fire. The two kids were home alone because their mother ran to the grocery store.

"Good job." Don patted me on the back.

"Right back at you." We bumped fists.

After speaking with the captain for a few minutes, I returned to my truck to find my guys in a heated debate with the men of Rescue Two.

"Nah, fuck that! A bet is a bet!" Steve, one of the guys from Rescue Two, yelled.

Fuck. Steve had a point.

"Harvard, you believe this shit? We saved their asses, and they're still trying to hold a bet over us," Corey said.

"First of fucking all, you didn't save shit!" Steve spat. "Second, we always knew the supposed tough guys of Rescue Four were a bunch of pansies."

"Watch your goddamn mouth, Steven. We'll make good on the bet," I interjected. They may have won the bet, but there was no way I was about to let them talk shit about Rescue Four.

"Yeah, what he said," Don added. "We can handle anything you throw at us."

"All right." Sean, another Rescue Two man, stepped forward. "We'll let you know what you have to do."

"When?" I asked, folding my arms across my chest.

"Oh, we'll find you. We know where you reside."

I gave Sean a look but didn't say anything. I shrugged as if it were no big deal, before telling the rookie with us to pack up the hose so we could leave. This scene wasn't our fire to handle all the paperwork on, so we didn't need to hang around any longer.

"I can't believe they beat us here!" Corey said, slamming the passenger door.

That had been the bet. Weeks ago, guys from Rescue Four bet Rescue Two that we could beat them to any fire, anytime, anywhere. And while I wasn't on shift at the time of the bet, it stood for all shifts. We lost this round, and now it was time for us to pay up. I knew the guys of Rescue Two wouldn't let us live this down.

"I'm gonna need a beer after this shift," Corey commented.

"Copy that," I agreed.

Chapter Two

Angela

"Heads up. Rescue Four just walked in."

I looked up from behind the bar just as they entered. Individually, these guys could stop traffic, but together they were enough to give a normally healthy woman a heart attack. The first to enter was Corey with warm brown skin that held gold undertones. He stood at about six-feet, and by the way the black T-shirt he wore clung to his body, you knew he was in the gym at least five days a week. Next to enter was Don, who was about an inch taller, and just as muscular with olive skin and dark hair with a scruffy beard. The first two were enough to make any girl swoon, but I felt the blood rush to my ears when the third and final Rescue Four man came into my line of sight. The one they called Harvard, although his real name was Eric. He stood the tallest of the three with creamy tan skin and dark hair that looked smooth as silk thanks to his Asian heritage. I once overheard one of the guys say that he was Korean. With his chiseled jaw, full lips that were almost pouty, and dark hooded eyes, he screamed sex appeal. He looked like he held the secrets of the world behind those eyes. His mysteriousness was coupled with the fact that out of all the firemen who frequented the bar, he spoke the least. Firefighters were a loud, proud lot. I knew them well. My father had been one for more than thirty years, and my older brother was one of them. I grew up around them.

But Eric had a steely calm to him, like he didn't have to announce who or what he was to the world. He knew who he was.

A trail of goosebumps rose along my arms when those dark eyes circled the room, finally landing on me. I was behind the bar, far from the door, but it almost appeared as if his eyes darkened when they slowly scanned down my body. His facial expression remained neutral and I forced myself to turn away, moving to help another customer.

"What's up, sugar?" Corey greeted a few minutes later.

I smiled. "How're you doing tonight, Corey?"

"Much better now that I've seen your beautiful face," he replied smoothly, perfect teeth appearing when he grinned.

Did I mention how much these men flirted? All except one, at least.

"Talking like that is going to get you in trouble."

"Trouble's my middle name."

"The usual?" Laughing, I pulled the rag out of the back pocket of my jeans to clean up a spill on the bar.

"Yup, make it five. We're meeting two more from Rescue Four."

"I thought you guys were traveling a little light tonight."

"Us three just got off. Thanks, sugar." Corey winked once I handed him the first of the three Coronas with lime he requested. He sauntered over to pass off the beers, and again my eyes collided with Eric's, almost as if he'd been staring at me.

A shiver ran through me when he took the proferred beer from Corey, his gaze still planted on me. His eyes narrowed and I felt as if I were in the crosshairs of a predator. Instead of fear, I felt my lower belly quiver as thoughts of the intentions behind those dark eyes ran through my mind. I finally managed to blink, and when I glanced back, he'd turned, facing the rest of the men at his table. I sighed. Even his profile was beautiful. I licked my lips as I watched Eric's Adam's apple bob up and down after he took a swig of his beer.

"You might want to clean up that drool you left on the bar," Stephanie whispered in my ear.

I snapped her hip with the towel in my hand. "I'm not above replacing you."

"You wouldn't fire me. Who else do you have to run this place while you're fantasizing about the hot firefighter?" She wiggled her eyebrows, and I tossed my head back, laughing.

"Get back to work," I ordered.

It was a Friday night, and *Charlie's* was hopping as usual. Being conveniently located between two fire stations meant that during evening shift changes, we were inundated with burly firefighters and the many female patrons who swooned after them. Coupled with the regular foot traffic we received at times, having two bartenders behind the bar wasn't always enough. I was grateful for it all. It's been eighteen months since I bought *Charlie's* from its previous owner. I did some construction work on the place to give patrons more room, added a Bluetooth jukebox, offered a few craft beers that were so loved by us millennials, and business was booming.

"What can I do for you, sir?" I asked the man who walked up to the bar. He ordered a rum and Coke. Once that order was done, I moved on to the next customer. It went on like this probably for close to an hour with Stephanie and I so busy we barely got a good look at who we were serving before we were pouring another drink.

"What can I get for ya?" I asked the patron, barely making eye contact.

"The usual."

A warm sensation moved through my belly at the sound of that voice. I locked eyes with Eric.

"F-five coronas with lime?" I stumbled over my words, internally kicking myself for sounding so lame.

A half-smile formed on those lips and he nodded, leaning down on the bar. I had to keep myself from watching his biceps bulge and strain again the T-shirt he wore.

"Coming up!" I infused my voice with the cheerfulness I gave all my customers. I felt his gaze on me as if he were touching me, while I uncapped the bottles and inserted the sliced limes.

"Thanks, sugar," I heard Corey's voice sound off from behind Eric. I lifted my eyes just as he put an arm around a now frowning Eric. "You know, this guy should drink free tonight."

Raising my eyebrows, I uncapped the final bottle. "Oh yeah, and why is that?"

"Harvard, you didn't tell Angela you're a hero?" Corey teased.

Eric just gave him a *shut the hell up* glare.

But Corey kept on going. "Harvard here saved a little girl today. Climbed a four-story building and brought her down."

My eyes ballooned. "Seriously?"

"Ye—"

"No, he's messing around." Eric tossed a deadly look in Corey's direction.

"Fuck no he ain't," I heard Don's booming voice come up behind both men and insert himself at Eric's left side.

"Corey's telling the truth. Rescue Four had to save Rescue Two's asses again today." Don and Corey both guffawed at that. Eric gave a light chuckle, and I had to avert my gaze. Something like not looking directly into the sun, unless you want your retinas to burn up. That's what it was like staring at this man for too long, especially when he laughed.

"Well, in that case, this round's on the house. Just don't tell Rescue Two about it."

Don and Corey grabbed all but one of the beers and headed back to their table.

"I'm good at keeping secrets." Eric's gaze lingered on me for a heartbeat, then he grabbed the beer I still held in my hand, his fingers grazing mine. My eyelids fluttered at the pulse of energy that ran through me at his touch. I looked up into Eric's handsome face to see his eyes widen ever so slightly. He felt it, too. He inclined his head toward me before turning to head back to the rest of his squad.

Picking up a stack of napkins, I began fanning myself with them. "Geesh."

I grabbed a bottle of water from under the bar, hoping to douse my internal flames before I returned to serving my customers.

"Talk about hot!" Stephanie said behind me. I turned to see her biting her finger as she longingly gazed over at the men who just departed from the bar.

"If you like that sort of thing." I shrugged.

"Oh please. Don't tell me you wouldn't leave this bar right now to go home with one of them. Especially Harvard. I've seen the way you look at him. And how he looks at *you.*" She wagged her finger at me, shaking her shoulders seductively, her blonde locks flowing around her shoulders.

"Oh please. The man barely talks."

"Even better! The strong, silent type."

"Get outta here. There's nothing there. Plus, I'm trying to see where things go with Marshall."

"Boring." Stephanie rolled her eyes. "You've been on what three dates with Marshall? That's not enough time to see where things are going?"

"Some of us like the slow build. You know, creating a solid foundation. Not everything's passion and hot sex."

"If you say so."

"There's a customer waiting on you." I pointed in the direction of a waving patron. Stephanie giggled before heading to the opposite end of the bar to serve customers.

Again, I was lost in the rush of the crowd until I heard a warm, familiar voice.

"Working hard, sis?"

My smile grew tenfold. "Sean! I thought you had a date tonight?" I leaned across the bar to hug my brother.

"I did, but we ended early. She had to work a late shift at the hospital."

"And you came to say hi to your little sis?"

"That and I needed to speak with the chumps from Rescue Four. I knew they'd be here tonight."

"Hmph!" I folded my arms over my chest, pouting. "You didn't think to come see me at all."

He chuckled. "Take it easy, Angela. Those chumps lost a bet, and I'm going to make them pay up."

I leaned over to look at the table where the guys from Rescue Four were laughing and talking. "Oh yeah? Well, they were bragging about how they saved your guys' asses today."

My brother's grin immediately dropped to a frown. "The day those cocky assholes have to save us is the day hell freezes over." My brother was pissed if the vein bulging out of the side of his neck was any indication. I couldn't help it; I burst out laughing. The rivalries between fire stations were something that mystified me, but I took pleasure in seeing my brother having his chain yanked.

"You want a beer?" I said between laughs.

"Nah, not yet. I need to handle something." And with that, he turned in the direction of the men of Rescue Four.

****

Eric

My head tilted backward as I took the last pull of my beer. My eyes surveyed the room, watching the women and men mingling around, likely scoping who they'd take home that night. That thought had my eyes floating back to the bar at the woman tending to customers. Angela. I drank her in without making it obvious. I felt a tightening in my groin when her succulent lips parted on a full-on laugh. Her head fell back, showing off her asymmetrical cut. Short dark brown with a few purple highlights was pushed from her forehead. Her skin the color of pecans glowed under the lights of the bar. She stood about five-five, but her presence was so much larger, with her bubbly and demonstrative personality. As the owner of the bar, everyone knew Angela, and it was her outgoing spirit that made this place what it was and kept people coming back.

Making a decision, I rose from my chair to head straight to the bar. Unfortunately, I was cut off when a large figure came between me and the bar.

"Going somewhere?"

I closed my eyes briefly and sighed before placing my empty bottle on the table

"What can we do for you, Sean?" I asked, as the rest of the guys stood.

Sean surveyed the five of us at the table and a smirk I didn't like appeared.

"It's not what you can do for me. It's what I'm going to do for you."

"Ah hell. Cut the shit and tell us what we owe you," Don interjected. He wasn't a guy who liked beating around the bush, especially when it came to losing.

Sean chuckled. "All right, gentlemen. Since you lost our little wager, we of Rescue Two propose that you attend a spinning class at the gym on Oakland this Tuesday morning."

My eyebrow spiked up. "Spinning?" I turned to look at Corey, Don, and the two other guys with us. They all wore the same skeptical expression I was.

"I'm not attending any goddamn spinning class," one guy muttered under his breath.

"Right? Not having my ass in the air like some pansy," Don added.

"Aww, the poor boys from Rescue Four afraid of a little spin class?" Sean taunted.

"We're not afraid of a damn thing. We also know you've got more up your sleeve." That was Corey.

Sean chuckled, indicating he indeed had more in store for us. "Now that you mention it..."

"Here we fucking go," Don mumbled.

"You will attend the ten o'clock class... in tutus."

"Get the fuck outta here!"

"Fuck off!"

"Are you shitting me?"

The chorus of curse words sounded off around the table. I shook my head. I knew it would be some dramatic bullshit. I was just as pissed as the rest of the fellas. Part of me was angry at myself since I was driving the rig this morning. The rig that got us to the scene just a couple seconds behind Rescue Two.

"A deal is a deal. Time to pay the piper."

"I got your piper right here!" Don grabbed his crotch, thrusting his hips aggressively.

That made Sean nearly double over in laughter. Here's the thing about firefighters—we're two things: assholes and competitive. The combination of which can sometimes be dangerous or get us into fucked up situations such as our current dilemma.

"Tuesday, ten o'clock at Oakland Gym. Wear tutus. And don't be late." He pointed his finger in our direction.

"Where the fuck are we supposed to find tutus?" Corey asked.

"Right? I'm not going to the damn tutu store to buy one," Riley, one of the other Rescue Four guys with us, yelled out.

"Don't worry. We'll drop some off at the station for you," Sean assured, still laughing.

"Yeah, I bet you pussies have spare tutus laying around," Don grumbled.

Sean laughed even harder at the targeted insult. "Tuesday," he added before sauntering off, still laughing.

"This is some bullshit. You know they're going to be in class, snapping pictures and shit. They'll blow those photos up and post 'em up at the Annual Ball or some shit," Corey fussed as we sat down.

I looked between all the men I considered my brothers. I grew up an only child, but these guys had become my family. I trusted them with my life, daily.

"We lost a bet. We pay up," I said. As soon as the words were out, the grumbling ceased. Don and Corey still looked like they were suffering from trapped gas, but they didn't dare refute my statement. We were Rescue Four men, and when we said we were going to do something, we did it, even if it meant we'd look like a bunch of suckers in tutus in a spin class. We'd own up to our loss, and then make sure to pay the favor back on the next bet, because I assure you we would not be losing another bet. Not on my damn watch.

"Who wants another beer?" Don asked.

Three hands went up, one of which was mine. Thankfully, I was off the next day and didn't have to worry about getting up early to fight fires.

"Let me," I told Don. Before he responded, I was halfway to the bar.

"Another round?" Angela smiled up at me and something funny in my chest happened. We've been coming to this bar more and more over the last few months. I've watched her since the first time I entered, telling myself to steer clear of her. I didn't do messy entanglements, and in case things didn't work out, I didn't want to find another bar for Rescue Four to hang out at after-shift. I knew all too well how clingy some women could get. But the more I showed up to *Charlie's*, the more senseless it became to try to deny this woman's appeal.

I leaned on the bar, drawing me closer to Angela. I watched her nostrils flare and her chest rise when she inhaled from my nearness.

"For starters, Angel..." I responded.

She hesitated. "Angela."

"What?"

"My name's Angela. I think you mistook—"

"No mistake. With a face like yours, you should be called Angel."

She dipped her head, but I caught the smile that parted her lips. "Firefighters are such flirts."

"Not all of us," I retorted.

"Yes, *all* of you." Her gaze drifted over my shoulder.

I turned to look back at the table where the rest of my squad was. They were now accompanied by three women, all of them sitting on one of the guy's laps. I grinned before turning back.

"Putting out fires is hard work. We need some type of outlet after hours."

"That's all women are to you? An outlet?" she challenged.

I raised my eyebrows, before letting my eyes scan down her face, the small amount of cleavage offered by her low cut sleeveless top she wore, those hips that flared out a little in the dark skinny jeans. She was about five-five and petite, but I knew we'd match perfectly.

"Not all women," I responded, taking the beers she placed on the bar and going back to the table. I did my best to adjust myself in my jeans without being obvious. It was only a matter of time before Angela and I ignited, and I couldn't wait.

Chapter Three

Angela

I grabbed my car keys from the wall mount and scanned the counters and stove to ensure I turned everything off before heading out the door. Moving through the living room, I picked up the remote and turned off the flat screen television hanging above the white brick fireplace. Grabbing my *Nike* duffle bag next to the door with my cycling shoes, towel, and a bottle of water, I was ready. Stepping onto my porch, I turned to lock the door. When I came down off the porch, I was greeted with a wave from my next door neighbor who was out for her mid-morning walk.

"Hey, Ms. Taylor. How're you this morning?"

Her smile creased her chestnut skin, glistening with sweat. "God woke me up this morning. Gave me the strength to walk on these old tired legs. Can't ask for much else."

I chuckled. "I guess not. You enjoy the rest of your walk."

"Thank you, baby. Oh, and thank you for that chocolate lava cake you brought over last week. It was so good, I had to stop Cheryl from taking the last piece. Was almost better than the cakes your mama used to make. God rest her soul."

A pang of sadness twisted in my stomach at the mention of my mother.

"I'm sorry, baby. I didn't mean to—"

"It's okay, Ms. Taylor. I'm just running late for my spin class," I interrupted.

"Well, then you go on. Guess we both need to work off that chocolate cake, huh?"

I grinned and gave her a wave, heading over to my electric blue Acura. My car was the one personal luxury item I've splurged on in the last three years. I preferred to drive in silence, letting my mind run through all the things I needed to take care of for the day before heading to the bar that night. Thankfully, there was plenty of parking in the gym's lot.

"Hey, Susie," I greeted as I rounded the front desk to sign in for my ten o'clock class.

"Hey, Angela. How's it going?" Susie studied the textbook in front of her. She was a college student at one of the major universities in the city and worked at the gym part-time.

"I can't complain," I answered, before heading off to the locker room to change into my cycling shoes. I was wearing my usual black biker shorts, sports bra, and a pink sleeveless tank top to the gym, figuring I would just change when I got back home. At five of ten, I exited the locker room to head to the class where the spin class was held. The previous class had already piled out and left the doors open to air it out before my class started. Seeing a few of my regulars, I waved and gave a couple of hugs out before moving to where the speakers and small entertainment center was set up. Plugging in my phone, I hit the music app to bring up high-energy playlist.

"Let's get this shit over with," a familiar male voice sounded off as he entered the room.

I turned around, and a laugh burst from my lips.

"You have *got* to be in the wrong place," I said to the group of men in front of me.

"Angela?"

"Ah, shit!"

Don and Corey belted out at the same time.

Without my consent, my eyes began searching the rest of the men with these two until they found him. Eric was amongst the group of firefighters, and right along with them, he was wearing a pink tutu over his workout clothing, but his strong, masculine presence couldn't be overshadowed even by the ridiculous ensemble.

"W-what're you all d-doing here dressed like th-that?" I stumbled out.

"Sean set us up."

"Sean?" I looked to Eric even though he hadn't given me that answer.

He remained silent, but his eyes did his talking for him, eyeing me up and down. I remembered our last encounter at the bar, just a few nights earlier. His eyes now held that same promise in them. He took one last look before climbing onto a bike in the front row, his eyes holding a glimmer of mirth.

"Time for class," was all he said, staring intently at me as if *I* was the one out of place.

The music started, taking me out of my mystified trance.

"All right, everyone on your bikes!" I announced into the microphone that was attached to an earpiece. "Make sure your feet are secured into the latches on the pedals. And ... 3... 2...1. We're starting off slow today," I began, my voice growing louder to be heard over the music. I climbed onto the bike in front of the room, facing the crowd of peddlers and directed the class as usual. We began seated to warm up, but by the time the second round of the hooks came for the first song, we were up off our seats, doing arm push-ups against the handlebars. By the beginning of the next song, we were down for a short rest and then up again, pumping our legs. Even though I was working just as hard in addition to calling out cues, I kept an eye on each one of the twenty-five or so participants. The usuals were used to my high-energy, fast-paced class, and while I suspected none of the firemen had attended spin class before, they all kept up with no complaints. Even while I tried to keep my eyes on everyone in the class, my gaze kept floating back to the man directly in front of me. Every time I looked at Eric, his gaze was squarely on me, pinning me. At one point, the look he gave me was so intense that I faltered and I lost my grip on one side of the handlebars.

Having been an instructor for three years now, I quickly recovered without too many people noticing. Embarrassed, I resolved to keep my gaze off of Eric for the remainder of the class. I failed miserably.

"Thanks, Angela. I needed that workout today," Sharon, one of my regulars, panted as I unplugged my phone.

"It was my pleasure. Why don't you bring Larry in here next time?" I laughed at the face she made. Larry was her husband, who she brought a few months back. She said he complained for days afterward.

"Never again. Larry can stick to his early morning runs now that he's retired."

I was amused at Sharon's exasperation with her husband. We talked for a few more moments until we both stopped upon hearing loud whooping and hollering coming from outside the room. Wondering what was happening, I made my way to the main gym room to see my brother and two other men from his fire station cracking up and taking pictures and filming the men from Rescue Four.

"I knew they'd show up eventually," Don stated loudly.

"Don't worry, someone was taking pictures of you in class, too," Sean laughed.

I continued to watch as Sean and his crew followed the Rescue Four men out the door. I covered my mouth, laughing to myself.

"Something funny?" That deep voice penetrated my senses. Although my temperature had begun to decline from my workout, I felt myself get all hot and bothered again.

I spun around to find Eric staring down at me. That same acute gaze drinking me in. My mouth suddenly felt dry.

"Shouldn't you be with them?" I looked down the length of his body to see he'd removed the tutu, leaving him in a workout T-shirt and a pair of shorts that stopped an inch above his knees.

His eyes flitted up to the entrance where I surmised the men were still being berated, before falling back to me.

"I'm right where I need to be."

My mouth went dry and I cursed myself for leaving my water bottle in my gym locker. A silence fell between us, which was so unlike me. Often, I could keep up an entire conversation on just my end alone, but my words seemed to get all jumbled up in Eric's presence. I felt like a deer in headlights, or like the prey in the crosshairs again, when his eyes lingered on me.

"Did you enjoy class?" I finally managed to get out.

"I did."

"Good. Good." I clapped my hands for some reason. "That's my goal. Make sure everyone has fun and burns lots of calories, of course."

"Goal accomplished. Do you have another class to teach?"

"No."

"I'll walk you out," he offered.

"Uh, I have to go get my bag from the locker room."

"I'll wait."

A giddy feeling filled my stomach, and I nodded, hurrying off to grab my duffle bag. Checking my hair in the mirror, I sighed. After such a sweaty class, my curls were limp, weighed down by sweat. I made do and fluffed the sides of my hair as much as possible, grateful that I just got my cut trimmed and purple streaks refreshed over the weekend. Wiping my face of the sweat with a facial wipe I kept in my bag, I then coated my lips in a clear gloss I had on hand before going back out. A smile touched my lips when I saw Eric still waiting for me.

"Do you teach here every Tuesday?" he asked as we proceeded to the door.

"Every Tuesday and Thursday morning at ten a.m."

His head tilted as if he was storing the information away for the future.

"We also have kickboxing classes, step aerobics, and of course a full weight room and cardio machines like most gyms. But we've got specialized personal trainers who've worked with some of the most famous people in the entertainment industry. That's the spiel they tell us to give everyone," I laughed as if it was an inside joke. "The gym has been open for less than a year, but I like the atmosphere. I've taught spin at other gyms in the city, but this place is by far my favorite." I clamped my lips shut to keep from rambling on anymore. It seemed I found my ability to talk in his presence, and I mentally kicked myself for it.

"I'm over here." I pointed to my car.

"And I'm right there." He nodded to the car next to mine.

"Fire engine red. Fitting color for a firefighter," I joked.

"I guess so." Again the smile that reminded me of the sun came out, and I lowered my gaze, wishing I had my sunglasses with me.

"I like the pool. At the gym," Eric added. "I divide my cardio between swimming and running to give my knees a break."

"Yeah, I've had a few participants in my cycling class say they needed to switch because of knee or hip issues from running. You know, they say running on pavement for long periods of time does it. I read that orthopedic doctors are finding they have to do two hip or knee replacements on older patients because those things only hold up for like ten to fifteen years, maybe twenty. And..." I trailed off when I noticed his amused expression. "Sorry, I tend to ramble. It gets worse when I'm nervous."

His head shot back. "I make you nervous?"

I rolled my eyes. "Oh come on, don't pretend like you don't have the whole sexy, brooding firefighter thing going on."

When he threw his head back and laughed, I had to squeeze my thighs together.

"You've never been told that?"

"No, I don't think I have."

I gave him a sideways look. "I think you're being modest."

He shook his head, grinning. "You work here and then work the bar at night?"

I shrugged. "It's only a fifty-minute class, and I don't go into the bar until around three or four, sometimes later."

"But you're there 'til what? Like two in the morning?"

I shook my head. "Between three and four."

"You don't leave by yourself, do you?" he asked, brows dipping into a V, expressing his concern.

"I usually have at least one other employee close up with me."

His look remained skeptical.

"Some nights Sean waits with me while I close up."

"Sean, from Rescue Two? The one who just clowned all my guys?"

I laughed. "That's him."

"You two..."

"Are related? Yes, he's my brother."

The crease in his forehead released as relief washed over him. "Good to know."

"Why's that?" My voice had dipped a little lower to just being this side short of seductive.

"Because when I take you out, I don't have to worry about him thinking I'm trying to steal his woman. Though, I wouldn't give a damn if that were the case."

My jaw dropped. "Sooo, you're asking me out? On a date?"

"Yes, Angela. I am asking you out on a date."

I think I swayed a little bit when I heard him say my name for the first time.

"When?"

"Tomorrow night."

No hesitation.

No contemplation.

"I have Wednesdays off."

"I know."

"Where?"

"That's for me to know. I'll pick you up at six?"

I nodded. "No, wait."

He frowned.

"You don't know where I live."

"I'll pick you up from *Charlie's*."

"Okay, that works."

"Six o'clock."

"I'll see you then." I gave him what I thought was one last smile, but he had other plans. I pressed the button for my locks, but when I went to open it, his large hand covered mine. I felt his warm breath on the back of my neck and the heat from his body along my backside.

"I got it," he said in my ear, pulling the door open for me to get in. "Wear something comfortable, to walk around in."

Turning, I looked at him, confused.

"For tomorrow night."

I nodded and then shivered when he ran his thumb along the inside of my wrist before releasing my hand just enough to allow me to get in the car. Instead of shutting the door, he leaned down, resting one arm on the roof of my car.

"Drive safe, Angel."

Another shiver. I was liking my new nickname, but only if it came from his lips.

"I will."

He stepped back, watching me as I started the car and pulled out of the parking space. I took a peek in my rearview mirror and saw those dark, hooded eyes still watching me. The first thing I was going to do when I got home was to take a cold shower. Unfortunately, my phone rang a few moments later, interrupting my thoughts about Eric.

I sighed when the name of the caller popped up on my car's bluetooth screen.

"Hi, Marshall," I answered.

"Hey, Angela, how're you?"

"I'm well, just finished teaching spin class."

"That's good. I was calling on my break to see if you wanted to go out again tomorrow night. I know Wednesday and Sunday nights are your only evenings off."

"Yeah, uh, I can't tomorrow night."

"Oh." Disappointment filled his voice.

"Maybe next week?" I injected my voice with false hope.

"Sure. Sure, next Wednesday will be fine."

"Okay, that's great. Listen, I just got home and need to do a ton of stuff before I go in tonight."

"A-all right then. I guess I'll talk to you later."

"Bye." I felt guilty for rushing him off the phone like that. Marshall was a good guy—an eighth-grade English teacher who tutored over the summers. The few dates we went on were decent, but none of them compared to the feelings experienced in Eric's presence. And while I'd told Stephanie passion wasn't that important and building a solid foundation with someone was, I'd be a fool to actually believe it. Besides, it's not like Marshall was my boyfriend, and Eric and I were just going on one little date. I'm sure after our date we would both realize there wasn't much between us besides physical attraction. I avoided dating firefighters for that very reason. But for some reason, I couldn't find it in me to turn down Eric's offer.

Chapter Four

Angela

I checked my gold wristwatch again. I wore it because I liked the way it looked against the sleeveless white flowy top I wore, with a pair of skinny sky-blue jeans that were ripped at the knees. On my feet, I wore a pair of platform white, strappy sandals. I wasn't sure how to dress for the evening since Eric didn't tell me where we were going. I hoped I dressed appropriately for our evening out. It was about ten 'til six, which meant I had just enough time to freak out about our impending date.

I checked around the bar to see Stephanie and Walter behind the bar serving the happy hour customers who've begun to trickle in since our four o'clock opening. I liked having the bar closed during the day. It left me some free time in case I needed to come in and do paperwork, pay bills, make orders, or anything else with less of a distraction. I checked my watch again.

"Keeping time?"

A chill ran down my spine. I turned on the bar stool I was sitting on and my breath caught as Eric's tall, muscular build came into my line of sight.

"Just making sure I was on time," I lied. "I hope this is okay. I wasn't sure what to wear." I held out my arms, displaying the outfit I chose.

"It's perfect." His eyes perused the length of my body, a whisper of a smile forming on his lips.

Suddenly, I felt warm despite the air conditioning in the bar. I, too, scanned his body and was relieved to see he wore a pair of dark blue jeans and a V-neck black T-shirt.

"Now, are you going to tell me where we're going for the evening?"

"Are you worried?"

I paused, taking in the smile that lingered on his lips, as his dark eyes studied me. I could get lost in those dark pools, and the mischief swimming in them. In a husky voice, I asked, "Should I be?"

His grin widened and he stepped forward, running a long finger down my jawline. "You can trust me. I'm a firefighter."

"I bet those same lines have been used on many women right before they dropped their panties for you."

I noticed a few patrons glance our way when Eric let out a belly laugh at my comment.

"But they all were left satisfied, Angel. Shall we?" He held out his hand for me to walk ahead. When I did, his other hand went to the small of my back and that warm sensation I normally felt whenever he spoke occurred, only tenfold.

I bet they were. If his touch had me feeling like this, I couldn't even fathom what the main event was like. "Thank you,"

I stated, my voice sounding hoarse, as he held his passenger side door open for me.

"My pleasure." He closed the door and rounded the front of the vehicle to reach the driver's side. "It'll take about thirty minutes to get where we're going due to rush hour. I figured we could have dinner there unless you wanted to do a sit-down dinner."

"No, I'm game for whatever," I answered honestly. I liked the idea of him keeping our date a secret for as long as possible. And despite the quip he made earlier about being firefighter, I did feel safe with him. Don't get me wrong, I wasn't stupid. I told a friend I was going out on a date tonight and I'd give her a call by a certain time, just in case. But as I eased back into the leather seat of his car I wasn't worried or in fear of what Eric had planned for us.

"Is it too hot in here for you?" he asked his eyes on the road. "I can turn up the AC."

I took that as an opportunity to stare at his profile. I've always had a thing for men with strong jawlines, and Eric's was beautifully chiseled.

"It's perfect," I mumbled.

When he glanced at me out of the corner of his eye, smirking, I knew that *he* knew I wasn't referring to the temperature.

"No, I'm fine," I tried to cover up my little flub.

"How long have you owned the bar?" he inquired, turning his attention back to the road.

I continued to stare at him. Hell, since he already knew I was looking, might as well get my fill. "A little over a year and a half."

"You've always wanted to bartend?"

I shook my head even though he wasn't looking at me. "No, I went to school for restaurant management. Well, I got my associate's degree in cooking and then my bachelor's in restaurant management. I did that for three years after college. Worked at one of the most exclusive restaurants in the city as a supervisor, working my way up to become a manager."

"What happened?"

"Hm?"

"I mean, what made you leave that to open the bar?"

"Oh. Well, I enjoyed the job at first and gained lots of experience, but I realized that I enjoyed interacting with people more, you know? As a supervisor or manager in a restaurant, the only real time you get to spend with customers is if there is a complaint. Otherwise, you're overseeing the kitchen and waitstaff, putting out fires behind the scenes, or doing a bunch of paperwork. The job can be very demanding, and you work lots of long hours. It got kind of humdrum after a couple of years, and then I had the opportunity to quit, so I did."

"Why's that?"

"Why's what?"

"Why'd you have the chance to quit?"

"Oh, um..." I paused, pulling my lips in, mulling over my next few words. I dropped my gaze down at my hands in my lap. "My parents died. They left Sean and me their life insurance and some investments." I cleared my throat. "I decided I wanted to go back to what I found fun, so I started bartending as I'd done in college, and when the owner of the bar said he was thinking of selling I didn't give it a second thought. I bought it, and the rest is history."

"I'm sorry about your parents. Were you close with them?"

I peered up at him. "They were my best friends."

He gave me an empathetic look. My heart jolted against my ribcage.

"They died in a plane crash. They took a trip for their thirtieth wedding anniversary and were taking a small plane to an island destination in the Caribbean, and it crashed." I stopped talking before I did something completely embarrassing like start tearing up. I was a talker, but I rarely talked to people about my parents. My head lifted when I felt a strong hand cover mine and squeezed, comfortingly. The balm of his touch was something I've never felt before. I wanted to pocket that feeling so I could pull it out on sad nights to keep the tears from missing my parents at bay.

"Ready to go in?"

I turned to stare out the window at the crowd entering underneath the neon sign ahead of us. "The fair?" I asked.

"You seemed like you'd like the fair."

My somber mood of a few moments ago evaporated as I gazed up at the lights and huge Ferris wheel. "I've wanted to get here all summer, but no one would come with me."

"You were just waiting for me. Don't move." He cut the engine off, got out of the car, and came around to hold the door open for me.

"Thank you." I swooned a little when he held my hand to help me down from the SUV.

"It's been so long since I've been to a fair," I commented as we entered the fairgrounds.

"Are you hungry or did you want to ride the rides first or play games?"

"Umm." I looked around and went to point but realized Eric still held my hand in his. I felt like a kid in a candy store. "Cotton candy, then the Ferris wheel, then that target practice game, then maybe those chili dogs." I added the last one a little sheepishly.

"So be it," Eric chuckled, pulling me by the hand toward the cotton candy stand. "Did you grow up in Williamsport?" he asked in between bites, as we walked.

I swallowed the mouthful of the super sweet and fluffy candy, and my eyes surveyed the passersby as they walked around the fairgrounds. I noticed a few couples, walking hand-in-hand, similar to Eric and me. The weather was in the eighties but thankfully it wasn't humid.

"Yup. My parents met in the same neighborhood they raised my brother and me in. We went to the same schools they went to growing up. The only time I moved away was to go to college in Boston. My mother told me going away to school was a good opportunity to find out who I was and what I wanted. She was right. I discovered that I'm just a Williamsport girl, so afterward, I came back home and never regretted it." I continued to talk about my adventures growing up and my family. It felt good sharing the happy memories of my parents with someone. Usually, I kept them hidden and locked away in my heart, only pulling them out when I was alone at night. To most people, I was the bubbly, spirited girl who rarely stopped talking or could be a listening ear when needed. I didn't let too many people know my sadder moments though. Eric rarely interjected, save for a probing question here and there. At times, I was in awe that he seemed to be listening.

"This line is pretty long," I commented. We were waiting for our turn on the Ferris wheel.

"Do you mind if I run to the restroom while we wait? It's right over there."

"No, of course not. I'll hold our spot."

He gave me a skeptical look. I found it sweet.

"Go. We'll be waiting here are at least another fifteen minutes in this line."

He inclined his head and turned toward the restrooms. I watched him walk away, taking in the bulges of his strong arms in the T-shirt and his long legs. My tongue snaked out to lick my bottom lip when I thought about the contours of his body hiding beneath his clothing. I fanned myself with my hand and then chastised myself for such lustful thoughts in public. About a man I barely knew. It was then I realized how much talking I was doing on our date so far. I talked so much about myself, I neglected to ask him anything. I bit my lower lip, feeling foolish.

"So much for being asked out again," I mumbled.

"Angela?"

I turned to the male voice that just called my name, and my stomach dropped. *Shit. What's he doing here?*

"Marshall. Hi," I greeted, trying to infuse my voice with a cheeriness I wasn't feeling at the moment.

"What are you doing here?" he asked, the dark brown skin of his forehead wrinkled in confusion.

"You know... just having fun at the fair."

"You're here by yourself?" He glanced over my shoulder. Seeing I wasn't with anyone, his gaze returned to me.

"No," I answered honestly, suddenly feeling silly for feeling guilty. "I'm here with someone."

"Oh." His face was a mask of confusion as he turned his head, again. "A male someone? As in a date?"

I swore I heard a slight edge in his tone, but I brushed it off. "Yes, I'm on a date with someone."

He remained silent for a moment, peering down at me from his five-foot-nine height. His confusion gave way to understanding and then his eyebrows pinched in what seemed to be anger.

"I thought you had to work tonight. When I asked you out yesterday—"

"I never said I had to work, just that I wouldn't be available tonight." I lifted my chin to meet his gaze. I didn't lie to Marshall, and we never discussed exclusivity. I didn't want to hurt him, but we were still in the "getting to know one another" phase, and well, I was having doubts as to whether or not I wanted to take it further with him.

"Well, where's your date now? Doesn't seem like he's much company at the moment," he countered, a little snark in his tone.

"I'm right here," a deep voice responded just behind Marshall.

My stomach lurched at the sound of his voice. There was something underlying in his tone. Something that didn't bode too well for Marshall.

"Something I can help you with?" Eric positioned his body between Marshall and I.

I attempted to take a step back to give him more room, when I felt a long arm around my waist, holding me in place.

Marshall's eyes traveled up the full length of Eric's body, and he unwittingly took a step back of his own.

"I was just talking to my, uh, friend."

Eric gave a tight smile. "I see. Thanks for keeping her company while I was away."

Marshall was being dismissed.

"Yeah, okay." He paused, then turned his eyes to me. "Angela, I'll give you a call sometime this week," he said before tucking his tail and walking away.

I peered up at Eric to see his jaw tightly clenched as he watched Marshall's back. I swallowed, hating the awkwardness of the moment.

"You should tell him not to bother calling you," Eric said.

"Huh?"

He didn't respond to my inquiry.

"We're getting close." He nodded toward the front of the line, jaw still rigid. I turned, and sure enough, it was almost our time to be seated onto the Ferris wheel.

Minutes later we were on the Ferris wheel being secured in. As soon as we were seated and buckled in, Eric asked me about something and I went on to answer, giving him another long, drawn out spiel about some aspect of my life. When he put his arm around my shoulders as we reached the very top of the Ferris wheel, I leaned my head against his shoulder. The awkwardness of Marshall's appearance evaporated. We fell into a comfortable silence, looking over the river running along the east side of Williamsport. I couldn't think of a time when I felt this safe and comfortable with someone I barely knew.

****

Eric

"Thank you for taking me out. I had a wonderful time."

To my surprise, Angela smacked her free hand across her forehead, eyes squeezed shut, mouth twisted up. "That sounded so lame and cliché."

My hands twitched and I couldn't stop them from reaching up and cupping her face. "Sounds like the truth to me." I brushed my lips against hers.

We were standing on the porch of Angela's two-story home. I insisted on driving her home instead of dropping her off at the bar where I picked her up. It was well after ten o'clock at night, and there was no way in hell I was about to let her find her way home on her own.

Her arms came up, gripping my wrists. "It was the truth. I mean it *is* the truth," she giggled, and that funny thing in my chest happened again.

"Good. As long as you had a good time."

"I did. I hope you did, too. I know I ramble a lot, so I apologize if I talked too much."

I frowned, giving her an incredulous look. "Talked too much?"

"Yeah, I tend to do that. An ex of mine broke up with me because he said I talked too much and that most guys don't like that sort of thing."

"He was an ass."

She gasped before letting out another round of laughter. "You're right; he was an ass."

"I enjoy the sound of your voice."

Her tawny brown eyes gazed up at me, a doe-eyed expression emerging. "You do?"

"What's not to like? It has an airy, melodic sound to it."

She gave me a shy smile before lowering her lashes. I loved that I could make her feel shy. I've watched her in her element at the bar, welcoming every patron who visited, there didn't seem to be a shy bone in her body. Dancing, serving up drinks, and conversation in one fell swoop. She has a magnetic energy about her that most people wanted to be around.

Pulling her face closer to mine, I took her lips. I lined her bottom lip with my tongue before going all in, allowing myself to get acquainted with her taste. Her soft hands tightened around my wrists, and I pushed my body in closer to hers. When she moaned into my mouth, the sensation shot straight to my cock.

Shit. I rarely had this much of a reaction to a woman so soon. It was time to say goodnight. I reluctantly pulled back.

Her surprised eyes looked at me, questions swirling in them. Instead of answering them, I asked one of my own.

"The guy at the fair... what's the story with him?"

"Oh." Her eyes widened as if she forgot all about him. "We've gone out on a couple of dates. He asked me to go out tonight, but I'd already said yes to you."

I poked out my lips and stared at her contemplatively for a second. "That's too bad."

Her eyes drooped, a sullen expression appearing on her face. "I wasn't leading you on. He and I aren't—"

"I meant, that's too bad for *him.*"

Her head popped up.

"I was raised to be a gentleman. Ordinarily, that would mean being okay with you dating Matthew—"

"Marshall."

"I don't care."

Her mouth snapped shut.

"But I'm not feeling very gentlemanly or patient when it comes to you."

Her eyebrows shot up. "After only one date?"

"My parents were married after only knowing each other for two weeks. We move fast in my family."

She dipped her head but not before I caught her grin.

"Don't worry," I moved in close to her ear, "I'll give you a little more than two weeks." I pressed one last kiss to her lips, unable to stop myself, and then paused to rein in my unruly emotions. I meant it about not feeling very gentlemanly. My brain was screaming at me to stake my claim already right here and now, but I knew that would be moving entirely too fast for her comfort. Summoning all the strength I had at my disposal, I let my hands drop before taking a step back, putting much-needed distance between us.

"Go inside." I jutted my head to the door.

She hesitated but eventually turned and used her key to unlock the door. She flicked on the light just inside the door, illuminating the living room.

"I need to give you my phone number so you can text me that you got home safely."

I stared at her for a moment before pulling out my phone. I scrolled to the contact section and typed in the name "Angel" before handing it to her to put her number in.

Her face lit up when she saw the nickname.

"I'll text when I get home," I stated when she handed me back my phone.

I waited for her to go inside and shut the door behind her before I bounded down the stairs and crossed the residential street where my car was parked. Inside my car, I just sat, staring at the relatively small home, adorned with dark grey paneling, white painted wooden porch, complete with a swing on it. The house was no more than a stone's throw away from neighbors on either side, leaving little room for a yard, like most of the houses and neighborhoods in this city. In a city with the population of more than four million people, space could be difficult to come by. There was something comforting about this home. Instinctively, I knew it was the woman who lived in it. Yes, she talked a lot, but that was fine with me. I enjoyed listening. I wasn't much of a talker myself, not with most people anyway. I was always more about action than talking. Guess that was why my job fit me perfectly.

You'll know when you know. My father's words echoed in my head. He'd been talking about how he decided to marry my mother. I had half a mind to call him and have him describe what he felt because I'll be damned if it wasn't something similar to what I felt at that moment, as I sat and stared hard at Angela's house.

For the first time in a long time, I was looking forward to something other than fighting fires.

****

"Well, look what the cat dragged in. Hey, Corey, I thought we said we were done letting strays just walk up in here!" I could hear Don's boisterous voice all the way in the back where I sat cleaning my equipment.

"No shit!" Corey chimed in.

I wondered what the fuss was all about. Standing, I placed a fire extinguisher, hatchet, and other equipment back in the storage area where we kept them.

"They're still letting you bums fight fires, huh?" The voice made me pause in my tracks. I was grateful and excited the owner of that voice was back. However, the last time we spoke—over six months ago—the conversation didn't go well at all. In fact, we almost came to blows. I was never one to hide, so I again moved to go out to the garage where a few of the rookies were cleaning off the rig, while Corey and Don stood around, welcoming Carter back to the station.

"Harvard, bring your ass over here. Look who the hell just walked into Rescue Four," Don laughed, clapping Carter on the back.

"Welcome back, man," I greeted with my hand out. I waited for a heartbeat to gauge his reaction, but before I knew it, Carter had wrapped me up in a warm hug. It only lasted for half a second. We weren't the touchy-feely type around here, but that brief embrace was enough.

"Feels fucking good to be back," Carter replied, his blue eyes circling the station, savoring everything. He stood about an inch taller than me at six-foot-three, but the expression on his face gave away his boyish admiration for where we stood. "Not much has changed, I see."

"You've only been gone six months. You know how slowly shit changes around here," Corey spoke up. "But we were about to run some drills. Perfect time to see if you've still got it," he challenged.

"You can't lose what you were born with," Carter replied.

"That's the spirit. Let's show these rookies how it's done!" Don yelped.

That was my cue to start giving out orders. "Rookies, back the rig up and then grab your gear. We're running drills."

"Still the unofficial lieutenant, I see," Carter said.

"Unofficial."

"Don't you think it's about time you made it official?"

I looked at him but said nothing. I've been thinking about it. The lieutenant's exam was months away, and I still hadn't committed myself to taking it. Instead of answering, I went over to the wooden table sitting in front of the flat screen television on the wall and picked up the clipboard to begin filling out names for the drills we were about to run.

Carter pulled me aside. "Hey, Harvard, I want to speak to you later on when you've got some time."

"Sure thing. After these drills."

"Thanks."

"Now, get your shit and put it on so we can show these rookies what real firefighters look like." We both laughed and headed out to the back of the station house where the mock obstacle course was set up. About ten years ago, some of the older guys at Rescue Four set up this obstacle course complete with rope ladders, mock fire hydrants, and all types of other shit to train on during the downtime. It was the responsibility of the men at the station to maintain the equipment for future use. I went and retrieved my stopwatch. We spent the next forty-five minutes running drills, timing one another, and showing the rookies some things that weren't taught in the academy.

Just as we were heading back inside, the siren in the station house went off, alerting us to an incoming call.

"Class B fire at Mike's Auto Shop," a voice came through the walkie-talkie I grabbed on instinct from the counter. A whirlwind of activity started around me as each man began grabbing their equipment and rushing to the rig. I threw on my gear the same way I've done hundreds of times, barely flinching at the nearly hundred pounds of equipment I was now carrying. Knowing the keys to the truck were in the rig, I ran to the driver's side door, just as the garage door was raised. Closing the door behind me, I went to start the engine and... nothing. *What the fuck?*

"Where the *fuck* are the keys?" I bellowed.

Don echoed my question, and one of the rookies called back, holding the keys in his hand.

"Toss 'em!" I yelled. "You stay your ass here!" I pointed at the rookie. "Never fucking take the keys out of the rig. Carter, get your ass in here!" I yelled. I didn't give the disappointed rookie a second glance. Seconds later, I saw Carter climbing in the back of the rig with all his equipment on. I wasted no time peeling off, as Corey to my right pulled the lever for the horn, alerting the entire neighborhood we were on the move. I was honking the horn on the steering wheel, still pissed at the rookie's mistake. It was an unspoken rule. We *never* removed the keys from the rig, unless it was during shift change. Looking for keys could cost us time—time that could be spent fighting fires or pulling someone out of the flames. It may seem minor, but in this job, even the little things mattered. I left the rookie at the station to ponder his fuck up, and let Carter come on this ride because, despite his absence in recent months, I trusted him with my life and the life of every man in this rig.

When we pulled up in front of the auto shop, I hopped out of the rig and quickly assessed the situation.

"Corey, you and Kyle man the hose. Don, grab the hatchet. Carter, you're on me," I threw out orders left and right. We were the first truck on the scene. I surveyed the scene and saw the police with a young male in custody, handcuffed behind his back. That wasn't my main concern at the moment, however.

"Anyone inside?" I asked the cop and the young boy, who presumably started this fire.

"Nah, man, I ain't set anyone on fire," the boy who appeared to be no older than sixteen answered, squirming in the officer's grasp.

I didn't know if I could trust his answer, though. On the one hand, he could be lying. On the other hand, there may have been someone inside that he didn't know about.

A round of sirens brought my attention behind me where I saw another rig pulling up. I made my way over to the captain of that rig and told him the situation.

"Your men are going to be on the hose while we go in." He nodded in agreement and then ordered his guys to take over hosing down the fire. It appeared to be a little more under control than when we first pulled up. I had my guys grab the fire extinguishers to use inside instead of the water hose.

"Carter!" I called.

"Right here," he answered.

I didn't need to say much more than that to continue inside the entrance with Carter behind Don and me and Corey and Kyle behind him. I steadied my breathing and lowered my face mask to utilize as little of the oxygen from my tank as possible. Our tanks were supposed to last up to sixty minutes, but in a grueling fire where we're working overtime, it could run out in less than twenty. Thick smoke coated the air, and I used my hands as my eyes, feeling for the walls, cars, canisters and anything else that was in the shop. I felt an arm to my left and knew that was Carter. I've come to know the feel of everyone after doing this hundreds of times over the years.

"Check to the left," I told him.

I heard a noise in front of me. Something fell or got knocked over. I knew it wasn't one of my guys who did it since they were behind me.

"What the fuck was that?" I yelled, then got quiet to listen for it again.

"A fucking cat!" Don yelled out at the same time I heard the meowing sounds.

"I got it!" Carter called out.

We made our way to the opposite side of the auto shop, Don and Corey putting out flames with the fire extinguishers as we moved. Thankfully, no one else was inside, just as the kid said. Twenty minutes later, I was lifting my face mask over my head as we stood outside the auto shop.

"I think he belongs to the owner," Carter stated, holding the frightened cat up.

"Pretty sure that's him over there." I tilted my head toward the man who was now talking with police, or rather yelling at them to let him get to the kid who now sat in the backseat of their car.

"I'll take it to him." I took the cat from Carter, who hissed at me. "Oh yeah? I don't fucking like you either," I growled back. I hated cats and the thought of us risking our lives to save a damn cat caused me to chuckle. But when I saw the owner of the shop's face when he saw what was in my arms, my attitude changed.

"Thank you!" The man was almost in tears. "He was a gift from my wife. She died earlier this year," he explained, cradling the fur ball as if it were the only thing that mattered to him.

"Our pleasure, sir." I inclined my head at the officer before turning and walking back to the truck. Corey was overseeing the rookie who came on this run while he put the hose away, while Don and Carter put the extinguishers up.

"Who's hungry?"

"I am!"

"Fucking starving!"

"Grub time!"

They all shouted at once.

"It's your first day back, you get to pick where we eat," I told Carter.

He grinned. "Lorenzo's."

"Of fucking course," Don stated as he shut the side doors of the rig.

"Best pizza in the city!" Carter replied.

"Up yours, Carter. Best pizza in the city is DiMaggio's, and I don't wanna hear any shit from you either," Don pointed at me, causing me to laugh.

"Fuck you, and Lorenzo's it is," I replied.

I called back to the station and had the rookie we left there order two pies from Lorenzo's, one plain and one filled with sausage and pepperoni. By the time we got back and took off and stored all our gear, the food was delivered, and we sat down at the table to eat. The rookie who was left behind was made to restock the equipment in the truck while we ate. We spent the next forty-five minutes recounting tales of the last six months to Carter to catch him up on what he missed. By the time we were done, I was stuffed and ready to call it a night. I was working the overnight shift, which meant another night on the bed that could barely be described as a cot on the second floor of the station.

"Hey, can I talk with you?" Carter asked, catching up with me in the hallway.

"What's up?"

"Thanks for letting me go on that run today. I know it wasn't protocol."

"Don't sweat it. The rookie fucked up, and I knew you'd be in position."

Carter looked at me before lowering his head, not wanting to reveal too much emotion. At the station, telling a man he was "in position" is one of the biggest compliments you can give. It said that he was reliable because he was always where he needed to be. It was akin to telling a man you trusted him with your life.

"I know the last time we spoke, I was really fucked up. You were telling me what I needed to hear at the time and I didn't want to listen. I said some shit..." He broke off.

"I've only got two questions for you."

He waited.

"Are you clean now?"

"Hundred percent."

"You plan on having my back and every other man's back like you did today?"

"Every single time."

"That's all I need to know." I clapped him on the shoulder. "You and I are good."

No hard feelings. We yelled and cursed at each other, and on the rare occasion even fought—it was what brothers did—but at the end of the day, I'd walk into a burning building knowing these men stood shoulder to shoulder with me.

Chapter Five

Eric

"Did you lose another bet?" Angela's smiling face asked.

I'd just stepped into the spin class with a few others who were now positioning themselves on their bikes. I made a beeline for Angela as she prepped the music on her phone for class.

"I don't consider it a loss since I got a chance to see you again." I grinned at the bashful face she made.

"I'm starting to think you have a crush on me." She placed her hand on her hip.

"More than a crush, Angel."

Her eyelids fluttered and the partial smile she wore expanded. I had to clamp my hands into fists to keep from grabbing her face and tasting those lips again.

"I signed up at the gym here," I told her. It was the first thing I did when I got off my shift that morning. I've been working crazy hours since our date the previous week, and save for a few phone calls, we haven't gone out again. I made time to see her today.

"That's great! You're in for a treat today. I just made a new playlist last night. This one's even more intense and high energy."

"Oh yeah? I'm looking forward to it." I admired the view as she walked over to her bike and climbed on. She wore a pair of grey biker shorts, sports bra, and a black tank top with the words "Shut Up and Train" written on the front of it. My eyes panned down her smooth, shapely legs. I grinned when an image of those legs wrapped around my waist came to mind.

"All right! Let's warm up those legs. You should be pedaling. Make sure your feet are secured onto the pedals. No accidents today!" her voice boomed into the microphone, interrupting my thoughts.

I did as told and began pedaling, but my mind was on memorizing every inch of her exposed pecan-colored skin. I already knew how soft her skin was, and now my body was screaming at me to feel it again, this time totally skin-to-skin. *Patience,* I told myself.

By the time we were on our first round of standing up on the bikes, her skin held a light sheen of moisture. I ran my tongue along my bottom lip, imagining it was her soft skin. I followed along with the instructions she threw out, standing and sitting when told, pedaling faster and harder when encouraged. And increasing the resistance when ordered to do so. Angela was a tough instructor. The workout was grueling, just the way I liked it. But the best part of the workout was when Angela stood up on her bike and leaned over, giving us a peek of her cleavage. I didn't even care if I was being blatant. My need and desire for her were growing by the minute.

"How was it this time around?" she asked, dabbing the sweat from her neck and chest with a towel.

Lucky towel.

"Better than the first time."

"Yeah, it takes a couple tries to get used to the hard seats," she commented, still a little breathless.

"What're you doing now?"

She poked out her lip, eyes rolling upward as she pondered my question. "Nothing until later when I have to go to the bar to do some paperwork and open up."

"So you have time to grab a cup of coffee? My treat."

"How's a girl to refuse an offer like that?" she teased.

"I'll wait while you grab your stuff."

She dashed off toward the women's locker room to grab her duffle bag. Five minutes later she was back, hair fluffed a little, and a new coat of lip gloss adorned her pretty, full lips. I had to shake the thoughts of what those lips would feel like underneath me, pressed to mine as I thrust in and—

"Thanks for waiting," she stated, interrupting my little fantasy.

Down boy, I mentally chastised myself.

"No problem." Placing my hand on the small of her back, I guided her toward the double doors. We walked next door to the Mom and Pop coffee shop. It was late morning, so the shop only had a few patrons milling around.

"What're you drinking?"

"Small iced vanilla latte," she answered.

I chuckled at her drink order. "One small iced latte and small regular brew for me," I ordered from the barista.

"Would you liked that iced as well?"

"Oh no, his kind doesn't do iced drinks, sweetie," Angela interjected.

"My kind?" I looked down at her.

"Firefighters. You all wouldn't be caught dead drinking iced coffee."

"You got me there."

"I grew up around firemen. I know how you all are."

I smirked, recalling she'd said her father was a firefighter, just like Sean, her brother.

"Oh yeah? How are we?" I asked as we retrieved our drinks from the other end of the counter and walked over to an empty table by the window.

"A bunch of tough guys. Who make crude jokes and constantly take the piss out of one another, but you've all got one another's backs when it counts."

I stared at her over the lid of my coffee cup as I took a sip. "Pretty accurate assessment."

"And you're all notorious playboys."

I lifted an eyebrow. "Think so?"

"You said it yourself. Said you all needed an outlet and that outlet was women."

I stopped just before we sat at one of the tables. I read the question in her eyes. The one she obviously didn't want to ask.

"You think I'm using you as an outlet?"

"You tell me," she retorted.

"I have plenty of other numbers in my phone I can call if I just wanted an outlet. None of them would I go to a spin class for or invite out to coffee afterwards. Okay?"

She paused, assessing me until she finally nodded. I pulled out the chair for her to sit.

"How come they call you Harvard?" she suddenly asked.

"Take a guess."

She poked out her lower lip and squinted, as she peered at me across the table.

I sat back and let her run through the possibilities in her mind.

"No way!" Her mouth shot wide open, excitement etched on her face. "You went to Harvard?"

I dipped my head.

"Graduated?"

"Yup."

"What'd you study?"

"Finance and sociology." I leaned in across the table. "And if you tell anyone that second part, I'll deny it with my life." Most of the guys knew where I went to school and that I studied finance. They didn't know I double majored in sociology as well.

"They won't hear it from me." She pantomimed zipping her lips and throwing away the key. I laughed at how goddamn cute she appeared doing it. Moments later, a pensive look covered her face. I could see the wheels of her mind moving. She had such expressive eyes. They practically screamed her feelings before her mouth did.

"You want to know how someone with a finance degree from Harvard became a firefighter."

She blew out a deep breath. "Yes. I mean, no offense, it's just not the first thing you think of when you hear the word firefighter. I'd expect someone with your educational background to be working in the financial district. Not that firefighters aren't smart. Hell, my father was a firefighter, and my brother is one, and they're two men I admire most, so I'm not—" She broke off when I grabbed her hand across the table.

"No offense taken, Angel." I brought her hand to my lips, unable to keep my hands or lips off her for too long.

"To answer your question, I did work in finance for a few years after graduating, kind of like you. However, I realized wearing a monkey suit and saving a billion dollar company pennies on the dollar every day wasn't my life's calling." I went on to explain to her the day I decided to apply to the fire department.

"I went for a run in the park and was stopped by fire sirens whizzing by. I followed and then watched as the men pulled a young child out of a burning home. That day I remembered my desire to be a firefighter as a kid. I was right in the middle of my applications for my MBA, but couldn't figure out what was stopping me from finishing them. That day I realized why. Crunching numbers wasn't my calling. A few months later, I was training at the academy. Toughest shit I ever did, but well worth it."

"Were your parents surprised?"

I snorted. "More like disappointed as all hell. They still haven't completely forgiven me, honestly. If it were up to them, I'd ditch the fire protective gear for a tailored suit."

"I imagine they're worried more about your safety."

"I suppose." I shrugged.

"You don't think so?"

"I do. I'm just more worried about enjoying my life. Sitting behind a desk eight to ten hours a day isn't for me."

"I guess we both have career changes in common, huh?"

"What do you enjoy so much about bartending?"

Those tawny eyes lit up. "What's not to love? I get to meet all types of people. Hear about their days, their careers. Some come there in an awful mood after a bad day at work, and I get to figure out how to cheer them up. I know some people think a bartender's only goal is to get you liquored up so you'll tip well or keep buying, but I enjoy getting to talk to complete strangers about their lives."

She continued talking about the bar and the different people she came across in her time as bartender turned owner. I was caught up in the sound of her voice, fueled by the passion she held for what she did. I watched her lips move as she talked, remembering how soft they felt against my own.

"You know you can tell me to shut up, right?" I heard.

I paused. "The only time you need to shut up is when my mouth is on yours. Got it?"

Another head dip. *Fucking adorable.*

"But I'm dominating the conversation."

"And I enjoy listening."

"Are you sure? Because—"

I reached across the table for her hand. "I'm not someone who says one thing but means another."

"Okay."

"Now, finish telling me the story about the guy who quit his job."

A satisfied smile spread over her face. "You were listening."

She continued talking about a patron who came into the bar after quitting his job, and I kept listening. We sat in the coffee shop for more than an hour, but it felt like only five minutes. By the time we stood up to leave, my body had begun to remind me that I haven't gotten more than two hours of sleep during my overnight shift. I planned on heading home and sleeping for the next six to eight hours before I was scheduled to be back at the firehouse that night.

"I'm parked up here." Angela pointed as we walked out the door.

"I'll walk you." I stepped around her so I was on the outside of the sidewalk, closest to the street, while she was on the inside.

"Thanks for the latte."

"Thanks for the spin class," I joked.

The sound of her laugh had that funny feeling in my chest going off again. Once we reached her car, I watched her tongue dart out to moisten her lips, and that was it. I moved in closer. My arm reached out, pulling her into me, and I dipped my head, capturing her mouth. The sweet taste of the latte combined with her own sweetness caused a primal surge to rush through my body. Our tongues clashed and the thought of having gone this long in life without this feeling formed a knot of regret in my belly. *Life won't be the same after her.* I pulled away from her kiss-swollen lips with that thought on my mind.

Leaning down, I brushed my lips against hers. Still keeping my hands around her face, I pressed my forehead to hers.

"You're in trouble," I growled. Hell, we both were in trouble.

"We all could use a little trouble." Her voice was breathless.

I stole another quick kiss before releasing her and stepping back. "You probably should go now before I do to you everything my body is telling me to." I smirked at the way her facial expression grew stunned. But in her smoldering eyes, I saw her desire grow. A reflection I'm sure mirrored my own.

"Get in." I gestured to her car behind her.

Bowing her head, she turned to get in.

"Hold on. What are your plans for this Sunday?" I would tell her to break them if she did have something planned.

"Nothing. Well, I was going to do some baking and take it to my neighbor's for her weekly bridge meeting. I'm off on Sundays."

"I get off around five on Sunday. There's a jazz festival in the park this weekend. You said you enjoy live jazz music."

My heart sped up when she smiled. "You really do listen when I ramble."

"Every word."

Her lashes fluttered as she blinked. "That sounds fun, but I'd like to make dinner if you don't mind?"

I stepped closer. "You sure? I don't want to put you out."

"It's no trouble. I love cooking. Is there anything you don't eat? Allergies or just don't like?"

I shook my head. "If you make it, I'm eating it."

"Okay."

Damn. That smile. I cupped her face, stealing another quick kiss just because I could.

"Six o'clock?"

"Dinner will be ready at six. Don't worry about bringing anything."

"See you then." Backing away, I watched as she got in her car and pulled off, waving.

I suddenly recognized what the feeling in my chest was. It was the same feeling I got whenever the alarm sounded in the fire station. The same feeling that got every cell in my body jumping and ready for action. Except, around her it was actually more intense.

****

I parked in the garage of my building. I was lucky to live in a place that offered parking, instead of having to park out on the street. My legs felt too heavy to take the stairs to my third-floor condo like I normally did. Instead, I opted for the elevator. Leaning back against the wood paneling of the elevator, I closed my eyes, remembering the feel and taste of Angela's mouth.

Suddenly, Sunday felt like it was much too far away. The dinging of the elevator as it landed on my floor, forced my eyelids open. I stepped off and made a left, moving toward my door when I saw a familiar face.

"Eric. What a surprise to see you here."

I sighing heavily as I lifted my head. "Brandi, I live here."

She giggled and covered her mouth in a way that was meant to be appealing, but it just annoyed me. "I know that, silly. I just meant that it's been a while since we ran into one another." Moving her petite frame closer, she began running her pointer finger up and down my abdomen.

I grabbed her wrist, not tightly, but enough to halt her movement. She peered up at me, surprise etched on her pretty face. Releasing her hand, I took a step backward.

"Work keeps me busy." That was the truth, but I certainly could make time when I wanted, and for Brandi, I hadn't wanted to. She moved into the building a year ago, and a few months later we started a short fling. It wasn't anything serious. I got bored soon after, which led to more infrequent hookups.

"Well, I'm sure they allow you some time off at the fire station." Her lips formed into a pout, brunette hair falling over her shoulders.

"Some," I commented. "Listen, Brandi, I'm tired. I had a long shift. I'll see you around." And with that, I sidestepped her and moved toward my door—no promises to call or try to see her at some other time. As far as I was concerned, it was a done deal.

When I shut my door behind me, relief flooded my body. I bought this place after graduating college while starting my first job. I was making six-figures back then and believed my salary would only grow as I moved up the corporate ladder. My condo wasn't large by any stretch, and I lucked out purchasing it while the surrounding neighborhood was still relatively inexpensive. In the decade since then, gentrification had made prices soar, and affording this neighborhood on my firefighter's salary alone would've been a stretch. Luckily, I was always good with money, having put down a large enough down payment, my mortgage wasn't too bad and could easily be managed on my current salary. I saved a good amount of my previous salary and made some good investments.

Toeing off the sneakers I wore to the spin class, I dropped my duffle bag containing my work uniform by the door. My condo had an open floor plan and hardwood floors which was what drew me to it in the first place. I decorated it in mostly a mix of greys and black. I padded over to my kitchen area, pulling my fridge open for a bottle of water, before heading down the hall to my bedroom. I was so tempted to stretch out on my king-sized bed, but remembering I came from a workout prevented me. Grabbing a fresh pair of boxer briefs and my towel, I made my way across the hall to the bathroom where I showered and did a quick shave of the new stubble that was coming in. Tapping my face with some aftershave, I was ready for bed. I glanced at my clock and had about six hours before I needed to be back at the station. I climbed into bed, the last thing I remembered thinking about was the kiss I shared with my very own angel.

Chapter Six

Angela

"Don't you have a hot date tonight?" Stephanie asked me just as I was finishing the count of the bottles of Jack Daniels.

Turning my head, I peered at her over my shoulder from my squatting position. "Yes, I do, but I needed to come in and take count."

"I could've done that. You should be home prepping for all that hotness!"

I stood, placing my hand on my hip. "Get your mind out of the gutter. We're having dinner, and he's taking me to a jazz festival." I told Stephanie about my date with Eric after she hounded me for details when she saw him pick me up for our date the previous week. It felt good to gush to someone else about the new interest in my life. I could feel the butterflies in my stomach every time I thought or spoke about him.

"The only place he'd be taking me is to pound town!"

I gasped. "You have such a filthy mind!"

"I know, right?" she laughed.

"Yeah, well keep those filthy thoughts off of Eric and on someone else," I warned.

"Protective already, huh?"

I buried my face in my hands. She was right, I was experiencing a twinge of jealousy at the thought of another woman thinking of him the way *I* was thinking of him.

"It's all right. I get it. I mean, those dark eyes that look almost black—"

"Until you get close enough to see they're dark brown, and depending on his mood they darken or lighten a little. And he has the smoothest skin with yellow undertones, but his cheeks flush with red when he's exerting himself in spin class. And his Adam's apple. I never really found them appealing before, but now I find myself wanting to—" I stopped, remembering where I was. I saw I held Stephanie's rapt attention. I cleared my suddenly parched throat. "Anyway, there are eight bottles of the Jack Daniels left, two cases of that new brown ale we tried. I don't think that one was too popular, so I'm not going to order it again. Oh, and tell Susan to give me a call when she comes in, please?"

"Sure thing," Stephanie answered, going back to wiping down glasses as she was before.

"I think that's it. Give me a ring if you need me, okay?"

"I think I've done this once or twice before."

"Okay, okay. I'll leave you alone now. Don't forget about Susan," I reminded her as I shoved the clipboard with the count back under the bar, and wiped the dirt from the floor off my knees. Giving my employees one last good-bye, I headed out the door for my fifteen-minute walk home. It was another warm day, but not too hot, so I opted to walk to the bar instead of drive. By the time I made it home, it was just after two o'clock, giving me enough time to start cooking the meal I planned for the evening. I chose a Tuscan chicken recipe and debated on making mashed potatoes or mashed cauliflower as one of the sides. Although I liked going with the low carb option, I decided that mashed potatoes would be my best bet for the night.

I skinned and dropped the potatoes in boiling water to let them cook through, and began chopping spinach to make part of the sauce with the chicken. I spent the next hour or so cooking, first pounding chicken breasts until they were as thin as I wanted them, then cooking them in the pan, and finally whipping heavy cream to make the sauce. After letting the potatoes cool for a few minutes, I got out my butter, salt, chives, and homemade chicken broth to make the mashed potatoes. Once all of the cooking was done, I quickly chopped some vegetables and lettuce, making a salad as the final side. I made one of my favorite salad dressings with freshly squeezed lemon juice as the base. Once the food was all prepped, I stuck the salad in the fridge, put the chicken and potatoes in the oven to keep warm, and then headed down the hall to grab my towel from my bedroom to shower.

Sunday was usually my wash day for my hair, so I grabbed my bottle of shampoo and conditioner that I loved to give my hair its weekly spa treatment. After shampooing, I lathered my short strands in conditioner and tied a plastic bag over it, allowing the conditioner to penetrate my strands, especially the pieces that I colored. They needed a little extra TLC. Next, I lathered up and then shaved my legs and underarms since I'd be wearing a sleeveless dress this evening. Once I rinsed my hair out and hopped out of the shower, I pat dried my body using my towel but left it in the bathroom as I walked to my bedroom and sat on my bed to slather on lotion and then some of my favorite shimmering body spray. I loved the way it made my skin look all dewy. I dried my hair using the diffuser to keep it from looking too limp. I finished dressing, looking myself over in my full-length mirror. I loved the way the sleeveless A-line electric blue dress swayed as I moved. The front stopped a couple of inches above my knees, while the back came down to just brushing my ankles. I opted to pair the dress with my tan, strappy sandals. The heels on the sandals were only about three inches. I wanted something manageable since we'd be walking around the festival later that evening.

Grabbing my favorite floral-scented body spray, I gave myself a few spritzes just as my phone buzzed. I looked at it to see I received a text from my close friend, Janine. She and I met in college, and although she remained in Boston, we still managed to be a part of one another's lives.

Bestie: **Matt dumped me!!**

I kept myself from rolling my eyes, but just barely. Janine and her on-again, off-again boyfriend were always going through some drama. The problem was she wanted to get married and he so obviously didn't. For the life of me, I couldn't figure out why she clung to him.

Maybe it's for the best. I responded, knowing that wouldn't go over too well, but she needed to hear it.

Bestie: **For the best?? I LOVE him!**

I sighed, as I replied that she was too good for him. After a few of these exchanges, I finally told Janine I had to go but that I would call her the following day and let her vent all she wanted about her man troubles. My phone buzzed again, but I didn't get a chance to read her response because I'd placed the phone on my coffee table in the living room while I went to the kitchen to take out the plates and bowls for our meals. I glanced up to see the time was 6:01, just as the doorbell rang. I smiled. *I do love a man who knows how to be on time.*

When I opened the door, the air rushed from my lungs. The first thing that hit me was his scent—some woodsy cologne mixed with what I knew was his natural scent. Those piercing eyes met mine, wrinkling slightly around the edges as his lips parted into a warm smile. A few strands of his dark, cropped hair fell over onto his forehead. Broad shoulders had the white Lacoste shirt he wore sitting like it was made just for him. Black jeans and loafers finished out the look.

"Hi."

He leaned down, and instinctively I tilted my head upwards, readying myself for what was to come. My eyelids drooped, and a tingling sensation went through me when our lips connected. He took my lips, owning them, and I gladly let him. An arm reached down around my waist, pulling me in, and I ran my hand against his hard chest. He was the one who broke the kiss first. We both stood there, transfixed on one another for an extra moment, until Eric held up his free arm.

"I brought a bottle of wine for our dinner." He held a bottle of red wine.

"That'll go perfectly with our dinner but I told you, you didn't need to bring anything."

He gave me a look. "I couldn't show up empty-handed."

My lips twitched at the gleam in his eyes.

"Come in," I said, stepping to the side to allow his entrance. I shut and locked the door. "Let me give you a short tour." I took one of his hands in mine, and when his strong fingers wrapped around my hand, I nearly stumbled at the way my body reacted. I peered up at him to see his eyes on our interlocked hands, and I knew he felt it, too.

"This is obviously the living room. A friend of mine came in and helped me redecorate once I took ownership." I held out the hand that had the bottle of wine, giving him a view of the space. His eyes observed the tan sectional filled with cream and brown pillows, the square dark wood coffee table sitting in the middle filled with magazines and candles, and the fireplace directly across from the couch, above which hung the massive flat screen television. Since redecorating over a year ago, this place has felt so much more like my own home as opposed to my parents' house. I released a breath I didn't even realize I was holding when he blinked and smiled in obvious approval. I didn't care to entertain why this man's approval of my home mattered.

"Down the hall is the master bedroom and bathroom. Upstairs are two more bedrooms, and over here," I led him farther inside, "is the dining area. Where we'll be eating tonight."

"Thanks for the tour. What do you mean by took ownership?" he asked a few moments later.

"Oh yes. This was my parents' home where they raised Sean and I. They left it to me after..."

"Ah." He nodded in understanding.

"I redecorated to make it feel more like mine, ya' know. Not that my parents' style wasn't great, but it was..."

"Theirs."

"Right!" I agreed with his correct assessment. "I wanted something a little more my own. Plus, every time I came home and saw all their furnishings and decorations it made me miss them that much more. Sean was the one to suggest I redecorate. I was pissed at first, but then talked it out with my friend, Janine, and she made me see the error of my ways. She even came down from Boston for two weeks to help me figure out what I wanted and shop with me. She's an interior designer, so it was perfect. By the time she left, I felt like I had a completely new place. I loved it before…" I trailed off, realizing I was doing it again. I peeked up at Eric to see his keen eyes on me as if waiting for me to continue.

Pulling my hand out of his grasp, I waved it dismissively. "We can talk about all of that over dinner. I hope you brought your appetite."

I set the bottle on the medium-sized circular table with a black cherrywood finish and matching chairs.

"I made Tuscan chicken, mashed potatoes, and a salad for dinner."

"Sounds delicious."

"Sit, I will pour the glasses of wine and fix our plates."

"Let me help with the wine at least," he insisted, grabbing the bottle from the table and putting his other hand at the small of my back to maneuver me toward the kitchen. "Just show me where the bottle opener and your glasses are."

I opened one of the drawers of the counter. "Here's the bottle opener. The glasses are on the top shelf of the cupboard right above your head."

He easily reached the top shelf of the cupboard, taking down two wine glasses. I moved to the dining space, placing the salad and dressing at the center of the table, along with two bowls. Next, I plated our food and just as I was about to take the plates to the table, a hand on my arm stopped me.

"Let me," he insisted, removing the plates from my grasp and walking them to the table where our glasses, half-filled with wine already sat. I was almost bowled over when he stood behind the chair with my plate, pulling it out for me, waiting for me to sit.

"Thank you."

"Thank you for cooking dinner. It looks delicious."

"It was nothing. Mm, this wine is pretty good." I held the glass up in front of me. I usually went for white wine, but this was a dry sherry that I thought complemented our dinner quite well. I leaned over to put salad in each of our bowls along with the dressing I prepared.

"This is delicious. You made the dressing?"

I laughed that he sounded impressed. "Yeah, just some lemon, garlic, avocado, and a few other things blended. I'm glad you like it. How was your day?" I asked after a few moments of eating in silence.

"Was pretty slow today at work."

"That's a good thing, right?" A day with minimal fires or emergencies sounded good to me. Apparently, Eric didn't think so.

He snorted. "Trust me, you do not want to be sitting around the station with a bunch of firemen who have nothing to do."

"Oh man, I can only imagine the trouble you guys can get into."

He laughed, wiping his mouth with a napkin. "Don, he's the prankster of the group. We're all sitting in the kitchen at the table eating lunch, talking smack. Our usual. Don gets up as if he's making a phone call. A few seconds later he runs into the kitchen, squirting something on the floor behind him, and then halfway up one of our newer rookie's legs then runs out. Seconds later we see flames rushing up the trail he left behind right up to the rookie's leg. It was lighter fluid."

I gasped. "No freaking way!" That sounded dangerous, but Eric was laughing about it.

"The rookie had his protective gear on. He wasn't in any danger, but he did freak out until I leaned over and dumped my coffee on his leg, putting out the fire."

"That's what you all do in the firehouse? Light one another on fire?"

"Sometimes. You don't want to know the other things we can get into."

I laughed some more as he told me a few of the other antics of the guys in his station. The poor rookies seemed to get it the worse, which was always the case, I figured.

"Are you close to your parents?" I asked during one of our lulls. I wanted to find out more about him besides his being a firefighter.

"Not particularly." He gave a one-sided shrug. "I mean, I love them, and they love me, of course. I visit them a couple of times a month."

"Do they live in Williamsport?"

"No. My dad finally convinced my mom to move out to the suburbs of Collingwood. It's only thirty minutes outside of the city. Close enough that my mom can commute back in three times a week for work."

"What does your mom do?"

"She's a professor of linguistics at Williamsport U."

I wrinkled my forehead, impressed. "Wow. Williamsport U is one of the top universities in the city."

"So I'm told."

I giggled. "What about your dad?"

"He works as an executive at Townsend Energy."

"And you're an only child?"

He nodded.

"They probably had a lot of hopes and dreams pinned on you."

"They did. Townsend was the company I worked for out of undergrad. I got hired through my dad's connections, although I had the education and internship experience for the job. It seemed like the perfect fit."

"Until you had other plans."

"Right."

"How much of a rift did your career change cause?"

"My dad refused to speak to me for months. My mother spoke to me, but it was minimal. It took a few years for them to come around, and even still..." He trailed off.

"But you're a hero. No, I mean it," I insisted when he snorted. I put down my fork, grabbing his wrist. His eyes moved from my face to my hand. A wave of need shot through my belly at the sharpness in his gaze. "I-I just mean, no disrespect to your parents. But you run into burning buildings and save lives. You may not make the big bucks like someone working in the executive suite at Townsend but what you do is so much more valuable." I squeezed his arm for emphasis.

He stared at me for a long while, his dark eyes burrowing into mine, drinking me in. A dizzy feeling came over me at the intensity of his stare. That spark of electricity that always threatened to ignite whenever we were close rose up, consuming us both.

"Are you finished with dinner?"

"Yes." My tone was low, breathy.

Rising from his seat, he came around to where I sat. Before my mind could register what was happening, he pulled me up to stand in front of him, strong hands holding me at my waist. His lips were on mine a second later, and I willingly opened up to receive whatever he was trying to give.

His tongue swept my teeth and then my tongue, tasting me, savoring me. His fingers dug into my sides, pulling me deeper and deeper into his spell. Knowing I'd topple over from the vigor of this kiss, I wrapped my hands around the hardness of his triceps, using his body weight as an anchor to hold me up. I moaned into his mouth, our lips smacking against one another. I needed to come up for air, but the kiss was too good.

Breathing could wait.

I didn't need it.

All I needed to survive was more of this.

More of him.

I was lifted off the ground and placed on the table. I wrapped my legs around his thighs and gasped when I felt the third leg in his pants. I moved back, staring at him, asking without words if that was what I thought it was. He smirked with a promise filling his dark eyes. The seam of my panties became moist with my need for him. He pulled me in again. I closed my eyes and sighed into his ravenous mouth, knowing this was wrong. But how could something wrong feel so right?

His strong hands on me.

His lips caressing mine.

I knew we shouldn't be doing this so early on. We were only on our third date... if we counted the coffee shop as a date. Each caress of his lips or swipe of his tongue left me falling deeper and deeper under his spell. One I wasn't sure I ever wanted to come out from under. Just when I decided to throw all caution to the wind, he pulled back, hand still holding onto the back of my neck, our foreheads pressed together. We both panted loudly.

"You're making it hard to take things slow."

"Who said you need to take things slow?" I practically purred.

"You did, Angel. Your body wants to, but your mind's still wrestling with it." He gazed into my eyes before taking a step back. "Go freshen up. I'll clear the table so we can head over to the festival."

I stood there for a second attempting to regain my equilibrium. Blinking, I oriented myself, and saw Eric taking our empty plates to the kitchen as if it was the most natural thing in the world. He looked at me expectantly, and I remembered he told me to go freshen up. I smoothed down the edges of my dress, almost embarrassed at how carried away I let things get on my dining room table!

I headed toward my bathroom and reapplied the light pink lip color I donned earlier, fluffed my hair out, and spritzed myself with some of my floral spray. When I re-emerged, the table was cleared, and Eric stood by the entrance way.

"Thank you for clearing the table."

"You cooked. Only right I should help clean up. Ready to go?"

"Yes."

He led me out the door, pausing for me to lock up behind us. When I turned, I noticed him staring at my legs. A shiver ran through me. I really shouldn't have been so caught up in this man. It was very early on. I've never had this type of draw to someone this soon. I bet he was used to women throwing themselves at him. *I mean, just look at him!* Six-feet-two inches of hard, solid muscles, covered by beautiful smooth, tanned skin with a face to match.

"You okay?" he asked, getting in the car just as I sighed.

"Of course." I kept my gaze directed at my hands in my lap.

He paused, leaving his key in the ignition but not starting it. Strong fingers gripped my chin, turning my head to look him in the eye. There was silence for few moments as he just stared into my eyes.

"You're uncomfortable about what happened," he stated.

"Not uncomfortable. If anything, a little too comfortable. If you weren't the one to stop us, I'm pretty sure we would've... you know." I felt so foolish admitting that out loud.

"That's a bad thing?"

I swallowed the lump in my throat. "I don't know. Just...what does that say about me?" I hated to sound like a prude, but I've never been intimate with someone I wasn't already in a committed relationship with.

"It says you've got good taste."

I laughed, despite not wanting to.

He placed one arm on the steering wheel and rested the other against the headrest of my seat, leaning in close to me. He was so near, I could feel the body heat emanating from him. That same feeling I had in my dining room began to emerge again.

His voice was low but laced with steel when he said, "I won't take you until you're ready. I could tell you were having doubts. And doubts lead to regrets, and when I finally do take you for the first time, there won't be with any regrets. Because once I make you mine, there won't be any take backs." He waited for me to accept what he was saying.

I nodded, and he pressed a kissed to my forehead before starting the car.

It took a while before my erratic heartbeat calmed down. I shifted the car's vent toward me to get the direct blow of cold air. This man couldn't be a firefighter—he's way too good at stoking the flames.

****

Eric

When I do take you...

My own words echoed in my mind over and over again. Even though every word I said was true, I cursed myself for sounding like a goddamned lame ass. It's been a couple of years since I was in a serious relationship. I was enjoying the single life and didn't think I was ready to settle down just yet. But a couple of dates with Angela and I was ready to say fuck the single life. That's why I completely put a halt to our previous night's kiss before it went too far. I could sense her hesitation. I even felt the exact moment she decided to say "fuck it" and was all in. I knew then it was my responsibility to put a stop to things. I was more than ready and willing to pick her up and pin her again the nearest wall, or countertop, or bed, whichever was closest and most convenient. But, I also knew that she'd have regrets afterward, and that's something I wouldn't let her take on.

"Harvard, I called you last night. Wanted to see if you were in the mood to meet me at *Charlie's*," Corey began, interrupting my thoughts as I walked into the kitchen. I saw his missed call and knew that's probably what he wanted.

"I was out last night." Grabbing a plate from the cupboard, I went about fixing a plate of the eggs, bacon, and toast that had been prepared, not realizing how quiet it'd gotten behind me. When I turned around, I saw Don, Carter, and Corey staring at me.

"What?" I asked as if I didn't know. Sitting down, I ignored their snickers and began eating my breakfast.

"Don't fucking *what* us," Don quipped.

"What Don here is trying to say is, what's her name? What does she look like? Do we know her?" Carter laughed.

"You bastards are worse than middle school girls." I pointed my fork at the three of them. A chorus of laughter sounded off between them as they pulled out chairs.

"Come on, Harvard. If you don't spill something new, Donnie here's going to go crazy. Probably lighting someone or something else on fire," Corey laughed. "We're bored as fuck without any fires. It's been a slow week."

That was true. It was a slow week. We got a few calls, mostly for small fires and a couple of car accidents, but for men like us, those types of days dragged on. We all wanted to be where the action was, or we got antsy.

"First of all, my damn love life is *not* going to be used for your fucking fodder around this station."

"Fodder?" Don looked puzzled.

I rolled my eyes. Don was always playing as if he didn't know what certain words meant.

"Gossip," Carter responded, his gaze pinned on me.

"Oh. Whatever, man, give us something. Is she hot?"

"Come on, Donnie. You know Eric only messes with beautiful women."

"Corey, you call me Donnie one more time, and you won't have to worry about women, fodder, gossip, or any-fucking-thing else. Got me?"

We laughed at Don's fake threats.

"Harvard," Carter started in a tone as if he was a school teacher dealing with an unruly child, "All we're saying is, you're our brother, and as such, it is our responsibility to make sure any young woman you're gallivanting around with is suitable. Right, fellas?"

"Yeah, what the fuck he said." Don pointed with his thumb in Carter's direction.

I looked at the three men, who reminded me of children, anxiously waiting to be dismissed from school on a Friday afternoon.

"Okay, you wanna know?" I asked after swallowing the last bite of my breakfast and wiping my mouth.

They glanced between one another and then nodded.

"She's..." I leaned in and held up my fork, jabbing it in their direction with every word I said. "None. Of. Your. Fucking. Business." With that, I stood up and took my plate to the sink.

"Ah, man, this must be serious. We never withhold this type of vital information from one another."

"Whatever, Corey." It was true. We've each done our fair share of talking about the women we dated and bedded. But this time around, I didn't feel like sharing what was happening between Angela and I. One reason was that these guys knew her. They frequented her bar and the idea of them knowing what went on between us didn't sit well with me. An image of Angela—breathing heavy from our kisses, as she sat on her dining room table, legs wrapped around my waist, eyes wide after having just felt the size of my hard-on—had me swallowing deeply. When I thought of her kiss-swollen lips, and then the acquiescence in her eyes as she decided to give in to the chemistry between us made me shift my positioning in my chair. No. I sure as hell wasn't about to share that moment with these guys. And I damn sure wasn't about to confess the sheer amount of strength it took for me to drop Angela off at her door after our date, place another kiss on her lips, and then walk away after she went inside, alone. All that, after feeling her body against mine as we walked and danced at the jazz festival. Nope. I'd never hear the end of it. But more than that, I wanted to protect what we were building. This felt entirely too important to expose for fire station gossip.

"Whatever, man. Since Harvard's not talking about his love life, let's talk about something that matters. You hear who our new captain is?" Corey asked, looking around the table.

I shook my head. There were a few different names floating around the station as to who was going to be our new captain. Unfortunately, in the fire department, things like replacements could happen slow as hell or quick as lightning. Just depended on what the upper-level department heads were doing. And since there'd recently been a shake-up with the Fire Chief, new positions had been slow to be replaced.

"I hear it's Graham," Carter spoke up.

"Graham? Fuck outta here!"

"You gotta be shitting me!"

"The hell?"

Corey, Don, and I spoke in unison.

"You mean Graham Waverly?"

Carter nodded.

"Shiiiit," Corey cursed.

Graham Waverly did not have the best reputation as far as Rescue Four was concerned. He was captain over at Firehouse Station Three a few years back when part of our station's area was redistributed to theirs. Graham had been the biggest proponent of the change. Since then, Rescue Four has held a grudge against Graham Waverly. As I said, firefighters are highly competitive, and the idea of knowing part of our district was taken away from us, thereby causing us to get fewer calls, was a *huge* problem.

"He better not bring his ass in here thinking he runs shit," Don mumbled.

We all chuckled at the look of anger on Don's face.

"When's he supposed to show up?" I asked Carter.

"Today, I hear."

"All right. In the meantime, let's run some drills and clean our equipment. It's been slow the last couple of days, and you know what that means."

A series of grunts and scraping chairs echoed as we stood. A slow couple of days usually led to all hell breaking out. It was summer after all, and things never kept quiet for too long during the summer.

****

"Heads up. He's here," Carter stated, tapping my bunk as he moved past me.

I rose up, peeling my eyes open from the short nap I was trying to get in. It was later that afternoon, and I was working a twenty-four-hour shift. I was attempting to get in a little shut-eye wherever possible. I had a feeling I'd be getting very little sleep that night.

Hearing footsteps around me I got up, tucked my navy blue, Williamsport Fire Department shirt into my standard department issued black trousers, slipped on my black boots, and headed down the steps. When I reached the middle of the stairs, I could make out the top of the new captain's greying head as he moved toward the kitchen. By the time I reached the bottom step, I could make out the speculative glare Don was giving the new captain. I followed him, and we stood at the kitchen's entrance, silently watching as our new captain wordlessly went over to the counter, grabbed one of the mugs from the cupboard, and poured himself a cup of coffee. By that time, the new captain had an audience of about six guys, who just stood around observing him, scoping out his behavior. Bringing the mug to his mouth, he turned and acknowledged each man with a slight tilt of his head. Only the rookies returned the nod, much to the chagrin of the older guys, including myself.

I observed the captain, who appeared to be in his mid-forties, sandalwood colored skin, and eyes that were slightly darker and sharp as a tack. He appeared to be the type who only needed to see something once to have it committed to memory. He also had the look that most older firefighters had in their eyes—as if they've seen a hundred lifetimes in the decades they've been on the job, and they had.

"Where's my office?" his gruff voice asked, looking around.

"Upstairs, Cap." That was one of the rookies.

Sucking teeth and mumbling ensued that from Don, Corey, Carter, and a few of the older guys. Rookies had so much to learn. Captain already knew the answer to his question before he asked. He was testing us to see who'd break this little showdown first. Of course, it was the same fucking rookie who took the keys out of the rig the other week. I glanced over at Don who gave me a look. I nodded, conveying I was already assigning this rookie cleanup duty for the next week for his latest gaffe.

"I'll be upstairs," the new captain informed, moving past us with his coffee mug in hand. For his part, he didn't appear intimidated or put off by the cold shoulder he just received. That boded well for him. Captains couldn't show weakness, not if they expected this group of roughnecks to follow them into the flames.

A few hours later the new captain received his first ride with Rescue Four when we got the call for a three-alarm fire. As soon as the alarm sounded off at one in the morning, I was up, ripping the blanket off of my body, whipping my feet over the side of the cot and directly into my boots, which were strategically placed where they'd be easily accessible. Less than three minutes later, I had my fireproof pants on, suspenders up, and was sliding down the pole right behind Don, Carter following right behind me, and the new captain behind him. I glanced at Corey, who was now relegated to the back of the rig because the captain always sat up front, passenger side.

I reached for the keys, relieved to feel them in the ignition already. Seconds later, we were in the rig, sirens blaring, charging out of the garage and making a left toward the fire. I focused on the road but could hear the captain using the walkie-talkie to communicate with headquarters. They'd gone to a private radio line to communicate, which usually happened when someone had been injured. I pressed my foot on the gas, pushing the rig to get us there faster. We were three blocks from the fire when I saw smoke billowing up toward the sky. Huge plumes of black clouds hovered over a five-story brick building. From the looks of it, it was some warehouse.

The captain grunted beside me. I didn't know him well enough to understand his grunts and moods just yet, but if he was thinking what I was thinking, it looked as if this fire was going to be a doozy.

"Roger that," he said into the walkie-talkie just before we jumped out of the truck. Ours was the first truck there, soon followed by two more rigs.

"Kim, you, Alvarez, and Williams find a way in. Rookie, you're with me. When I move you move. Got it?" The captain didn't bother waiting for the rookie's reply. He referred to myself, Don, and Corey by our last names. Nonetheless, we grabbed our hatchets and the hose, then hooked it up to the nearest hydrant, but we didn't immediately turn the hose on. The fire was now shooting outside of the fourth story windows. Observing the area, I saw people in nightgowns and sleeping attire crying across the street. I knew there was a high chance that people were still inside. It was one in the morning, and in all likelihood many people were passed out from smoke inhalation or trapped inside.

"Don, Corey, let's go!" I yelled, running toward the first entrance I saw, lowering my mask over my face. I entered on the first floor and yelled at a few people I saw coming down the apartment building's stairs, pointing toward the exit. A few of them cowered in fear. In addition to people being terrified of fires, seeing large, bulky men in facemasks can be jarring in the middle of the night. I often have to cajole frightened children and even adults, letting them know I'm there to help them not harm them. Of course, I didn't always have time to play nice, so yelling out orders and directions ended up being my go-to method most of the time. They may not like my tactics at the moment, but in the end, I've never met a person I pulled out of a fire not say thank you for saving their ass.

"Anyone in here?" I yelled, banging on each door I came to. Corey and Don were doing the same behind me.

"All clear!"

"Clear!"

Both men yelled once we cleared the first floor. I led the charge up to the second floor, which was coated with a thick fog of smoke. By the time we arrived, we knew the fire started on the fourth floor of the building. There was already smoke on the second floor which meant the fire had burned down to the third floor and soon down to the second, soon enough consuming the entire building.

"All clear!" I yelled out when we cleared the second floor. Thankfully there were no people trapped, but I knew the next two floors were going to trick us. As we made our way up the nearly black stairwell, which would carry us to the third floor, I steadied my breathing a much as possible. There was a great deal of noise that could be heard on our two-way radios.

"Fourth floor is completely consumed! Copy?" I heard the captain's voice.

"Roger that!" It was meant to be a warning. We were not to go up to the fourth floor. We were already on shaky ground on the third floor. I heard the heavy breathing of Corey and Don behind me. We knocked on doors of the apartment.

"This one's locked!" I shouted when I came across a closed apartment. I checked over my shoulder to make sure no one was behind me and swung my hatchet into the door, making a hole big enough to stick my arm through to reach the knob and unlock the door.

"Fire department! Anyone in here?" I yelled out, doing my best to make my way through the living room, then down the hallway to what I presumed were the bedrooms. I check one room, looking around as best I could, and saw an empty bed. When I cleared that room, I started to head to the one across the hall only to be nearly knocked over by Corey.

"I got one. She's unresponsive," he informed me.

I got on my radio. "Coming out with a female. Unresponsive."

"Don!" I called, making sure he was with us.

"Yeah! All clear," he announced.

I helped Corey with the woman, carrying her legs while he had her upper body. We went back down the stairs, the same way we came up. It took us mere minutes to get back down to the first floor and then out the same entrance we entered. Corey and I carried the woman across the street, taking her to the awaiting paramedics. Out of the corner of my eye, I watched Don run to the rig and begin helping the rookie who stayed back with the captain with the hose. By now the other two rigs had their hoses turned toward the fire and were now putting it out. In Williamsport, firefighters were required to put out every fire we encountered. While in many cities around the country, firefighters were allowed to let the fire burn, in our city, the houses were too close together to let that happen. The fire could quickly jump from one house or building to the next, and before we knew it an entire block could be up in flames.

Once paramedics took over CPR on the young woman, Corey and I grabbed a second hose off our rigs and connected it to another hydrant and joined the other guys to battle the flames. We fought that fire for the better part of two hours. It made its way down to the third and second floors, much of the inside collapsing under the melting power of the fire. By the time we turned our hoses off, and the last ember burned, my throat was sore and voice hoarse from yelling so many directions at the rest of my guys or following our captain's instructions.

Once assured the fire was completely out, we were given the all clear to go in and check the first and some of the second floors. The third and fourth floors were destroyed, and there was no safe way anyone could enter let alone walk on those floors.

For the next half an hour we made our way through the first two floors, ensuring that no one had been left behind. I had a feeling, however, that not everyone had made it out of this fire alive.

"She's going to be okay," one of the paramedics came over to Corey and me to let us know. The woman we pulled out was taken to the nearest hospital after she regained consciousness still at the scene. The 'medics just got a report from the hospital that she suffered smoke inhalation and some first-degree burns, but after a day or two in the hospital, she'd be okay.

"Hell of a job," I said, clapping Corey on the back.

"Thanks for the help, bro," he returned.

We did the customary fist bump when we made a save, then headed to the rig to load our gear back on. By the time we returned to the station, my body felt the weight of the physical and mental exertion it just exercised. You would think I'd be tired, but these were the times where my mind was still racing, going over and over what I'd just done. While it was close to four in the morning, none of the men were going back to sleep anytime soon. So we did what we always did. We parked ourselves in the kitchen, at the table, and ordered some food. There were a couple of twenty-four-hour food places within blocks of our station. We ordered breakfast food, as no one felt like cooking. We'd leave that for the next shift that was scheduled to relieve us at nine a.m.

"Good job out there today."

I lifted my eyes to see Captain Waverly standing at the head of our table, sincerity in his eyes as he looked pointedly at all of us.

"They pull anyone out of there yet?" Don asked after a few heartbeats of silence. We all knew there'd be at least one body coming out of that building in the morning. Fires that started in the middle of the night, when people were asleep, often had the most casualties.

"Not yet. Fire investigators are going to be scoping it out in the morning."

"I'll head over there in the morning also," Don commented.

The captain gave no argument, just nodded and pulled out his chair to eat with us. A silent respect had begun to form between the new captain and Rescue Four. He'd done a hell of a job taking over and commanding us and the other rigs that showed up at the scene. While he still had a ways to go to prove himself, on his first day in action, Captain Waverly was looking like he just might make it at Rescue Four.

Chapter Seven

Eric

I felt refreshed, sitting up from my six-hour nap. It was just after six o'clock. After my shift, I ran some errands, went home, and passed out after taking a shower. Now that I was up, I figured I'd hit the gym for a strength training workout. Although I was going to Angela's spin class every Tuesday and Thursday I had off for the last few weeks, that wasn't nearly enough of a workout to keep me in the condition I needed to be in to do my job. I figured I could grab something for dinner after the gym, but I somehow found myself at *Charlie's* once I finished my workout. I haven't seen Angela in two days, and although we've spoken over the phone and via texts, it wasn't enough interaction for me.

It was a Thursday night, and the music was blaring as soon as I walked into the bar. There were even a few people dancing in between the tables. My eyes scanned the room, first to see if anyone from Rescue Four was there. I tossed my head in a nod, acknowledging two Rescue Four guys who were talking with some firefighters from a different squad. One of them gestured for me to join them, but I gave them an "in a minute" signal before I turned my attention toward the bar. The edges of my lips curled upwards when I saw what was taking place behind the bar. That moment I realized Ed Sheeran's "Shape of You" was playing out of the jukebox, and my girl was behind the bar giving a show.

I moved in closer but still kept my distance so she couldn't see me over the crowd standing around the bar. Angela wore a sleeveless, floral, flowy top and a pair of skinny blue jeans. Her hair was styled in its usual cut, short strands falling over her forehead on one side. She was holding up a steel shaker, shaking it over her shoulders to the beat of the music. Effortlessly, she moved her hips in time to the beat and then did a spin before pouring the shaker mix into two margarita glasses and passing them over the counter to two female patrons. Tossing the shaker somewhere under the counter, she and the blonde bartender turned to one another and did a shimmying shoulder move, moving in and out from one another. The crowd of patrons clapped and whistled at the show.

"Who's next?" Angela called, still dancing.

A customer called out a drink order, and Angela danced her way over to the glasses and used a tap on her side of the bar to fill the glass with one of the specialty beers she served, then placed a paper coaster on the bar and the glass on top.

"I'm in love with the shape of you!" she sang along with the music. She, along with the other bartender, kept the show up for the remainder of the song, raising their hands to clap over their heads.

"Thank you, thank you!" They both clasped each other's hands and bowed to the applauding patrons.

"Don't forget to tip your bartenders!" she joked.

I moved in closer to the bar as more patrons moved away, making their way back to their tables, drinks in hand.

"Nice show."

I heard a slight gasp as Angela spun around, her lips parting into a wide smile when her eyes landed on me.

"When can I get one of those in private?" *Preferably with you wearing nothing but my scent.* I left that last part out when I bent over the bar and whispered the question in her ear. I leaned back to see her dip her head, a shy smile forming on her lips and a slight blush in her cheeks.

"I thought you were resting?"

I grinned at her ignoring my question. "I did. Then went to the gym and was going to pick up something to eat but ended up here instead."

"Can't stay away, huh?"

"Not for too long," I admitted, finally pulling her in for a kiss. My entire body relaxed on a sigh at the feel of my lips on hers. Any concern I had that day drifted away.

"Been way too long since I felt that," I murmured against her mouth before pulling back.

"Are you hungry? We do offer some food."

I hadn't even thought about food once I stopped inside the bar. I was so anxious to see her and then mesmerized by the show she was putting on that my hunger had fallen by the wayside, but now that it was mentioned my stomach began growling.

"That sounds like a yes to me," she laughed. "What're you having?"

"Turkey club." I held up my hand before she could hand me the menu, not needing it.

"Coming up." She wrote down my order and then dipped from behind the bar to hand it off to the part where the small kitchen was. I watched her hips sway, and her ass move from side to side in the jeans.

"I'd sure like to get a private show of that," a guy sitting two stools down from me commented.

I peered at him, and he held up his beer to me, grinning. My top lip curled upwards into a snarl.

"She's taken," I responded, voice tight with underlying possessiveness.

The guy's eyes widened briefly before he nodded. "Hey, no harm, bro."

"I'm not your fucking bro." I was rarely this short with people, but he pissed me off.

"Hey, your sandwich should be ready in about five minutes. I told 'em to put a rush on it." Angela appeared in my line of sight, breathless as if she rushed back.

When I turned my gaze back to her, the anger that I was just feeling ebbed and all that remained was the damn tingling in my chest again.

"How was your night? You had a long shift yesterday." There was a worry in her voice, although she tried to hide it.

I eyed her, noting the slight crease in her forehead, and could tell she was holding something back.

"You heard about the big apartment fire," I stated.

Her shoulders slumped as she blew out a harsh breath. "I saw it on the news. They're saying a woman and her two children died."

I sighed, having heard the same news before the media got ahold of that piece of information. The woman and her children were on the fourth floor of the building, right next to the apartment where fire investigators believe the fire started. They'd likely been sleeping when it started, and either had no way of getting out once it spread or had passed out and possibly died from smoke inhalation. I hoped like hell it was the smoke inhalation that got them first because burning to death is quite possibly the worst way to die. I did my best to push thoughts of the small children out of my mind.

"Yeah, Rescue Four was there," I answered honestly.

"One turkey club sandwich." A man brought a plate out from the kitchen area, setting it down in front of me on the bar.

"Come sit with me while I eat." I knew it was kind of busy at this hour but I felt selfish. I wanted her full attention.

When Angela nodded, I blew out a breath I didn't know I'd been holding.

"Hey, Jimmy, can you help Steph behind the bar for a few?" she asked the man who just came out.

"Sure thing. Take your time."

"Thanks, Jim."

With my plate in one hand and a glass of water in the other, I followed Angela to one of the empty booths. I waited for her to sit, admiring the way her jeans hugged the curve of her hips and lean legs.

"I missed you in spin class today. And Tuesday."

I nodded, wiping my mouth from the bite of sandwich I took. "This is good," I said, looking at the sandwich.

"Thank you. I have my cook make them with my special mayonnaise recipe instead of the regular stuff."

"It's delicious. But yeah, I missed it, too. I'm getting used to spin class," I teased. It was more so *her* I was getting used to. "What are your plans for this Sunday?"

Her eyes moved upward toward the ceiling. "I'm doing a little housecleaning and then having lunch with my brother and nephew at home, but I'm free in the evening."

"Nephew?"

Her smile grew, and her eyes lit up. "Yeah, Sean has a six-year-old son. Light of my life."

"I didn't know that." For some reason, the idea of Angela swollen with our child came to mind.

"Yeah. Jeremiah," she said, interrupting my thoughts.

"If you're not too tired afterward, I'd like to take you out. There's a movie playing in the park. I'll even spring for the popcorn." I wiggled my eyebrows, causing her to laugh.

"That sounds like a good deal. Won't you be too tired after work though? Don't you have an overnight shift on Saturday night?"

"I do, but I'm never too tired to take you out." I finished the last bite of my sandwich, savoring it.

"You are a charmer."

"My mom used to say the same thing."

"I bet she did," she giggled.

We talked for a few more minutes, catching up on one another's day. I opted not to go into too much detail about the apartment fire. I didn't like the fear I saw in her eyes when she initially asked about the fire. It was the same look I sometimes saw my mother, and even my father, give when they asked about my work—which wasn't often. We talked more about our common appreciation of old-school R&B music and the jazz festival we went to instead. Before I was ready for her to leave, Angela had to get back to work. That was my cue to take my ass home. I needed the rest before I had to get up for another twenty-four-hour shift the following day.

"All right then. Thanks, f—"

Whatever she was about to say was cut off by my lips on hers. I didn't care that we were in a very public place. We hadn't gone public with our relationship, but the combination of my growing need for her, and what the schmuck from earlier said about wanting a private show, made me possessive. I wanted to leave my mark on her, in front of others, so they knew to keep their distance. So, that's what I did.

I pulled her into me with one arm, her hips pressed against mine. I took my time, feeling the plushness of her mouth, exploring the feeling of our tongues coming together. She tasted sweet, sweeter than any dessert I've ever had. I did my best to commit her flavor to memory. When she moaned into my mouth, I decided it was time to end the show there. I might've wanted to brand her with my taste for others to see, but I wasn't about to give a fucking peep show.

"I'll pick you up at five on Sunday." My voice was thick, full of pent-up emotion and need.

"I'll be ready."

My cock jumped in my pants at the promise behind those words. I don't even think she knew what she was promising, but my body did and responded in kind.

"It's going to be a long two days," I commented, pressing my forehead against hers.

Even her giggle made my body react. At that point, I released her. Suddenly, remembering I hadn't paid for my food, I pulled out my wallet from my back pants pocket. A soft hand covered mine.

"It's on the house." Her voice was just above a whisper.

"You sure?"

"Positive." She moved in, pressing a kiss to my cheek. "I have to get back." She turned and walked away. My eyes trailed her from behind as she pivoted and tossed a wink at me over her shoulder before ducking back behind the bar.

Reluctantly, I headed out the door to my car. Most nights, the only place I wanted to go was home after getting off work. Even when I'd gone out with a woman or went to hang out with the guys after work, I always looked forward to going home alone. I found comfort in my solace most nights, but at that moment, I knew things were changing when I wished that she was coming with me.

****

Angela

My head popped up from the homemade tomato sauce I was mixing over the stove when I heard the sound of my doorknob turning and then the door pushed open.

"Angela, you home?" a deep baritone voice rang out.

I sighed in relief, grabbing the edges of the apron I wore and pulling it over my head to toss it on the counter. Quickly rinsing my hands off, I patted them dry with a dish towel and made a beeline for the living room.

"Aunt Angela!" my nephew, Jeremiah, called out.

"Hey, sport!" I greeted, giving my little guy a warm hug. When I released him, I held him by the shoulders, examining him. I looked over the cinnamon brown color of his skin, which mirrored his father's, and the honey-colored eyes he inherited from his mother. Although Jeremiah was only six, his height was in the age range of an eight year old, revealing that he'd likely be tall like both his father and grandfather.

"Hmmm, I think you've grown at least three inches since I last saw you," I joked.

He giggled, displaying his missing front tooth. "You saw me just last weekend."

I stood, pressing my hand to my chin and giving him the suspicious eye. "Are you sure? It felt like longer than a week."

"I'm sure! Dad brought me, remember?"

I laughed at the way he looked at me as if I was the one who was the child.

"That's right, sport. It's coming back to me now. You made me promise to make your favorite spaghetti and meatballs when you came back, right?"

His little face lit up with pleasure. "Right!"

"You're in luck, kid. It just so happens I was making my famous spaghetti and meatballs when you showed up."

"Yes!" he cheered. "Hey, Dad, Aunt Angela made me 'pisghetti!'"

"Oh yeah? How about you go wash your hands before you eat your 'pisghetti." Sean and I both laughed at his joking of his son's pronunciation. Jeremiah ran down the hallway toward the bathroom.

"What's up, big brother?" I asked, swatting him with the dish towel I still held in my hand.

"It's about time you acknowledged me. I've been standing here for ten minutes, just being ignored while you butter up my son."

"Oh shut up." I pulled him in for a hug. "You're lucky I acknowledged you at all. How many times do I need to tell you to knock before you come in?"

"Why do I need to knock? You ain't doing anything in here."

I turned, hands on my hips. "How do you know?"

"Because I do. Anyway, you knew we were coming over. I figured you'd be in here cooking."

"Only because I love my nephew. And I know my poor baby probably hasn't had a home-cooked meal since he was last with his mama."

Sean waved his hand, dismissing my comment. "Get outta here with all that. I'm working on my cooking skills. I made us some scrambled eggs this morning."

I frowned.

"The hell is that look about?"

"Poor baby probably has a scratched up throat from all the cracked shells you left in those eggs."

"Don't play me, Angela." He pointed a finger at me, trying to appear stern.

Laughing, I proceeded to the kitchen.

"Smells good in here though. Thanks for hooking my lil' man up," Sean stated as he moved farther into the kitchen behind me, toward the refrigerator.

"What are you doing?" I turned from my tomato sauce to see my brother leaned over at the waist, head in the fridge.

"Why did you make so many sandwiches? Jeremiah doesn't like sandwiches," he stated, ignoring my question. "And why'd you cut up all this fruit?"

"Will you get out of my damn refrigerator with your big head!" I pushed him at the shoulder, forcing him to stand, and shut the door.

He frowned down at me, arms folded.

"All clean!" A smiling Jeremiah entered the kitchen holding up his hands in the air as proof he washed them.

"Thanks, sport. Can you do me a favor and set the table like I taught you?" I asked, handing him a couple of Solo cups.

"Yeah!" He nodded his head before dashing out of the kitchen with the cups.

Ignoring Sean, whose eyes I felt on me, I took down three plates for our lunch.

"Who're the sandwiches for?"

"None of your business." I placed spaghetti noodles on each of the plates.

"For Eric?"

I stopped myself from turning toward my brother. "You heard, huh?"

"Who didn't hear with the display you two, apparently, put on at the bar the other night."

I sucked my teeth. "It wasn't a display." I figured news of Eric and I would've made it back to my brother by now. I knew there were a few firefighters in the bar that night, as there usually are. And one thing I've realized is that nobody gossips like firefighters.

Sean tutted. "That's not what I heard. You two were practically dry humping by one of the booths."

I turned sharply, facing Sean, pointing the wooden spoon I held at him. "Stop being ridiculous. You know me better than that."

"I'm just saying, Angie, out of all the firefighters, you go and date a guy from Rescue Four. The competition."

I rolled my eyes, trying to keep from laughing. "How are they your competition? Last I checked, you both work for the Williamsport Fire Department. Heck, for all you know, you could be transferred to Rescue Four and work with those guys someday. You might wanna be careful who you piss off," I warned. Sean had recently put in a transfer, seeking a new station. Although he loved his current house, he'd also passed the lieutenant's exam the previous year, and since his fire station already had three lieutenants, to progress in his career, he needed to move somewhere else.

"I—"

"Cups are done. What's next?" Jeremiah interrupted Sean's retort.

"Here, buddy. But be careful. Take one plate at a time to the table." I watched, smirking as Jeremiah carefully held onto the paper plate I'd just given him, slowly creeping toward the dining area with it.

"That's not gonna happen," Sean finally stated, once his attention was back on me.

I shrugged. "If you say so."

"I do say so, and I also say I don't like hearing news about my sister and who she's dating from anyone besides her. Especially when it concerns her dating a firefighter."

The way he spit out the word firefighter, caused me to rear back, frowning.

"Why did you say it like that?"

"I'm just sayin', I know how we are. We meaning firemen," he added when I scrunched my face up at the word "we."

"We're loud, brash, and sometimes we're players."

I gave him a look.

"Okay, more than sometimes."

"Eric's not like that."

He let out a humorless laugh. "Wrong." He pointed at me. "Eric's exactly like that. Don't think just because he's quieter than the rest of us that he's Prince Charming. That man lets the bevy of women he leaves behind do his talking for him."

I raised my eyebrows. "You sound as if you admire him."

"Fuck you, Angie."

"Ohhh! Daddy said a bad word," Jeremiah shrieked.

"Dammit," Sean mumbled under his breath, but it was too loud.

"Another one! That's two dollars for the swear jar."

I covered my mouth, laughing. Sean's been trying to do a better job of not cursing when he wasn't at work. Having a son who looked up to him and copied just about everything he did, he wanted to set a good example. The swear jar was something Sean came up with to hold himself accountable.

"I'm gonna go broke messing around with you two. Let's go eat."

"Wait, why me? I didn't do anything."

"You got me in here cursing around my son."

I shook my head at my older brother. We sat down to eat, and Sean cut up the garlic bread and handed the bread basket to Jeremiah for him to dig in. Within minutes the only thing that could be heard around the small room was the smacking of both Jeremiah and Sean's lips as they ate. I ate much slower, savoring the flavors of the Italian seasoning, garlic, and tomatoes in the sauce, along with the delicious bread I'd picked up from the farmer's market the previous day.

"Can I have more, please?"

"Dang, boy, can you swallow what you have in your mouth before speaking?" Sean scolded.

I felt lighthearted watching my precocious nephew gobble down my food. I loved moments like this—serving others either at the bar or home, and watching them delight in what I'd made for them.

"I'll tell you what, sport, how about I give you and your dad the leftovers so you can take them home. That is unless you don't want the lemon pound cake I made for dessert?"

I almost fell over at how wide Jeremiah's eyes grew when he heard what I made for dessert.

"You're gonna have to roll the both of us outta here," Sean groaned.

"Don't act like you don't want any cake either. It's on the counter by the sink, covered in the tin foil. Bring out just two plates, though. I don't want any," I told him as he headed to the kitchen.

"You sure? You know me and this boy can finish a whole cake in one sitting."

My lips turned downward at the sound of that. "I hope you aren't letting my nephew eat all that sugar in one sitting."

"Nah, I said we *could* finish a whole cake in one sitting, not that we *would.* We'll leave some for you."

"No, you all can take that home with you, too. I had some of it earlier."

Sean shrugged. "Suit yourself."

Minutes later, Jeremiah and Sean ate their cake while I got up to retrieve some more of the fresh squeezed lemonade I made for lunch.

"Are you excited for school to start next month?" I asked Jeremiah.

He nodded, thankfully swallowing his cake before answering. "I'll be in first grade."

"That's right. My boy's in the gifted and talented program, too!" Sean cheered, holding up his hand. Jeremiah slapped it, and the two broke out into the personalized handshake they created for just the two of them. I adored the relationship between them. It reminded me of Sean and my father. Sean had emulated just about everything my father had done, right down to his career choice.

"You two remind me so much of you and dad," I stated a later on, as we sat out on the porch, watching Jeremiah tossing a football with another little boy from the neighborhood.

Sean let out a chuckle. "Dad always said, I wouldn't understand pure love until I had a kid of my own. I get it now."

"I bet," I sighed. Talk of my father made my heart heavy. I missed both my parents so much sometimes it felt like they just died.

"You okay?"

I nodded. "Fine." I stood from the step I was sitting on. "What are you two doing the rest of the day?"

"Probably head over to the pool. Jeremiah's been loving his swim lessons this summer. He's less afraid of the water. It's so dope watching him get excited about swimming underwater and all his new tricks."

"Aww, my little sport. I can't believe how big he's getting."

"They grow up fast," Sean sighed. "A'ight, we're about to get outta here before it gets too late. Thanks for lunch, lil sis." Sean pulled me in for a hug and kiss on the cheek.

"Anytime. Can't have my sport starving."

Sean frowned at me, his eyebrows nearly meeting as his forehead creased. "That's cold. I feed my son."

"I'm just messing with you." I slapped him on the arm.

"Jeremiah, come give your aunt a hug and say thank you for making us lunch."

"We're leaving, Daddy?"

"Yes."

"Going to the pool?" His brown eyes sparkled with hope. I was reminded of the community center our parents used to take Sean and I to during the summers for swim lessons.

"I told you we were."

"Yesss! Aunt Angie, you wanna come?"

"Thanks, sport, but I can't hang out today. Maybe next time, okay?"

He came over and wrapped his arms around my hips, pressing his head against my belly. "'Kay. Thank you for the 'pisghetti and cake!"

I lowered my head, pressing a kiss to the top of his low cut hair. "Anytime."

I waited, watching as Jeremiah told his little friend good-bye, and for my brother to load him and the food they took into the car before I waved and stepped back inside. For some reason, my mood soured after talking about my parents. I had wonderful friends, but I didn't feel like unloading on any of them to express how empty I felt without my parents. My whole life my parents were my world. Hell, even Sean had commented on how close I was a few times, telling my mom and dad that they needed to cut the chord. But I wasn't babied by my parents. We just were close. I moved back in with them right after college, and never felt the need to live on my own. They left me the house in their will since, at that time, Sean had purchased his own home for his then-fiancee and Jeremiah's mother.

I spent the rest of the afternoon trying to shake off my mood, not wanting to carry it with me throughout the rest of the day. I was looking forward to spending time with Eric that evening, and I did my best to remember that. No one wants a pouting, sad date. I didn't have much to clean up after lunch since Sean insisted he and Jeremiah do the cleaning since I cooked. I put away the now dry pots and pans and then proceeded to pack up the sandwiches, fruit, and chips I bought to surprise Eric on our date. I liked the movie in the park idea and thought instead of going out for dinner afterward, we could just eat it while we enjoyed the show. That was yet another thing I loved about my city. There was always something to do, especially during the summer months. I would have to fix my sour mood before six o'clock when Eric showed up.

Chapter Eight

Eric

As soon as she opened the door, I could tell something was weighing on Angela. She greeted me as warmly as she had any other time, but the shine in those tawny eyes was dimmer than usual.

She smiled. "Hi."

"Hello," I returned, leaning down to press a kiss on her lips.

"I thought instead of finding something to eat before or after the movie we could have dinner picnic-style in the park." She held up a white wicker picnic basket.

"I should've known you'd be making something. I didn't want you to go through the trouble."

"No trouble at all. We both need to eat right?"

"Right. Let me." I took the basket from her arms so she could lock up.

"It's a perfect night for a movie in the park. It's cooled off since this afternoon," she stated as I started the ignition.

I placed the basket in the backseat so we had enough room as I drove.

"How was your day?"

I took my eyes off the road for a second to see her flash me a smile that didn't quite reach her eyes. Instinctively, I grabbed her hand for comfort, bringing it to my lips and then placing it on my thigh as I drove.

"It was good. My brother and nephew came over. I made his favorite dish...'pisghetti."

"'Pisghetti?"

She laughed lightly. "Yeah, Jeremiah still has a little trouble pronouncing spaghetti. Anyway, I made them lunch, lemon pound cake included, and they took the leftovers home. I hate leftovers. But don't worry, I made us strawberry cheesecake tarts for our dessert. Two desserts in one day is going to have me tripling up on my spin classes this week." She lightly patted her flat stomach.

"I have a few other ideas in mind to help you work those calories off."

She giggled.

She talked more about her nephew, Jeremiah, and her brother. It was apparent how much she loved them.

It took us about twenty minutes to get to the park and find parking, but I paused just as I was about to turn off my car. Instead, I turned to her, again noticing the sadness in her eyes.

"You want to tell me what's wrong?"

She appeared shocked. "Nothing's wrong. Why, did I—"

"You didn't do anything. I get the sense you're a little off tonight."

"I'm sorry, I—"

"You don't owe me an apology. But I don't like seeing the sadness in your eyes."

She blew out a deep breath, turning toward the windshield. "It's my parents."

"Your parents?"

"Yeah, seeing Sean with Jeremiah always gets to me. It reminds me of how my dad and Sean were together, and how much my parents loved Jeremiah. They were so excited when they found out they were going to be grandparents. I remember my mom mentioning how much she couldn't wait until I had kids. She planned to spoil them rotten," she chuckled.

When she paused, I covered her hand, which still rested on my lap.

"It's ridiculous... they died almost two years ago. I should be over it by now."

I snorted. "There is no expiration date on grieving for the people you loved. It's okay to be sad."

She gave me a half smile through watery eyes. "And now I've ruined our date."

"Nothing's ruined. We're still together." I passed her a tissue from the box I kept in the glove compartment. She dabbed at her eyes with the tissue in her free hand. I still held onto her left hand in my lap.

"How about we take a drive?" I suggested.

"What about the movie?"

"There'll be other movies."

"I'd like that." Her voice was low, filled with a sweetness that pulled at my heartstrings.

"Why do you have this?" she questioned, pointing to the scanner I'd taken out of my glove compartment.

We drove around for the better part of an hour. I asked her about her parents, and she divulged all about them. If the light in Angela's eyes when she talked about them was any indication, they seemed like great people. Her sadness transformed to happiness as she talked about the different family vacations they went on. Her voice growing shakier when she talked of the last trip they took to the Bahamas. The one that'd killed them.

"It does bring me comfort knowing they died together. I don't know if either one of them would've survived without the other," she'd said when speaking of their death.

"It's a police scanner," I answered her question, pulling it from her hand. We were parked at a spot that was about ten miles outside the city. It overlooked the surrounding suburbs and part of Williamsport.

"I know what it is. I just want to know why you have it?"

Smirking, I leaned my head against the back of my seat. "I'm sure your brother and father had one."

She laughed. "They did and do. I know most firefighters carry them. Why?"

I gave a one-shoulder shrug. "To keep up with what's happening."

"Even when you're not at work?"

"Especially when I'm not at work. I don't need it then, I have my walkie-talkie at work. I often turn my scanner on when I'm driving in to hear what's going on or get updates on what happened while I was out."

"You guys are addicted." She shook her head, smiling. I was grateful her mood seemed to lighten.

"You hungry?" she asked.

I almost forgot about the food.

"Sure."

"I made turkey club since I know you liked the last one. This time I used an avocado sauce instead of mayo. Or I made a roast beef and cheddar melt. Which one would you like?"

"Roast beef."

She reached back and grabbed the picnic basket, handing me the sandwich and pulling out paper cups and a bottle of champagne.

"You came prepared."

"Always." She winked. "Let's listen." Her head jutted toward the scanner.

"Really?"

"Yeah, I wanna hear what goes on between you guys."

I laughed. "We save the dirty talk for the station. Not over the scanner." I flipped the switch, turning it on. After a few moments of static, we heard voices come through.

"Let's get in the backseat to get more comfortable."

I waited for her to climb in the back, before going after her. I positioned myself to one side, and Angela slid in between my splayed legs, making herself comfortable. She fit like a glove. We ate our sandwiches and fruit, listening to the scanner.

"What's a 10-88 mean?" she asked between bites.

"It's a code for a type of fire. A 10-88 is a relatively small fire. Probably only a one alarm."

That went on for the next two hours, us listening to the scanner and her asking questions about what this code or that code meant. I didn't mind the questions; I genuinely appreciated her interest. Now and then she would intersperse her questions with a memory of her father talking about a run he went on with her mother late at night.

"He rarely talked about the big fires with us, though."

"Most of us don't." That slipped out of my mouth before I had a chance to think better of it. That was unusual for me since I always measured my words before speaking.

"Why is that?" Sitting up, she stared at me expectantly.

"We just don't want to bring our work home. Most people try to separate work from their personal life. No different with us." That wasn't the complete truth. A bad day for someone who worked a nine to five could mean being yelled at by their boss. A bad day for a firefighter could mean a person dying in your arms due to burns or smoke inhalation. Every man wanted to keep his personal life separate from that. The home was our respite from the sometimes dark world of our careers. No matter how much we loved the job, everyone needed a respite.

She continued to look at me as if the answer hadn't satisfied her, but she didn't push the issue.

"I worry about you," she said, voice low. "I used to just worry about Sean, but now I worry for your safety, too." She grabbed my hand, wrapping it around her waist, tightly.

"No need to worry about me." I tried to sound lighthearted about it.

"Are you kidding me? You run into fires for a living. How can I *not* worry?"

Bending down to place a kiss on the top of her head, I ran my thumb along her forehead to smooth out the worry lines.

"Keep scrunching your forehead like that, and you'll get early wrinkles."

"Don't joke about this, Eric." She sat up and fully turned to me.

I sighed, sitting up and cupping both sides of her face in my hands. "Nothing's going to happen to me."

"How can you be so sure?"

"I work for Rescue Four. We protect one another. We're the guys everyone else sends in when a man is trapped inside. You know what that means?"

She shook her head.

"It means that I work with the best of the best. If I'm in trouble, I know I've got the department's finest coming in after me. I have my own personal insurance policy as a Rescue Four guy. All right?"

Her gaze pinned me, soaking in my words and picking them apart. Finally, she nodded. I pulled her into me, fusing our mouths together. She sighed into my mouth. I tasted the sweetness of the fruit she ate after her sandwich. It mixed with her sweet flavor, and the more I tasted, the more I wanted. She made me greedier than I've ever felt. I pulled her onto me, so she straddled my lap. Even through my jeans, I felt the heat from her center. My groin tightened as my need for her grew. She moaned into my mouth at the same time as her hips started rocking into mine. Feeling the bulge in my pants, she began rubbing herself against it. I moved my hands from her face to her hips, pulling her onto me even more. I kissed a trail down her neck, sucking on the soft flesh there and licking it. She let out a loud moan and her body began to tremble. She was about to orgasm. I needed to see the expression on her face when she came. I pulled back.

"Eric," she whispered and I swear I almost came in my jeans.

"Let me see you come, Angel," I encouraged.

And she did. Head thrown back, eyes closed tightly, she came. And it was the most beautiful sight I've ever seen.

****

Angela

I panted and huffed as I stood up, hunched over the handlebars, legs pumping, doing my best to keep up with Cynthia's instructions. It was Wednesday morning, and I decided to take Cynthia's spin class this week. I meant what I said about needing to up my exercise routine after all the sweets I had eaten over the weekend. Plus, with extra energy to burn off, I needed the outlet. Eric and I were going out later that evening, and he was taking me to his parents' home for dinner. It was his father's birthday, and they were having a family dinner to celebrate. To say I was nervous would be an understatement.

"That's it, Angela! Show 'em how it's done!" Cynthia yelled out, causing a few of the other spinners to laugh and cheer.

I laughed and pumped harder, turning up the resistance on the bike when she instructed us to. I was in my zone, heart-racing, feeling good. A good sweat always had a way of making me feel as if I could conquer the day. And that feeling was just what I needed to tackle this date head-on. By the end of class, I was feeling spent in that really great way. Each of my muscles were singing to me, and I wanted nothing more than to stretch them out and then head home for a small lunch and a bath to calm my nerves and look my best for my guy.

"I'm probably overreacting," I mumbled to myself as I sat on one of the gym mats in the corner to stretch. In all likelihood, I was overreacting. Families often loved me. The boyfriends I've had over the years all brought me home to meet their parents, and they fell in love. Of course, the relationships never worked out in the end, but it wasn't due to family strife. I was a natural at making people warm up to me. I could do that again, especially when it came to someone who's become so near and dear to my heart in such a short period of time.

I smiled to myself, just thinking about Eric, as I moved into a downward dog position. I groaned as my heels strained to make contact with the floor, stretching my calf muscles.

"It'll be fine," I stated, continuing to talk to myself. By the time I was finished with my stretches, I felt much better about the night ahead.

"Long time no see."

Turning from the stack of mats, I found Marshall standing behind me. A surge of guilt hit me in the gut. I ignored his last two calls, and this was the first time we've seen each other since that night at the fair.

"Marshall. Hey. How are you?"

"I'm well. I see you're doing okay."

I nodded. "You know, just enjoying what's left of summer."

"Same here. Trying to, at least. Did you receive my messages?"

I did my best not to avoid eye contact, though my guilt nearly forced me to hang my head in shame. "I did. I've just been busy."

"With that guy you were out with?"

"Yes." No sense in lying about the obvious.

"You're seeing him now?"

"We're getting to know one another." That sounded way too casual for what was going on between Eric and I. No, we haven't defined our relationship as boyfriend-girlfriend just yet. It's been close to a month since we started dating, but it felt like we were a lot further than that in the "getting to know one another" stage. That was even funnier, seeing as how Marshall and I dated and talked for nearly the same amount of time, and yet, the connection I had with him was nowhere near what Eric and I had.

"I thought you and I were getting to know one another."

"Right. We were. Are. Were."

He frowned at my confused statements.

"Marshall, you're a great guy. It's just that...well, the feelings and chemistry aren't there between us."

"There's more to a relationship than chemistry."

"I know that," I retorted, feeling defensive all of a sudden.

"And I know I'm not some macho six-foot firefighter who women swoon over, but I won't dog you out like—"

"Dog me out? Wait, how do you even know what Eric does for a living?" I haven't spoken to Marshall since the night he saw us together on our first date.

"I came into the bar one night. I saw you and him at one of the booths. A couple of the other firefighters were there talking about their fellow firefighter dating the owner."

I blinked, feeling somewhat caught. "I didn't see you that night."

"I know. I left after I saw that kiss between you two. Looked like a lot more than just getting to know one another."

I tilted my head back, angling a sideways look at Marshall. I didn't like the accusation I heard in his voice at all.

"I never would've thought you'd fall for one of them. You know how they run through women. I thought you were smarter than that."

"Whoa!" I was taken aback by the harshness of his tone and insulted. "I could've sworn you just called me stupid. But I'm sure that's not the case because I know *you're* smarter than that."

"I didn't call you stupid. I just—"

"Insinuated it."

"I just meant that I thought what we were building was something real. And you traded it in for a roll in bed with a firefighter. For what? A fun story to tell your girlfriends?"

I could feel my anger rising, my heartbeat quickening, and my hands balled into fists at my side. How dare he insult what Eric and I have? Marshall knew nothing of went on between us, nor was it any of his business!

"Marshall, I'm going to excuse everything you've just said and intimated about my character. My intent was never to hurt your feelings. You and I were just in the 'getting to know one another' phase, and now that is over. This *will* be our last conversation. You have a nice life." With that, I sidestepped Marshall and headed to the women's locker room to gather my belongings, not bothering to give him a second thought. I was not about to ponder for a second longer on his words. I knew all too well about the reputations firefighters held of being players and breaking hearts left and right. I also knew Eric wasn't above any of that, as well. The man looked good, and he knew it, but I could feel right down to my toes that what was happening between us was deeper than a woman going all heart-eyes emoji over a good looking firefighter, and him playing me. There was something real between Eric and me, and I had every intention of finding out what it was, even if it meant the possibility of getting my heart broken in the long run.

Chapter Nine

Eric

"Hey, Captain, you wanted to see me?" I knocked on the open the door to alert him of my being there.

The captain's head popped up from the files on his desk. He didn't exactly smile, but his lips turned upward into a grimace that I'm pretty sure was supposed to come off as a smile.

"Yeah, Kim. Come in." Captain referred to all of the men in the station by our last names. Considering it's only been a few weeks since he signed on as our captain, we all were still feeling him out, as he was us.

"Shut the door," he ordered.

I did as told and moved to sit in the hard metal chair across from his desk, which reminded me of the ones teacher's used in the classroom. His desk was covered in files and stacks of papers.

"You hear they think that apartment fire from the other week was set intentionally?"

I wrinkled my forehead. "Not an electrical fire?"

He shook his head. "No, but that's what the department is letting the media run with for now. If it was arson, they want the suspect to think he got away with it."

"Don knows?"

"He's been working with the police. Helping the investigation."

I nodded. Don might be audacious and loud at times, but he wouldn't broadcast this type of news. He was one of the best fire investigators in the department. More than a decade ago, the city decided to have an investigator at every station. Don has been Rescue Four's for the last few years.

"He's got it under control. But that's not what I wanted to talk to you about. I know the guys are still feeling me out..." He paused.

Sitting back in my chair, I folded my arms across my chest. I hoped like hell he wasn't about to ask me something stupid like trying to help him get in good with the rest of the guys. That'd severely decrease the respect I had for him. He had more than twenty-years in this department. He should know how the hell the rules are played. You wanted respect among the guys, you earned it. No two ways around it. The number of bars you wore on your officer's suit didn't earn respect. Your battle scars did.

"But, I wanted to ask if you've considered taking the lieutenant's exam?"

"The exam?"

"Yeah, I see you haven't registered. Rescue Four needs lieutenants. The exam's in three months. Gives you plenty of time to study. I'm sure the test will be a breeze for you."

"I've been thinking about it."

"I suggest you do more than think about it." He stood.

"Copy that." I stood as well.

When Captain reached out his hand across his desk, I reached over to shake it. He held my hand firmly.

"The men around here respect you, Kim. They already see you as an unofficial lieutenant. Certain guys in this department have that look. You can tell early on they were meant to move up the ranks. You're one of 'em. You're going to make captain someday, Kim. Hell, maybe even chief. It's time you accepted that as your fate." He let go of my hand.

I took a step back, replaying his words, and the assuredness in his voice. *You're going to make captain someday.* I thought about the possibilities.

Captain Kim.

Chief Kim.

I liked the sound of those titles.

****

I pressed my thumb against the doorbell and heard it sound off in the house. It was just after six o'clock, and I've been looking forward to this time all day. I heard the click-clack of heels making their way across the hardwood floor to the door. Seconds later, my lips parted into a smile I couldn't contain. She wore a loose-fitting sleeveless floral dress that went all the way to the floor but had a slit that showcased her shapely legs. On her feet were a pair of coral, strappy heels that matched the color of the flowers on her dress. Her makeup was done lightly with a glossy lip.

"Goddamn," I said just above a whisper, right before swooping her in my arms to feel her lips. I ran my tongue along the seam of her lips, and as soon as they parted, I dove in, reveling in the taste of her. Her hand began stroking my chest, and I felt my groin tighten with need. Reluctantly, I pulled back and grinned at the dazed look in Angela's eyes.

"Thanks for getting me all hot and bothered before meeting your parents," she mumbled.

"Your fault for answering the door looking like my wet dream." I tipped her chin and kissed her again, unable to stop myself.

"Come in. I just need to grab a couple of things." She stepped aside to make room for me to enter.

"You probably should freshen up your lip gloss," I told her.

She gave me a mock glare before heading toward the hallway. I stopped myself from following her. It was taking all the strength in me to not rush her into bed, but her time was running out.

"What's that look for?" she asked, finally emerging from the kitchen.

"Nothing. What's that?"

She held a covered platter in her hand.

"These," she held it up higher, "are more of the strawberry cheesecake tarts you loved from the other night. You said your dad passed on his love of cheesecake to you, so I thought I'd make them for his birthday. I also made some with raspberries and other assorted fruit. And don't tell me I didn't need to make anything. I'm not about to show up to your parents' home empty-handed."

I held my hands up. "I'm not saying anything."

"Good."

"Here, let me hold those for you."

She eyed me. "And don't you try to sneak any."

I gave her an innocent look.

"Don't even," she reiterated. She grabbed her purse from the couch and her keys, which were hanging in their usual spot on the wall, and minutes later, I held my car door open for her. She insisted on holding the platter of tarts in her lap to keep them from sliding around the backseat for the duration of the thirty minutes it would take to get to my parents' house.

"Tell me about what your father does again?" she asked as we drove.

I glanced over at her. "He's the Chief Financial Officer at Townsend Industries. Meaning, he's the top finance guy at the company. All the finances run through him."

"That sounds like a huge responsibility."

"It is."

"And you worked for Townsend for a while after college, right?"

"Yup."

"Was he your boss?"

"No, not directly. He was my boss' boss at the time."

"I bet he liked working with his son. My dad was so proud of Sean when he completed the fire academy."

I nodded. "My dad was proud."

"Do you ever miss it? Working in an office, I mean."

I stopped at a red light and turned to her. "Never. Every day I go to work at the station, I pause and read the top of the marquee that tells everyone who we are, and I just know this is what I was meant to do."

"Even on the hard days?"

"*Especially* on the hard days." Reaching up, I moved a curl of her hair that fell over her eyes. We stared at one another, reading each other without words. A horn sounded behind us, alerting me that the light had turned green. I had half a mind to tell the person behind us to fuck off, but instead, I moved my foot from the brake to the gas and pulled off. We talked about my parents the remainder of the ride. I could sense Angela's nervousness, but she was putting up a good front. I didn't feel nervous myself, which was sort of strange considering this was only the second woman I've ever brought home to meet my parents. I've had girlfriends in the past, a few of which were long-term, but most haven't been serious enough that I considered anything permanent.

"How come your parents decided to move outside of Williamsport?" Angela asked.

I chuckled. "It took my dad years to convince my mom to leave the city."

"What finally did it?"

"One night my mom was leaving work, around seven-thirty, but it was winter, so it was dark out. She was mugged. Right outside of the building where her office is."

Angela gasped. "No!"

"Yup." I nodded, my hands tightening around the steering wheel. "They took her wallet, phone, and the tablet she had on her."

"Was she hurt?"

I shook my head slightly. "No, but she was shaken up."

"I bet she was."

"Yeah. After that, my father insisted they move and that she only work during the daylight hours. Since she's tenured, she's able to change up her schedule and reduce her teaching time."

"That's scary. Did the police ever find out who did it?"

"Yeah, the dumbass used her phone to take selfies. He uploaded to her cloud, and the police used the images to track him down. He was a young sixteen-year-old kid. He's on his second stint in juvie last I heard."

"At least he's off the streets."

"At least. We're here," I stated as we pulled up to my parent's house. My mother and father's vehicles were parked in their driveway, so I parked at the curb in front of their house.

"This seems like a nice neighborhood," Angela stated as she exited the car, looking around.

"Too quiet," I grunted, placing my hand on the small of her back.

"You would say that," she laughed.

"Seriously, no sirens within a five-block radius of this place. How on Earth is a guy supposed to sleep in all that quiet?"

She covered her mouth, laughing while holding the platter of tarts in her other hand. "You're going to make me drop these. That would not be a good way to start this evening."

I shrugged. "I'm just saying."

We reached the door, and I knocked. I had keys to my parents' home, but they were for use only in cases of an emergency. Out of the corner of my eyes, I saw Angela pat down her hair, and smooth down the edges of her dress.

"You look fine," I leaned down and said in her ear. I nipped her earlobe for good measure, causing her to giggle. At that same moment, my mother opened the door. Angela gasped. I looked down at my petite mother's stern face.

"Hey, Ma," I greeted.

I watched as her sepia eyes carefully assessed Angela from head to toe, pausing when they looked over Angela's hair. Her face didn't soften until she turned her attention to me. The edges of her eyes crinkled, revealing the age lines she's developed over time. Her dark hair was cut into a short style a few inches above her shoulders but framed her face. Some greying strands were apparent. I bent down, pulling my mother into a warm hug.

"Eric," she said, cupping my face with her hands.

"Ma, I want you to meet Angela." I stepped back, wrapping my arm around Angela's waist, pulling her to me.

"Hi, Mrs. Kim, it's a pleasure to meet you. Eric has told me so much about you. Thank you for having me over. I brought a little something for dessert," Angela started.

"Thank you," my mother responded rather curtly, before looking back to me. "Come in. It's been so long since you've been over to the house." She wrapped her arms around my free arm.

"Ma, I was here a couple of weeks ago."

"Much too long. A lot can happen in a couple of weeks. Anyway ..." she waved her hand around dismissively, "your grandmother is here. She's in the living room with your father. Go in and say hello. Dinner's almost ready. Oh, let me take those," she said to Angela, retrieving the platter of tarts.

I escorted Angela toward the living room where I first saw my father seated watching a baseball game.

"Happy birthday, Dad." I went to him, and we embraced. "Dad, this is Angela," I introduced.

"Nice to meet you. Happy birthday, Mr. Kim."

"Thank you. A pleasure to meet you as well." His reaction was different than the somewhat cold reception my mother had given Angela just moments before. He and I stood shoulder to shoulder when he turned, grinning at me. "Your mother was starting to think you wouldn't come."

I frowned. "Why would she think that? We're not even that late." I checked the watch on my wrist. It was a little after six-thirty.

"You know how your mother is." He waved his hand. "Say hello to your halmoni."

I turned. "Halmoni," I greeted my grandmother in Korean, bending down to hug her and kiss on the cheek in the comfortable chair she sat in. "Grandma, I want you to meet Angela."

"Hello, it's a pleasure to meet you."

My eighty-five-year-old grandmother may've looked frail, but her eyes held a keenness. She eyed Angela much the same way my mother had at the door. Thankfully, my grandmother's gaze softened, and she gave Angela a small smile.

"Thank you." My grandmother didn't like to speak much in English, so she kept her introductions short.

Just then the doorbell rang. I peered over at my father. "Who's that?"

He gave me a puzzled look, shrugging. "I have no idea," he stated but began moving toward the doorway to answer.

"Oh, your father got the door?" my mother entered the living room, questioning.

I nodded. "He said you weren't expe—"

"Look who decided to join us," my father's voice rang out, surprise in his tone.

I pivoted to see who stopped by and my eyes widened and then narrowed as I turned to my mother, who was already walking over to the new guest. On instinct my arm went around Angela's waist, pulling her into me.

"Son, don't be rude, say hello," my mother urged me.

"Hey." I nodded toward the woman standing by my father.

"Eric, I didn't know you were here," Lisa stated.

"It's my father's birthday," I retorted dryly. Lisa is the one ex of mine who my parents met. We grew up together and dated for a few years after college. Once I decided to make the career change to a firefighter, she—like my parents—was extremely disappointed, and practically begged me to reconsider. Not too long after, we parted ways. Another thing my mother has yet to get over.

"Well, I didn't know if you'd be working or something." Lisa's dark eyes went to Angela, assessing her. "Aren't you going to introduce us?"

"No."

"Eric," Angela admonished, her hand pressed against my abdomen.

"Angela, this is Lisa. Lisa, Angela," I begrudgingly introduced.

"Nice to meet you." Angela stuck out her hand.

Lisa hesitated, her gaze flickering toward my mother before she gave a limp handshake to Angela. It was then I knew my mother was conspiring with Lisa.

"Dinner's ready!" my mom called out. "Eric, help your grandmother to the kitchen," she ordered.

"I can help," Angela jumped in.

"No. Eric's got a handle on it," my mother cut in, rather abruptly.

I looked at her, tilting my head, silently asking what that was all about.

"You know how your grandmother doesn't take to new people too well," she explained before turning and heading back to the kitchen area. "Lisa, follow me please."

Watching the two women traipse down the hallway, I knew I wasn't going to enjoy the rest of the evening.

I helped my grandmother out of her chair and held her by one arm as she gripped her wooden cane in the other. We slowly made our way down the hall into the dining space. My father, like always, sat at the head of the long table. Moments later, my mother and Lisa emerged from the kitchen, placing plates and dishes at the center of the table. When finished, my mother sat at the opposite end waiting for everyone to sit. After I helped my grandmother to her seat, I went to hold the chair out for Angela.

"Thank you." She smiled up at me.

"Eric, be a gentleman and do the same for Lisa," my mother ordered.

I stood erect, gaping at my mother as if she'd fallen ill. "Lisa isn't my date."

My mother's mouth widened, and she was about to say something when Lisa finally spoke up.

"It's all right, Mrs. Kim." She went around the table and sat directly across from me, to my grandmother's left.

When I felt Angela's hand stroking my arm comfortingly, I had the biggest urge to lean in and kiss her. Just as I started to bend down, I heard my name called.

"Eric, that's a little inappropriate for the table, don't you think?"

The sharpness of my mother's voice had me looking at her sideways. I opened my mouth, but Angela beat me to it.

"I'm sorry, Mrs. Kim."

I glanced down at Angela.

"We have nothing to be sorry for," I directed my comment to my mother.

She pursed her lips but didn't respond. My gaze slowly left her and I pulled my chair out and sat.

"Everything looks and smells great, sweetie," my father commented.

"You did a wonderful job, Mrs. Kim," Lisa interjected, not letting anyone forget her presence. "Eric, is pork bulgogi still one of your favorites?" she asked, flipping her long, dark hair over her shoulder.

"Yeah," I replied, then turned my attention back to the table.

My father was right; the food looked delicious. My mother often made traditional Korean dishes for my father's birthday dinners, and this year for his fifty-ninth was no different. In the middle of the table sat dishes filled with mixed seafood stew, pork bulgogi, kimchi, and more.

"I hope you're not one of those women who doesn't eat pork. Or insists on eating a little because you're watching your figure."

"Ma!" I called, not liking the tone of her voice.

"It's okay." Angela wrapped her hand around mine under the table. "No, Mrs. Kim, I do eat pork, and everything looks so good, I wouldn't dream of insulting the chef by not eating."

Angela gave her a warm smile, one that was only minimally returned by my mother.

"Thank God for small miracles," Lisa mumbled but not low enough, looking toward my mother.

"What did you j—"

My response to her was stopped by a squeeze at my thigh from Angela's hand. My grandmother suddenly spoke up and began telling my father a happy birthday and how proud she was of him. She spoke in Korean, and I translated for Angela so she wouldn't feel left out. I didn't want her being the only one at the table who didn't know what was being said since Lisa also spoke Korean. My grandmother talked about how my father had become the embodiment of the dream she and my grandfather had when they came over from Korea all those years ago. My grandfather wanted to come to the U.S. for school, bringing his young bride with him. They had my father a few years after arriving in the U.S. They made a way for themselves, and my father lived up to all their hopes and dreams. It was the same speech my grandmother gave every year on my father's birthday, but it never failed to make him just a tad bit emotional.

When my grandmother finished, my father reached across the table, patting her hand and telling her in Korean how much he loved her.

"And thank you to my lovely wife for this beautiful dinner. And my son and his new, friend, Angela, for coming to celebrate with us. And you Lisa," he added.

We began spooning food onto our plates and in bowls. As usual, the food was great. Mom had made the kimchi with just a slight bit of spice to it. My father wasn't a fan of spicy food, despite how common it was in many Korean dishes. My father discussed the happenings at his job, often looking pointedly at me. He mentioned that he was thinking of retiring in the next few years. I knew he wished I still worked with him, but that was one birthday present I couldn't give him. For her part, Lisa kept interjecting with stories from our childhood, trying to jog some emotion from me, I guessed. It served to annoy the hell out of me more than anything. Lisa and I grew up in the same Korean community in Williamsport, but we weren't close as children, and in reality only dated because it was something both our parents wanted. We weren't compatible—I saw that as soon as I stopped living for my parents and started living for myself.

Toward the end of the meal, my mother stood. "I hope you all left room for dessert."

"I can help bring it out, Mrs. Kim," Angela began, placing her cloth napkin on the table, readying herself to stand.

"No, Lisa will help," my mother tossed back, moving into the kitchen without a backward glance.

That was the last straw.

"You sit down," I pointed at Lisa. My voice held a hard edge, daring her to defy me. Lucky for her, she didn't. I patted Angela's hand and got up, pushing through the swinging door to follow my mother into the kitchen.

"Ma, what was all that about?"

"All what?" She had the nerve to look at me with a confused expression.

"Ma, you know what. Why are you so rude to Angela? Why is Lisa here?"

"I'm not being rude. I just told her I didn't need her assistance. And Lisa is a friend of the family."

"Who conveniently pops by after years of not seeing her?"

"She was back in town," my mother argued.

"I'm sure. Angela has been nothing but be respectful and polite since we arrived and you've given her the cold shoulder."

"I have not. I've just been preoccupied with getting your father's dinner prepared and out on the table."

"And the comment about her eating pork or watching her weight?"

She waved her hand in the air. "I was just making sure the girl ate. So many women today are afraid to eat meat and all that. They watch one documentary on Netflix and next thing you know they've sworn off all meat and dairy products. It's ridiculous." She turned, cutting pieces of the chocolate cake she always made for my father and putting them on plates.

"Ma, Netflix documentaries? What are you even talking about? Can you just tone it down a little with the attitude toward Angela? She's my guest." I was doing my best to be as respectful as possible.

She shrugged. "Fine."

"I'm going to bring out the cheesecake tarts as well," I stated. I moved to the counter where the platter was sitting and removed the lid, exposing the little mini tarts. It was apparent that Angela had gone through a lot of trouble making these. Knowing that pissed me off even more at my mother's behavior. I heard the kitchen door open and then swing shut behind me. I sorted the desserts out on the platter and then carried them to the table.

"Ohh, look at these." My father's eyes grew bigger in excitement, staring at the cheesecake. "Are those strawberry cheesecake tarts?"

"With graham cracker crust," Angela answered, smiling proudly.

"I must try one of them. I don't know if my son has told you, but I have a thing for chocolate cake and cheesecake."

"He may have mentioned something about it." She winked at me.

"Yep, I—"

"We need to light the candles before it gets too late. Don't want it sitting out too long. That's how cake dries out," my mother began, shoving my father's plate with his slice of cake on it practically in his lap.

My father gave Angela and I a contrite look before smiling at my mother as she lit the three candles she'd placed in the center of the cake.

"Time to make a wish!" Angela clapped, causing my father to laugh.

"We don't make wishes in this house. We work for what we want." My mother stared pointedly at Angela. Between my mother's glare and Lisa's stupid giggle in the background, I'd had it.

"That's it. Ma, in the kitchen!" I stood and moved to the kitchen without a backward glance. "What is your problem?" I was doing my best to rein in my temper.

"I am not the one with a problem!" my mother protested. "Why did you let that girl come here with cheesecake of all things? Did you bother to tell her your father is lactose intolerant?"

I stared at my mother as if she had three heads. She was ordinarily one of the most rational people I've ever met. Except now nothing she was saying was making a bit of sense.

"No, I didn't think it would be appropriate to discuss my father's digestion issues," I stated flatly. "What is this *really* about? The truth."

"She's not right for you!" my mother burst out, hands waving in the air.

My head shot back at how adamantly she stated this. "How would you even know that? You've barely spoken to her the entire time we've been here."

"I just know. A mother knows these things. I can't believe the first woman you bring home in years is someone like *her*. Did she even go to college?"

I squinted at my mother, not believing what she was insinuating. "Ma, what do you mean *someone like her?*"

"I just meant—"

"She's black."

"No! Of course not," she insisted. "I mean, I don't know anything about this girl's background. Who knows where or *if* she went to college? What does she even do for a living? She has purple hair for goodness sake!"

I tightened my jaw, still not liking the distasteful tone my mother was taking on or the way in which she spoke about Angela.

"You need a good, ambitious woman like Lisa in your corner. She just got promoted to manager of her bank branch."

I sucked my teeth. "Are you even listening to me? Do you even hear yourself?"

"I am ... I just am worried about you. Ever since you quit your job at Townsend to become a firefighter—"

I erupted at the way she said, firefighter as if it was gum on the bottom of her shoe. "Are you fu—" I paused, remembering this was still my mother. "Are you serious? So this is about my career? You know what? I'm not fucking doing this." I stormed out of the kitchen, violently pushing the door open.

"Dad, thank you for inviting us. I wanted to give this to you once we had cake, but that's not happening. Here you go." I pulled the envelope with the card inside from my back pocket. Inside were two tickets to the opera. Both my parents loved the opera.

"Angela, we're leaving."

"Wait, what?"

"Why?"

"Eric."

I heard my father, Angela, and Lisa's voices. Ignoring their questions. I rounded the table to kiss my grandmother and tell her in Korean that we were leaving. I came back to the table to help Angela up, not addressing the funny look she was giving me, quickly escorting us out of my parents' home. So much for a great first meeting.

Chapter Ten

Angela

Well, that was a bust.

I felt the tension coming from Eric's mom as soon as she opened the door. However, I did my best not to let it get to me. I knew this was a big deal for Eric, bringing a woman home to meet his family. I thought it might be a little awkward, but I figured I'd be able to get his family to warm up to me. Obviously, that didn't happen, and now I was feeling bummed. Not only bummed but totally out of sorts. I was starting to fall for this man, but not being liked by his mother was a problem for me. I couldn't imagine being with someone who my parents didn't accept.

I sighed, lifting my gaze to realize we were just now turning onto my street. The entire car ride had been silent. I got the impression Eric was attempting to calm himself down or trying to figure out a way to let me down easy.

"Thank you for dinner. I can walk myself to the door," I stated, opening the car door. My movement was stopped by a large hand on my knee. I turned to glance back at Eric who wore a quizzical expression.

"Since when have I ever let you walk yourself to the door? Or open your own door for that matter?" His eyes drifted to my hand on the door. I let my hand fall from the handle.

"Don't move." He got out and rounded the car to open my door, just like he always did.

I'm going to miss this, I lamented as we crossed the street to my home. I left the porch light on to make it easier to see. Before I could put my key in the lock, Eric reached out, pulling my arm to turn me toward him.

"I'm sorry about my mother. I don't know what got into her."

I forced a smile. "It's all right. Hey, I'll see you around, okay?" I quickly turned to insert the key, but before I could turn the knob, I was spun around.

"See me around? I'm a pretty smart guy, so I know a brush off when I hear one. What the hell is that about?"

I shifted my gaze to a point over his shoulder, not liking the feeling rising in the pit of my stomach at the thought of not seeing him anymore.

"I was trying to give you an easy out," I admitted.

"An easy out?"

"Yes. Since things didn't go so well with your parents—"

"My mother, you mean."

I nodded. "Okay, with your mother, I figured that would be the end for us."

"Why the hell would you think that?"

"Well, you were kind of quiet on the ride over here, so I assumed you were trying to figure out a way to let me down easy. I don't want to cause any strife between you and your parents."

"And you won't. My mother's issue is her issue."

Blowing out a deep breath, I folded my arms across my chest. "Eric, family is important. I know how important it is and I don't want to be the reason you and your mother don't get along."

My eyes fluttered shut when he took a step forward, cupping the left side of my face with his hand. In spite of my will to remain firm, I leaned my head into his hand, parting my lips slightly when his brushed against mine. I felt bereft when, instead of deepening the kiss, he pulled his head back.

"You want to know what I've learned in the last seven years?"

My eyelids parted to see his serious expression.

"Family isn't just blood. Family is who we make it. My parents are my family. The guys at my firehouse are my family. And you...you're going to be my family." He growled the last part, before his lips took possession of mine. His hand cupped the back of my head, as our tongues dueled. I unfolded my arms, reaching them up around Eric's neck. He pulled me in tighter by the waist. Feeling his hardness press against my lower abdomen, I gasped.

"Let's take this inside," he murmured against my lips.

I hesitated, my brain still foggy from his words and that kiss.

"Angel, don't think I mind giving your neighbors a show. Open the door or I can pin you to the door and take you right here for all to see."

Holy shit! I gasped at his words, moisture pooling in my panties. I peered up into his eyes to see they'd darkened, his perfect jaw rigid with tension.

I nodded, then somehow fumbled for my keys in my purse. Once inside, Eric took the liberty of flicking the light on, shutting the door, locking it, and pulled me to him. His lips pressed to mine, again and again. I was lost in the softness of his lips, the hardness of his body, and the pulse of electricity that occurred whenever we touched.

"Which way to your bedroom?" he asked his lips still on mine.

"Down the hall and to the left," I breathed.

He bent down, swooped me up in his arms, and strolled down the hallway. Kicking the door open, he walked over to my bed and placed me in the middle.

"Where's the light switch?"

When I pointed to the switch on the wall by the door, he went over and turned the light on, illuminating the entire room.

"I want to see all of you," he explained. He pulled the T-shirt over his head, and my mouth went completely dry. I struggled to swallow, as I let my eyes drift down over the hard muscles of his chest and the rippling of his six-pack abs as he slowly made his way toward me. I bit my lower lip when his fingers grazed against the inside of my ankle, removing first my right, then left shoe. His hand trailed up my leg along the sensitive skin of my inner-thigh, until it met the seam of my panties. I was never more thankful to have worn a dress in my life. I widened my legs. He leaned down, capturing my lips with his, and I wrapped my hands around the back of his head.

"Ahh," I gasped when he began rubbing his fingers against my clit through my panties.

"I need you." His voice was hoarse.

Moving to sit up on my knees so that I was eye level with him, I held his hand to my core and responded, "Then have me."

From there it was a frenzy, each of us working to undress the other. I felt his hand on my back, pulling down the sides of my dress. My own hands went straight to his belt buckle, fiddling with it, trying to get it undone. I was unable to look down to see what I was doing because I was caught up in yet another one of his kisses. Thankfully, the belt came undone, and I went for the button and zipper of his jeans. By then, he'd pushed my dress down around my waist. He then laid me down again, and stripped me entirely of the dress, leaving me in my strapless bra and black, lace panties. He moved quickly to remove his jeans, but not before pulling his wallet out and placing it on the white wicker nightstand next to my bed. He stepped his long, muscular legs out of his jeans, kicking them aside. Wearing only a pair of boxer briefs, he moved over me on the bed.

He dipped his head again, stealing another kiss. "I can't get enough of the taste of your lips."

"I know the feeling," I laughed, raising up to meet his mouth again. Soon after, he broke the kiss off, moving over my jaw, kissing his way down to my neck.

"Mmm," I moaned when he bit my earlobe.

Taking my hands in his, he lifted my arms over my head and held them there as he kissed, sucked, and nibbled his way down to my breasts. Once there, he encouraged me to sit up so he could undo the back strap of my bra. My breasts spilled out, nipples tingling and awaiting his hot mouth. Thank God, he did not disappoint. He covered one hard nipple and used his tongue to moisten it, before biting down with his teeth, lightly. He gave just enough pain to make it pleasurable. An electric zap flowed from my nipple down my belly until it reached my core. I threw my head back and moaned when he did the same thing to the other nipple. My legs widened, knees bending, allowing me to raise my hips until my core met with the hardness in between his legs.

"Eric," I panted and moaned at the same time.

"Shh." He left a trail of kisses down my belly, stopping to tongue my belly button. My hips shot up, and I pressed my head into the pillow as the feelings of need grew even more intensely. The lower muscles of my abdomen clenched. I inhaled and exhaled in rapid succession, wanting him to move faster, to put out the fire he was stoking.

"Isn't it your job to put out fires?" I whined.

"Are you feeling hot, Angel?" The rumble of his deep laughter had me growing even wetter.

He sat up in between my legs, placing his palm to my core; the only thing between his skin and mine was the thin layer of lace.

"You are," he answered his question.

Feeling impatient, I went to sit up, reaching for him, only to be stopped by his large hand. He pressed me back down against the bed with one hand and began removing my panties with the other.

"Let me show you how I put out fires," he said, lips hovering above my core.

"Ohhh!" I groaned when his tongue made contact with my throbbing clit. He used his tongue to make love to me with his mouth. My toes clenched, and my feet dug into my mattress. I've experienced oral sex before, but nothing like this. My pelvis thrust up to meet Eric's mouth. He said this was how he puts out fires, but I could feel my body temperature rising with each passing second. I struggled for air. His mouth on me could sustain me for a lifetime.

I reached down, placing my hand on the back of his head, holding him in place, out of fear he would move and this marvelous feeling would end too soon. I swear I heard a muffled chuckle, but I was too far gone to know what was going on.

"D-don't stop!" I ordered, clenching my thighs tightly around his head. The fear of cutting off his airway didn't even occur to me. A feeling that began deep in my pelvis washed over my entire body, and I began shaking, my orgasm consuming all of me. I did my best to surrender to the orgasm, still feeling Eric lapping up the juices that flowed from me. I turned my head into my pillow, letting out the biggest moan I can remember ever doing. When it ended, I fell back against my bed, breathing hard and more satiated than I'd ever felt.

I opened my eyes to see Eric's stern face looking down at me.

"You're fucking fascinating to look at when you come." His voice was thick, full of awe. He moved, pushing down the black boxer briefs he wore, and the longest cock I've ever seen sprang out.

"Holy shit!" My eyes were glued to the thick, veiny snake staring back at me, pointed in the exact direction it was intended for.

Wordlessly, Eric reached over me for his wallet. He removed a condom, then sat back, hand holding the condom, reaching for me.

"Put it on me, Angel," he ordered.

I sat stunned for a moment, then with trembling hands, I retrieved the gold wrapper from him. Ripping it open, I removed the slippery latex, pinching the tip, and pausing to stare up at Eric. His eyes were sharp, waiting for me to finish this task. His chest rose and fell in rapid succession, telling of his eagerness. I dared to let my eyes fall from his and stare, again, at the monster between his legs. Swallowing, I reached out, placing the tip of the condom on him and then looking up at him, as I rolled the condom down, sheathing him.

Gripping both of my wrists in his hands, he pushed me back to the bed, kissing me as we fell. He moved his hips, aligning his cock with my opening. He bit my lower lip at the same time he breached my entrance. The fire that had burned low, after being nearly extinguished from my first orgasm, began to grow in my belly again. It was a slow burn though, due to Eric's slow penetration. He moved centimeter by centimeter, allowing me time to adjust to his length and girth. But time wasn't what I wanted.

"Eric, hurry!" I demanded in between kisses.

"You feel too good to rush."

I moaned in anguish at his reluctance to fill me up. I broke my wrists free of his grip, wrapping my hands around him, my fingernails digging into the skin of his back, urging him. He grinned down at me but continued, slowly, until our pelvises touched, and he filled me up completely. I had no idea what I was thinking, rushing him. I felt filled to the hilt.

A cocky expression covered his face.

"See what you get for rushing," he dared to gloat. He didn't wait for me to respond before he pulled out of me and then thrust back in, this time much quicker than the first time. Every bit of oxygen I had in my body was pushed out of me. He did it again, and again I struggled for air.

"Mmmm," I finally managed to get out. The feeling of fullness gradually ebbed into a deep sense of bliss. The more he thrust into me, the top of his cock rubbed against my clitoris every time he entered me. I continued to dig my fingers into the skin of his back, needing something to hold on to.

"That feel good?" he asked before biting down on my earlobe.

"Unh-hunh," I answered, too tongue-tied to respond with actual words. Lifting my legs, I wrapped them around his waist. We grinded against one another's body, wringing out pleasure I've never encountered before. Our lips smacked against one another's and the bed squeaked as Eric jolted it when he penetrated me. We moved in unison, creating our own little dance, which felt as if it had been made just for us. I don't know how much longer it took, but I felt that same welling up deep in my pelvic area and knew my orgasm was imminent. Breaking my lips from his, I moved my head back and opened my mouth on a silent cry as my second orgasm flooded every cell in my body.

Moments later, I felt our bodies move, rolling over until I was on top and Eric laid beneath me. Though I was spent, I knew he didn't orgasm yet, and I wanted to make him feel at least half as good as he made me feel.

"Ride me," he said.

Doing as requested, I braced my arms—which still felt like jelly from my orgasm—against his chest and sat up. Eric reached up, squeezed my breasts in each one of his hands, and pinched my nipples. I gasped at the pain-turned-pleasure of his ministrations. I began moving my hips, lifting and falling on his thick cock, squeezing my pelvic muscles to tighten around him.

"Shit," he murmured at the same time his hands tightened around my breasts.

I reached my hands down, bracing his arms to give myself some leverage, and continued riding him like my life depended on it. At that moment, I was pretty sure it did. The smacking of flesh against flesh echoed around the room, along with a mix of moans. A short while later, I felt him swell inside of me, and I looked down at him.

"Come with me," he growled.

I had no idea it was possible, but somehow his words managed to wring a third orgasm out of me. My climax ripped through me, my hips moving wildly against him, my hands gripping his arms tightly. Eric's hands remained on my breasts, squeezing as his body jerked. All the while, our eyes remained locked on one another's. It was the most intimate, passionate thing I've ever experienced, staring into my lover's eyes as we both came.

****

The following morning, I walked out of my bathroom, dressed in my black silk robe. My lips spread when I saw Eric still resting comfortably in my bed. His bottom half was covered in the light pink sheets on my bed, while his top half was bare, his broad back exposed, allowing me to ogle it. His spine rose and fell as he breathed. It was then that I saw a scar that ran about halfway down his back, curving around the side. When I moved in closer, I gasped, covering my mouth with my hand. A feeling of embarrassment overcame me as I saw higher up on his back were fresh nail marks, obviously from my doing the night before.

"What's the matter?" he asked, voice groggy with sleep.

"I didn't mean to wake you."

"I've been awake for a while. Even heard you singing in the shower."

I dipped my head. "What'd you think of it?"

"Don't quit your day job, Angel," he retorted.

Giggling, I swatted at him, only for my hand to be caught by his, as he turned over, pulling me onto the bed with him.

"I'm sorry about the scratch marks," I said, timidly.

"That's what had you gasping?" he asked, laughter in his voice.

I swatted his arm. "Don't make fun of me! I got a little carried away."

"I'll say."

I moved from his embrace, grabbed one of the pillows from my side of the bed, and hit him with it, causing him to roar in laughter. He easily yanked the pillows from my hands and wrapped me up in his strong arms to lay back against his chest.

"What's the other scar on your back from?" I asked before I could think better of it. I hadn't noticed it the night before, but now that I had my curiosity got the best of me.

"You really want to know?"

"No, I just asked to be polite." The sarcasm was evident in my tone.

I smiled at the deep sound of his chuckle, leaning back and relaxing my head against him comfortably.

"It happened on a call a few years ago. The guy was high out of his mind and had set a small fire in his house. We came to put it out, and he went crazy and stabbed me."

"Oh my God!" I gasped, sitting up and turning to him. "Really?"

He nodded. "It was mostly a superficial wound though it obviously left a scar. About a year ago I got a letter at the fire station apologizing. He was in jail and got clean."

I stared at him, my mouth wide open. He recounted the story as if it was no big deal. As if this guy hadn't endangered his life, not just by fire, but also physically attacking him. I hadn't even considered that someone would attack a firefighter. These were the good guys. The ones who came to help.

"You sound like you don't even blame him."

He gave a nonchalant shrug of his shoulder. "I mean, what am I gonna do? Still be pissed over a call that happened years ago? The guy apologized."

"But you could've been seriously hurt … or worse?"

He gripped my chin in between his thumb and forefinger, yanking me toward him, pressing a kiss to my lips. He pulled back. "Remember what I told you the other night in my car?"

I frowned, forehead creasing as I recalled that night. "You said you worked with the best of the best, and if anything happened to you, they were your insurance policy."

"Right. They have my back, and I've got theirs. Nothing's going to happen to me."

I wasn't able to respond before he engulfed me in another kiss. I moaned into his mouth, feeling myself falling under his spell, but I moved back before I could get too lost.

"Turn over and lay on your stomach."

He looked at me quizzically.

"I want to kiss it," I answered his silent question. I pushed him by his shoulder. He complied, and turned over, exposing his broad back to me. I sat back on my haunches, just examining the muscles in his back. Leaning over, I pressed a kiss to his scar, then another one, and another. I sighed with contentment, stretching up to wrap my arm around his lower back and lay my cheek on his upper back, laying half on top of him.

"What're we going to do about your mother?"

He made a snorting sound. "What about her?"

I lifted my head. "Don't say it like that, Eric. She's your mother. I know you're upset with her, but I do think she just wants the best for you."

"You're the best for me." He turned over, capturing me in his arms again and gripping my chin. "I meant what I said last night."

Him telling me I was going to be a part of his family came flooding back. Butterflies began moving in my stomach. I swallowed then sighed into his mouth when his lips brushed against mine. Once again, I lowered my head to lay on his bare chest. After a few silent moments, I laughed slightly, thinking about the other encounter I had yesterday at the gym.

"It seems your mother isn't the only one upset about us being together."

"Someone else is giving you shit?" The tone of his voice almost had me regretting my previous comment.

I shook my head to signal that it was no big deal. "It was just Marshall. He was at the gym yesterday and said some things. I think his feelings were a little hurt, which is understandable." I waved my hand around as if I was shrugging it off.

"What'd he say?"

"Eric, it was nothing—"

"What'd he say?"

I hesitated. "Just that he didn't expect me to fall for the games of a firefighter or something to that effect."

"What else?" he asked, forehead wrinkled.

"Uh, he said he thought I was smarter than that or something."

He gave me a long glare. I could see the wheels of his mind churning but couldn't read his facial expression.

"It's okay, Eric. No big deal. Like I said, he was probably hurt. And I mean, I didn't reach out to let him know that I was now seeing someone else—"

"Which you didn't have to since you two weren't a couple."

"Yes, but..."

"But nothing. Does he go to the gym regularly?"

"Yes, that's how we met." I paused. "Don't do anything. He got the message yesterday after I told him to have a nice life."

Eric's jaw clenched before he spoke. "I'm sure he did," he retorted, but his eyes were staring at something over my head.

I cupped his face between mine. "I'm serious, Eric. Leave him alone, and he'll go away quietly."

He turned those dark brown eyes, which often spoke more words than his actual mouth, back to mine. They wrinkled at the edges when his lips formed a half smile. Leaning down, he kissed me. "Okay, Angel."

I gave him a skeptical look, but he kissed me again, before pulling me into his arms, as he sat back against the headboard of my bed. I turned, so my back was against his chest again. We were quiet for a few minutes, just savoring the feeling of being in each other's arms. It wouldn't last all day. Eric had to go to work in a couple of hours and then I needed to open up the bar.

"You have a thing for white wicker."

I glanced around my bedroom, at the white wicker dressers and vanity, along with the headboard of my bed, which was white wicker as well.

"The picnic basket you used the other week was made of white wicker, too."

I chuckled. "Yeah, I have a thing for it I guess. I went on vacation a few years back, and the hotel room we stayed in was all white wicker. It was right on the beach. Since then, it reminds me of spending time on the beach. That's how I feel when I come into my room. It's my own little getaway."

"Where'd you go on vacation?"

I began telling him about my trip to Costa Rica that I took with friends as a college graduation present to myself. It was one of the most fun experiences of my life. We talked about other vacations we've been on until late that morning when I got up and made us both breakfast. Eric had to leave soon after that to get back to his place, shower, and change for work. I missed him before he even left.

Chapter Eleven

Eric

"So, you're finally doing it, huh?"

I glanced over my shoulder from the laptop on my lap as I sat on the edge of my bunk to see Carter standing over me, arms folded. His head motioned toward the screen of my laptop. I turned back around as he rounded my bed to stand in front.

"Yeah, it's about time," I answered, typing in the rest of my registration form for the lieutenant's exam.

"Damn right it is. When's the test?"

"End of October," I grunted.

"Gives you about three months to study. Little less," he commented, sitting down on his own cot.

"Can you believe it's almost a hundred dollars to register? And if I pay by card, they charge me an additional three percent fee," I scoffed.

"That's the Fire Department for ya'. Nickel and dime where they can. Well, that's most businesses and organizations for you, to be honest."

I peered up at a frowning Carter, whose mind had obviously drifted off to someplace else.

"You ever think about taking the exam?" I questioned. Carter had been with the department for as long as I had.

He grunted. "With all the recent shit I've been in? They'd probably laugh my request off the captain's desk."

"They wouldn't. You had some trouble, but you dealt with it."

"They won't see it that way. Not so soon, anyway. Its okay, man. Maybe in a few years when I've racked up all the commendations you have, I'll apply." He was teasing, but I could see the the want behind his eyes.

"Just make sure you save up to be able to pay for this registration process," I joked.

He chuckled. "I'll do that." It was funny because Carter was the wealthiest man in the fire station... hell, the entire *department*. He was born with the proverbial silver spoon in his mouth. And he walked away from it all to do what he loved. He and I had that as one of our bonds. We both turned down lucrative futures to put out fires.

"Hey, is Don around?"

"Yeah, last I saw him, he was cleaning his gear."

"Good." I nodded and finished up my registration before closing my laptop.

"I'm going to catch some sleep," Carter said, laying down. He was on the twenty-four-hour shift, so he was just coming up on his sixteenth hour at the station. The previous night had been a busy one.

I stored my laptop in my storage space, right next to my bunk before heading downstairs to seek out Don. I checked in the area where we kept our equipment, but he wasn't there. I headed right for the kitchen, knowing that nine times out of ten that's where he'd be.

"Heard you're registering for the exam," Don stated as soon as he saw me. He peered at me over the brim of what I was sure was his fourth cup of coffee. He, too, was working a twenty-four shift.

"Word travels fast."

"Nah, I just knew it was coming up and figured you're the most qualified. Plus, I saw Cap pull you in his office the other week."

I grinned. Don liked to play down how savvy he was, but the man had street smarts and book knowledge.

"Yeah, I just registered."

"Good. We need a lieutenant around here. Whip these damn rookies into shape."

"And to keep an eye on the more seasoned guys."

He grunted at that.

"Hey, anyway, I got a favor to ask."

"Shoot."

"You still have your friend down at the police department?"

"I have a lot of friends at the department."

"The one who runs IDs and can get you all types of information?"

He nodded. "Yeah. Why?"

"I need him to look someone up for me."

"It's a she," he corrected.

I gave him a look. He shrugged.

"Whatever, man. Can *she* look someone up for me?"

"This person causing you trouble?" Don's voice took on a serious note as he stepped closer.

"No, not much. I just need his address or possibly his whereabouts during the day. First name Marshall. I don't have a last name, but he works as a teacher over at the middle school on Henderson." I gave Don all the information I had on Marshall. I didn't want to ask Angela for more info to not arouse any more suspicion on her part.

"All right, man. Let me see what I can do."

"Thanks, man."

"You sure you're good, though?"

"Positive."

"Okay. I'll give her a ring now." He strolled off, pulling his cell phone out of his pocket. I appreciated he didn't ask for more information about why I was seeking this guy out.

With that settled, I reached for my cell phone, sending a text to Angela letting her know the guys and I planned on stopping by the bar tonight after our shift. That wasn't unusual, but I still wanted her to be in the know. I also didn't want to admit to myself that I was probably just finding any reason to reach out to her during the day. She's been on my mind since the moment I left her place. For once, I regretted that I had to get up and go to work.

I'll be waiting. Came back her text reply with a winking eye emoji. I had to make sure to wipe the stupid, school-boy grin off my face before any of the other guys saw me.

****

The three of us walked in the bar, and the first thing that hit me, as usual, was the energy. Patrons mingled, laughed, and danced to the tunes of "Good Life" by OneRepublic. The first place my eyes zeroed in on was behind the bar. And there she was, once again, the focal point of most of the patron's entertainment, dancing and serving drinks. A male bartender was with her this evening, but he was dancing right along with Angela to the music. I had to tamp down on the jealousy that ran through my chest at the sight of her laughing with another man. *It's her job.* It was also her personality—open, friendly, laughing, and welcoming. Who wouldn't want to be around that type of energy?

I answered my question when my feet picked up their pace headed in her direction. I didn't bother to see if Corey and Carter followed or if they went to find a table for us; it wasn't my concern at the moment. I took the space at the bar a woman just vacated after retrieving her drink. When Angela's eyes landed on me, my heartbeat quickened the same way it did whenever we got a call at the station. Her eyes smiled before her mouth did and for a second I was thrown back to the previous night when I first thrust inside of her. Then, her eyelids hung heavily, drained after the orgasm I gave her with my mouth. But as soon as I pushed up against her, those tawny orbs sparkled with fire and awe.

"And for you, sir?" Her voice was airy. She was flirting with me, but it wasn't the same, friendly flirting she did with her other patrons.

I had to adjust myself in my jeans before responding. "Four of the usual, Angel."

She raised an eyebrow. "I only saw you come in with Carter and Corey."

My lips parted, and I leaned farther on the bar. "You watched me come in?"

"I've been waiting for you," she admitted, leaning over the bar as well. Our lips were only a few inches apart, and with temptation like that, I wasn't one to resist. I took the liberty of leaning in even more and brushing my lips against hers. The kiss wasn't nearly long enough for either one of us.

My head spun to the right of me when a man whistled across the bar. "I'll take one of those as well!" he called, causing the few patrons around him to laugh.

"Like hell you will!" I shot back without hesitation or thought. The men laughed, but my frown remained.

"He's just teasing," Angela stated, bringing my attention back to her. "So, four of the usual?"

"Yeah, Don was taking a call outside," I responded to her earlier inquiry about there only being three of us.

"Ah." She nodded, her curiosity satisfied.

Seconds later, she placed four Coronas with lime slices sticking out the tops of the bottles in front of me. I hesitated to retrieve the beers, not wanting to take my eyes off her.

"You closing tonight?" It was a ridiculous question; she always closed.

"Yup."

"Which means you'll be done around three?"

"Possibly sooner if I can ge—"

"Make it sooner."

She gave me a curious look.

"I'll wait for you."

"You just got off work. You'll be exhausted by the time I finish closing up."

I stared at her, not even realizing my brain was working to memorize every aspect of her face. "I'll wait for you."

Placing money on the bar, I grabbed the four beers and turned, surveying the bar and looking for the rest of my crew. I found them seated at one of the corner tables, talking with a few guys from another fire station. I strolled over in their direction, handing Corey, Carter and Don—who'd apparently ended his phone conversation—each of their beers.

"I'm starving. Wanna order a round of wings?" Don asked.

Corey, Carter, and I all grunted our agreement. The other firefighters had gone back to their tables. Don strolled toward the section of the bar where food orders were placed. He was back within a few minutes, tapping me on my back.

"That call was from my friend with the police department. She gave me the info you were looking for." He pulled out a small piece of paper that he scribbled Marshall's information on.

I looked it over, noting his home and work addresses, including the community center he worked at over the summer as a tutor.

"Thanks."

"Should I even ask what you're going to do with that?" He nodded in the direction of my hand, as I placed the paper in my back pocket.

"Probably not."

We headed back to the table.

"Wanna tell us what's up with you and the owner of the bar?" Corey asked, nonchalantly, just as the food Don ordered was brought to the table.

Three pairs of smirking eyes were trained on me. "No."

"Aw, come on, man!" Carter cried.

"It's about time you gave us something. We're not gonna act like we didn't just see what happened at the bar. Don't say it's nothing! The Harvard we know doesn't do PDA," Corey challenged.

Letting out a deep sigh, I attempted to divert attention back to the food. "I thought you bozos said you were hungry." Nine times out of ten, it worked. Not this time.

"We can eat and talk. Spill it," Don added.

I narrowed my gaze at him first, then the rest of them. "I can't believe I call you guys my brothers."

"Brothers from another mother. And don't you forget it. Now spill," Carter laughed.

"Look, it's new. Really new, and I'm liking it. That's all I'm saying about Angela and I. Now mind your fucking business and eat your goddamn wings."

"Someone's sensitive," Corey sing-songed.

He was right, I *was* sensitive over my budding relationship. Especially after what happened with my mother. And while I didn't fear these guys wouldn't accept Angela like my mother hadn't, I didn't want to share her either. Not yet. I turned back toward the bar and smiled as Angela danced behind the bar again, serving drinks. When she looked up and caught my eye, I gave her a wink, and her smile grew even wider. The stirring in my groin happened again, and I began counting down the minutes until the bar closed.

****

"You've been up for nearly twenty-four hours," Angela commented, as we stepped up onto her porch.

"I suddenly got my second wind." My hand went to the small of her back.

She grinned at me over her shoulder. Instead of heading right to the door, as I expected her to do, she turned for the wooden swing sitting at the far right side of the porch. She sat and patted the space to the right of her for me to sit. I joined her, but my need to touch her became overwhelming, so I picked her up, placing her on my lap, nuzzling my face into the crook of her neck. Her sweet scent made me feel heady and my fingers dug into the flesh of her thighs.

I used my long legs to push off the porch and get us swinging, causing her to laugh. It was one of those perfectly warm summer nights. While sirens and car horns could be heard in the distant background, Angela's street was quiet. Quiet enough that you could close your eyes and almost pretend that instead of being in one of the nation's most populated cities, you were in the suburbs of Middle America.

"My dad built this porch and swing for my mom. I think I was about eleven or twelve. My mom loved sitting out here summer nights with her friends from the neighborhood, or with my dad after Sean and I went to bed. They were so much in love, even after years and years together and two kids." The wistfulness and sadness that was always there when she spoke of her parents was apparent.

I pulled her in closer.

"You see that house right there."

I lifted my head to see her pointing to a home across the street and two houses over. It was a moderate size home. The layout was different from Angela's home as it appeared to be a one-story home as opposed to Angela's two-story house.

I nodded. "Yeah."

"My father grew up in that house. His father was a sharecropper down south. He came up to Williamsport as part of the Great Migration and brought my grandmother and father, who was just a baby. They wanted my father to be able to live in a place without fear of being lynched or shut out of opportunity because of his race. My grandmother worked as a nanny, and scrubbed floors part-time. My grandfather was able to get a job in construction. They bought that house a few years later. They raised my father and his siblings in it. When my father grew up and married my mother, they lived there with my grandparents as my father had this house built. He became a firefighter in his early twenties, but on his time off he spent hours working with his father and others to build this house. Today my younger cousin owns that home, but she travels a lot, so she rents it out."

"Your father sounds like an amazing man. Your family's background sort of mirrors my own."

She sat up, looking at me. "How so?"

"My grandparents—my father's mother and father—immigrated from North Korea to the U.S. for a better life."

"Really? I assumed your family was from South Korea."

"My mother's family is. My father's parents were able to get out just around the end of the Korean War." I continued to explain the evolution of my family as they barely escaped Communist rule. I told her how my parents met their junior year of college and married within weeks of knowing each other.

"My grandparents, on both sides, were pissed, but they were relieved when my parents agreed to wait to have children."

We sat again, for a few more moments in silence, until Angela broke it. "All the circumstances our families have been through just to get to this point. All of that for you and I to be right here. Right now." She paused to sigh. "Do you believe in fate?"

It was a surprising question, but I didn't have to think about the answer. "Yes."

"Really? Why?" Surprise was evident in her tone.

"It comes with the job, I think."

"How so?"

"I've seen too much not to think fate, or something like it exists. When I've seen a man, who should be dead, come back to life. Or a woman narrowly miss being hit by a beam falling on her. Or a perfectly healthy child dies in a matter of minutes by a freak fire or accident. I don't know. It seems like there is something behind it all, directing the show. Maybe our destinies are determined before we get here."

Her head tilted up from my chest, where she'd again laid into me. "You think you and I are fate?"

That was another easy answer. Instead of giving a verbal response, I pulled her to me and brought our lips together. Heat rose in my belly and I moved to have Angela's legs straddle me, so I could stand up.

"What a—" she questioned, breaking free from the kiss. By the time the first word was out, I was at her door.

"Open it or—"

"My neighbors will get a show?" she retorted saucily.

"Exactly," I growled, nuzzling her neck again and then biting her earlobe.

She did as told, turning awkwardly in my grasp, with her legs still around me to unlock the door. Once she had it unlocked, I moved, turning the knob and pushing it open, then slamming it behind us. By the time we were halfway down the hall I had her dress stripped from her body and on the floor.

<u>Chapter Twelve</u>

Eric

I stepped out of my car of the gym's parking lot, preparing to head into Angela's ten a.m spin class. It's been about three weeks since the disastrous dinner at my parents' house, but I wouldn't change any of that considering how the evening turned out. Angela and I have seen each other just about every day since that night, save for two days when I worked twenty-four-hour shifts. We were growing closer after having discussed our family history. I knew I was falling for her, or maybe I've already fallen and wasn't totally willing to admit it to myself just yet. Either way, I could see this thing with us going the distance, and that was not a sentiment I took lightly. Hell, I haven't ever thought about any other woman like that, not even ex-girlfriends.

I stored my belongings in one of the lockers in the men's locker room, using my padlock before heading directly to the room where the spin class was held.

"Here he is, boys!" Closing my eyes, I inhaled as Don's voice, filled with humor, washed over me. I parted my lids to see Don, Corey, and Carter standing in front of me, workout gear on and all.

"What the hell are you doing here?"

Carter looked between the trio and was the first to step up. He came over to me, placing an arm around my shoulders.

"We're here to support you, Harvard. That's the type of men we are," he joked.

I shoved him off of me.

"Oh come on, Harvard. Don't be like that!" Corey started.

"Yeah, if it weren't for us, that douche over there would still be trying to put the moves on your woman," Don added.

I hated them, but at the same time, my eyes narrowed as my head pivoted toward the only other male in the class. He glanced over at us but quickly turned away when he saw us looking. I heard the cacophony of laughter from the damn goof troop and ignored them. I knew they were looking to bust my balls. Instead, I moved past them to see Angela just finishing her set up for the class. Her lips moved and those pearly whites shone when she saw me.

"I thought you decided to sleep in."

"Caught in traffic." I spent the night at her place again but had to run home to get my workout gear and uniform. I was heading head straight into work after the mid-morning brunch we planned to attend after this class.

Her smile grew. "Glad you made it in time." With that, the heavy bass of the music started pumping through the speakers. I took one last glance at her before moving to an empty bike in the front row. It wasn't directly in front of her where I usually like to sit, but it still gave me an obstruction-free view of her, which was all I needed to stay motivated during class. Not even five minutes into class I heard Corey yell from the back of the room to turn it up. His yell was followed up with grunts and whoops of agreement from his two sidekicks. I pulled my lips in, grimacing at the three of them, causing them to break out into laughter. Surprisingly—or maybe not so surprisingly—Angela took on the challenge. In fact, she turned the volume up slightly and directed us to stand as we cycled. Despite the commotion from the guys, my eyes zeroed in on her. For the next fifty minutes, I sweated and burned off the extra energy that always seemed to manifest itself when I was in her presence. When class finally ended, the smell of sweat and heat permeated the room.

"Great class!" Angela remarked, her pecan skin glistening with sweat. As if my reaction to her wasn't already a growing problem, I felt my mouth water at the thought of licking the sweat off her. I briefly wondered if we could skip brunch and head back to her place—since it was closer—for a doubles shower.

"And we had some special guests today. They weren't too bad themselves," she continued, holding out her hands toward the guys who bowed at the applause they received from other participants.

"I should've kicked them out for you," I told her, but I was eyeing my brothers from the station—two of which appeared to be getting two women's phone numbers from the class. And Don seemed to be easing over toward a third woman.

Angela giggled, and my eyes zeroed in on her once again. "They were terrific. They showed up to bust your balls, huh?"

I grunted.

"They're your family, too. You knew it'd happen sooner or later."

I peered down at her, noting the caring tone of her voice, and I remembered the words I said to her that night after having dinner with my parents.

"You handled their antics pretty well," I commented. Despite the rowdiness of the fellas, Angela commanded the class with ease.

"I enjoyed it. They were kinda fun."

I frowned.

"Aww," she started, wrapping her arms around my waist loosely, and reaching up on her tiptoes to kiss my chin, "don't be like that. You're still my favorite firefighter in spin class."

In spite of myself, my lips twitched, but I refused to let out the laugh that wanted to escape. Instead, I bent down to kiss her lips.

"Cut that shit out! There are kids around for Christ's sake!" Don's voice boomed.

I popped my head up, glaring at him, and wanting to wipe the dumb smirk off his face.

"Thanks for coming to class, guys!" Angela interrupted, her arms still around my waist.

"Anytime. Though, we just wanted to bust this guy's chops since he's so mum about you two," Carter admitted.

Out of the corner of my eye, I saw Angela's head pivot back toward me, but I kept my eyes focused the three assholes in front of us.

I pointed my finger at Carter. "You don't need to worry about my lady and I. But good for you for coming to workout. You were looking a little slow on that last call yesterday," I returned.

Don and Corey covered their mouths and let out whoops of laughter and a round of, "Oh shit!"

"If you say so, Harvard." Carter turned those blue eyes toward Angela. "Angela, you might wanna give this guy a little break at night, if you know what I mean. I had to practically toss him out of his bunk the other day when we got a call. Sleeping like a baby and I doubt it's from spin class." Carter's eyebrows wiggled up and down at the same time I took a step toward him, my possessive side coming out. But before I could complete my first step, I was stopped by Angela's arms tightening around my waist.

"My guy doesn't need any breaks. Not in class or anywhere else," she saucily retorted. The feel of her soft lips on my cheek after that comment soothed my rising temper. By then all the guys were laughing.

"Guys, we had plans to go to brunch after class, before the big guy has to head into the station. Want to join us?"

I turned to give her an incredulous look. She returned it with one of her own.

"I'm in."

"I'm always fucking hungry!"

"Grub time!"

I sighed as all three agreed to join us. My Angel reached up again, giving me a quick peck, and whispered, "It'll be fun." Looking down into those eyes, I doubted I'd ever be able to refuse her anything.

****

"Since you bums decided to crash my alone time with my woman, brunch is on you," I told the guys as we sat down at one of the tables of an American-style diner only a couple of blocks from the gym.

"Bullshit!" Don countered. "Let Richie Money Bags over there take the tab," Don grunted, jutting his head in Carter's direction.

"Richie Money Bags?" Angela asked, gaze bouncing between the four of us with confused eyes.

Carter dipped his head, obviously not wanting to speak up. That problem was solved when Corey, who sat directly across from Angela, intervened.

"Carter's last name is Townsend." He paused, giving Angela time to let the name register. A few seconds later she gasped as it came together.

"You're a Townsend? Like of Townsend Industries?"

"The one and only, toots," Don spoke up.

"Don't call my woman toots, asshole." I pointed a finger at him.

All three of the guys chuckled.

"This one's grown a possessive streak around you, Angela," Don laughed.

I looked down to my left, to see her grinning back at me. "I kinda have, too," she stated.

That funny feeling in my chest started happening again.

"Anyway," Carter interrupted our moment, "to answer your question, yes. I am a Townsend of Townsend Industries."

"Wow. Wait, isn't your dad a high-level executive there?" she asked me, the fingers of her right hand curling, as she gripped my workout shorts on my thigh.

"He is." I nodded.

"Did you two know each other before joining the department?"

I shook my head. "No. Young Rebel over here has probably never stepped foot in a Townsend Industries' office."

Corey and Don snickered.

"Let's just say, I made my own way." His voice had a heavy note to it, and it was obvious there was more to the story, but his response made it clear he didn't intend to give up any more information than what was already said.

Thankfully, he didn't have to as the waitress returned with the food we ordered. A plate with an omelet stuffed with chorizo sausage, red and green peppers, mozzarella cheese topped with salsa, and potatoes was placed in front of me. A plate of three fluffy, stacked pancakes topped with melting butter and a jar of syrup was placed next to it. My stomach began grumbling when the scent of the food hit my nostrils. We all dug into our meals.

"How is it?" Angela asked. A habit of hers, even if she didn't cook the food herself.

I leaned in, after swallowing a mouthful of pancakes. "They're pretty good, but your pancakes are better." Her eyes lit up. She genuinely got a kick out of making people happy by feeding them. And I got a kick out of seeing her happy. She could serve me sardines for breakfast, and I'd probably say they were delicious just to make her smile like that.

"Angela, I know I didn't hear you're cooking this fool pancakes!" Corey's voice intruded on our little moment.

"From scratch. With real buttermilk and everything," she answered proudly, popping another forkful of her vegetable omelet into her mouth.

"You think you co—"

"No! Hell no!" I pointed the knife I was using to cut my pancakes at Don.

"What? I was gonna ask if she could pass the recipe along to one of my lady friends. And throw in some cooking tips while she was at it."

"I'm sure." I gave him a disbelieving look. "You want your lady friend to learn to cook, pay for some cooking classes your own fucking self."

The table went up in laughter.

"Don't be like that, Harvard. Tabitha just needs a little bit of TLC when it comes to matters of the kitchen."

"Tabitha?" I questioned.

"Yeah. I've mentioned her, unlike you." His dark eyes shifted between Angela and I.

"Is it serious between this Tabitha and you?" Angela innocently asked. All of the men, except for Don, laughed loudly at that question.

"Oh no, doll. Donnie over here doesn't *do* serious," Corey added.

"Watch it with the terms of endearment," I supplied, glaring in his direction. He smirked but held his hands up in a surrendering manner. I heard Carter and Don snicker but ignored them.

"Why don't you do serious?" Angela asked.

"Don't listen to these schmucks, swee—" Don paused, looking at my stern face, before turning back to Angela. "Angela. I can do serious. I just like to have my pick of the litter. And anyway, Tabitha has the potential to be something serious. She is *seriously* stacked." He sat back and held his hands out in front of his chest, indicating the largeness of this Tabitha's breasts.

I rolled my eyes. "Fucking seriously?"

Don gave me an innocent, questioning look.

"We're in the presence of a woman. Not at the fire station. Tone it down a little, Don," Carter spoke up.

"I'm sorry, Angela."

She waved her hand around. "No offense taken. Who doesn't appreciate a good stack?" She quickly reached over me, forked some of my pancakes, and popped them into her mouth. "Right?" she mumbled.

The tabled erupted into laughter and agreement. I threw my arm around her, laughing myself. She might be the only woman I'd let eat off my plate with zero complaints.

"Anyway," she began after swallowing the pancakes, "if your Tabitha is interested in cooking, I wouldn't mind helping her out a little."

"Oh no, you don't want to meet his Tabitha or any of his ladies."

She turned to me, a wrinkled in her forehead. "Why not?"

"Just trust me. The women he entertains are a couple of fries short of a Happy Meal."

"That's fucked up, Harvard."

"No, *you're* fucked up," I countered.

"Oh shit!" Carter and Corey interjected at the same time.

"Is that any way for a lieutenant to talk to one of his subordinates?"

Angela inhaled loudly. "You made lieutenant?"

I eyed Don before turning to Angela. "No, he's just a fool."

"Fuck no I ain't. Harvard's taking the lieutenant's exam in a few months. And with his brains, we all know he's going to pass. Rescue Four has only had one lieutenant for two years now, and each station is supposed to have three."

"You didn't tell me that," Angela accused.

"It's no big deal. I'm just taking the test."

"It *is* a big deal. I remember how happy my father was when he made lieutenant. I was still young, but I remember his giddiness and my mama laughing as he kissed her all over her face. And Sean, he was so excited when he passed."

"Sean?" Carter questioned.

Angela turned her still star-filled gaze to Carter. "Of Rescue Two. He's my older brother." She turned back to me. "Oh my goodness! We have to make you some study cards. They always helped me in college. You'll be able to carry them with you wherever and study at the station, at home, at my place. Wherever." She waved her hands around animatedly.

I couldn't help the amusement I felt at seeing how excited she was over this. Pulling a pen out of the workout bag she carried, she jotted some notes down on a napkin on the table of things to pick up from Staples to help me study.

"I think you've got a winner there," Carter leaned over and stated, low in my ear.

I didn't even look at him to acknowledge the truth of his words. I was too busy staring down at the giddy Angel to the left of me.

****

"I thought we were stopping for food. Come on, Harvard. I'm fucking starving," Don grumbled as he dismounted from the rig.

"We are," I answered, glancing at him over my shoulder.

"Then what the fuck are we doing at a community center?" he asked, just as we reached the door.

I held it open for him.

"If there's not a large pepperoni and sausage pizza waiting inside for us, I'm setting your boots on fire." He pointed at me.

I laughed, not because I didn't think he was serious, but because I believed he would light my boots on fire.

"Come on, man. I'll spring for extra garlic knots later."

"You better," he grumbled, brushing past me.

I entered the center behind Don.

"Welcome, gentlemen. Can I help you?" the young receptionist asked.

"Yeah, we're here to see Marshall Jacobs." I leaned on the counter, noticing the young brunette eyeing both Don and I. We were dressed in department dark blue T-shirts, displaying the department's emblem, and our bright orange-yellow coveralls from the waist down with the standard red suspenders to hold them up. We were returning from a call. I'd dropped off the other guys and told them we were heading out to pick up a pizza. Since there was another rig at the station, it was customary that one or two of us would take one out to pick up food for the station.

Her head leaned over the counter, and she saw the huge fire rig that I parked in the lot.

"Are you gentlemen here to do a presentation for the students?"

"No, doll. But if you give me your number, I'd be more than happy to give you a call to set that up," Don responded, his voice dipping low.

The girl lowered her head as she blushed.

I just shook my head at Don's way with the women. How someone could be as crude as he was sometimes and still beat women off with a stick was beyond me.

"We just need Marshall for a moment." I gave her a smile I knew would charm the pants off most women.

"Thanks, doll," Don added before she even moved to pick up the phone.

Her blush revealed her intentions before her movements. Seconds later she was hanging up the phone and telling us that Marshall was on his lunch break but would be right out.

I straightened and moved closer to the glass doors that led toward the rest of the community center. Moments later, I saw a figure emerge, and I immediately recognized the man from the night of my first date with Angela. As soon as he stepped past the glass doors, his eyes landed on me, and a confused expression followed.

"Remember me?" I smirked. "I'm Eric. Angela's man. Let's talk, just you and me." I stepped closer, towering over him for a brief second.

"Donna, what's this about?" He turned toward the receptionist's desk.

My eyes remain trained on him, but the receptionist must have given him an unsatisfactory look because he soon frowned and planted his gaze back on me.

"It'll only be a minute," I added, stepping to his side, placing my arm around his shoulders. "Let's take this outside." I felt some reluctance when I pulled Marshall along, but eventually, he conceded.

"You stay here," I said over my shoulder to Don who'd begun walking behind us. He hesitated but then shrugged and went back to the front desk.

"Why are you here? How did you even know where I worked?" Marshall asked as soon as the doors closed.

"A man who gets straight to the point." I nodded, arms folded across my chest and planted my feet. "I like that. I'm here about Angela, obviously."

"She told you where I worked?" he questioned, accusation in his voice.

I stepped forward, crowding his personal space. "She doesn't know I'm here. And we're going to keep it that way."

His eyes narrowed slightly.

"I'm here because of an encounter I heard occurred between the two of you. She was reluctant to go into much detail, but I got the sense you insulted her."

"Now wait. If she's telling you I threatened—"

His rant was cut short by my chuckle and a firm hand on his shoulder. He glanced at my hand on him and then back to my hard face.

"Marshall, let me make one thing clear right now. If you would've threatened her, this would be an entirely different conversation. No words would be exchanged. You get what I'm sayin'?" I clamped my teeth together, causing the muscles of my jaw to flex at the same time my hand squeezed his shoulder. The thought of him threatening Angela had me on edge. I didn't take a step back until I saw him wince in pain from my contact. Marshall visibly exhaled.

"I don't like the implications of your actions. You berated her, and that's not something I take lightly."

"I didn't berate her."

"So you're calling Angela a liar?" My eyebrow spiked, daring him to lie.

"N-no. I just said what I felt."

"And you *felt* that she was stupid for seeing me, correct? Last time I checked calling someone stupid is an insult. Has the definition changed since the last time I checked Webster's?" I gave him a serious look.

His gaze casting downward was his only response.

"Didn't think so."

"Okay, I'm sorry for insulting her. I didn't mean it like that. I was just disappointed and I—"

I held my hand up. "Disappointment is understandable. She's beautiful, vivacious, and caring. Any man would be lucky to have her. *I'm* that man. And I don't like what belongs to me being disrespected. An apology is a good start—"

"Start? Start of what?"

A sideways tilt of my head revealed I didn't appreciate his tone at the moment.

"An apology is a good start, but also, you're going to find another gym. Cancel your membership and find another place to work out. Delete Angela's number, email, and all memory of her from your mind."

His jaw dropped. "You can't be serious? I paid for the year for my membership."

I shrugged. "There's only four and a half months left in the year. Workout at home, go to a park, take up yoga somewhere." I stepped closer. "I don't give a shit where you workout just don't do it in the same gym as Angela. And don't even *think* of taking a step inside of *Charlie's.* Whether she's there or not. We clear?"

He began shaking his head, and my already present frown turned into a scowl. His eyes widened when I bent down lower to get in his face.

"This isn't a request. I don't take trips like this during my work shift for shits and giggles. You had your chance with her, you blew it, and another man stepped in and did what you couldn't. You acted like a spoiled child who didn't get his milk and cookies by insulting her and by proxy insulting me. Typically, I'd blow off any insults directed at me, but not those directed at my woman. Do yourself a favor, heed this warning and make yourself scarce." I pulled back a little and watched the pensive expression on his face.

His eyes trained on me and he nodded ever so slightly. I tapped him on the shoulder and then moved to the door.

Opening it and sticking my head in, I called for Don. With one last glance at Marshall, I turned and headed for the rig.

"We better be getting pizza now," Don grumbled as we climbed into the rig.

I peered over him. He wore a sour expression, and I began laughing. "She didn't give you her number, did she?"

"Fuck are you talking about?"

"You know what I'm talking about. The receptionist. Despite all her blushing, she saw through your bullshit."

He turned dark brown eyes on me. "She's a fucking psych student in grad school at the university. Says I got some fucking issues and I mask it by using women. You fucking believe that?" he roared, pulling the seatbelt across his chest. "Fucking ridiculous!" he mumbled, intensifying my laughter as I started the rig.

"You said what you needed to say?" he asked after a moment of silence. His head was turned, watching Marshall as he entered the building and we pulled out of the community center's parking lot.

"Sure did."

"Still don't wanna tell me what it was about? What if Captain asks where we been?"

"What're you talking about? We're on a pizza run."

He grinned. "As long as you add my fucking garlic knots, mum's the word from me."

"Consider it done." I held out my fist and Don responded by giving me the fist bump.

Chapter Thirteen

Eric

"We headed to *Charlie's* after work?" Corey asked around the table as we ate our breakfasts. The usual series of grunts and "hell yeahs" sounded off as the guys agreed to our after-shift destination.

"Count me in. I saw this one filly there last week. Had legs like a stallion. I'm hoping she'll be there again tonight."

"See," Carter pointed his fork accusingly at Don, "that's why you have so many problems with women. You refer to them as fillies.'"

Don frowned, his forehead wrinkled. "Who said I got problems with women?"

"Me."

"I do."

"I've seen it."

Myself, Carter, and Corey answered.

Corey tapped me on the chest with the back of his hand. "Harvard, remember that one call we went on? We get to the fire. A mother and her twenty-something daughter are outside the house, distraught... until they see Don. A fight broke out as soon as both women ran to him for comfort thinking he was their boyfriend." The table broke out into laughter as Corey finished recounting that story.

"He had a mother and daughter who just lost their home fighting each other in the street over his ass," Corey said, fist to his mouth, laughing hysterically.

"Oh no. Remember when that girl...what was her name?" Carter tapped the table with his fingers, trying to recall.

"Samantha," I provided, already remembering this story.

"Samantha. That's it!" Carter pointed at me, excited. "Samantha. Yeah, she lasted what? All of two months before she was down here at the station scratching the word 'liar' into your car with her car key. We had to call the police on that one when she tried to throw a brick through the windshield of the rig."

"Fuck all of you!" Don yelled over the laughter at the table. "See if I offer to pay for another round of beers for you assholes."

"It's okay. You're gonna need that money to repaint or fix your car soon, probably!" Corey added, and another round of laughter ensued. The taunting probably went on for the next ten minutes. I added a funny story or two of Don's escapades with the ladies. It was all in good fun, and I've been in great spirits lately. It's been a month since we had brunch at the diner together, and I confronted Marshall. He followed through and rescinded his gym membership, claiming he had some medical emergency and couldn't use the remaining four months to get a partial refund. Angela told me about it after an employee, who knew the two dated a few times, told her. As long as he steered clear of her, I didn't give a shit what he did. In the meantime, Angela made good on her word and did her best to help me study for the lieutenant's exam, which was now just under two months away. And while I was perfectly capable of handling studying on my own, I was more than happy to let her help. I especially appreciated the way she rewarded me after getting a decent score on one of the practice exams. *That* was a good night.

"The hell are you smiling about over there?" Carter's voice broke through my thoughts.

The entire table was staring at me. Laughter danced in Carter's eyes, and I could tell he had a suspicion of where my thoughts had gone.

"None of your damn business." I pushed away from the table and stood, ignoring the snickers of the fellas. I placed my empty plate in the sink.

"It's the rookie's day to do dishes, right?"

"Rookie one or rookie two?" Don asked.

I didn't give a shit which one as long as they got done. But instead of saying that I stated, "Rookie two, I think." Rookie two was the rookie we left at the station a few months back after he took the keys out of the rig.

"No can do, Harvard. Rookie two called out according to the captain."

I turned back to the table. "Called out?" My incredulous expression likely mirrored the rest of the guys at the table. Firefighters rarely called out of work, but *especially* not while you were still in rookie status.

"Yup," Don simply answered.

"I'm not sure about that one," Corey added, stating aloud what we were all thinking.

"Rookie one's out back cleaning off the equipment. We can have him do the dishes."

I shook my head at that suggestion. "Nah, he's got enough on his plate." Rookie one, unlike the other rookie, was shaping up to look and perform like a real firefighter. He may even be awarded the privilege of being called by his actual name soon enough. "Leave him be. I'll do 'em later."

Three pairs of eyebrows lifted and I sighed internally.

"You're doing dishes now?"

I snorted. "Angela's got me in the habit. She does all of the cooking, so..." I shrugged, giving just a small bit of insight into our relationship. I've gotten a little more open with these guys about Angela since we all dined together. So far, they all kept what I did share just between us, which I appreciated.

"Well shit, if she always cooks as good as that cake you brought in for us, I'd probably be doing dishes, too," Corey added. Angela insisted on making one of her chocolate lava cakes for the station. I felt like a sissy bringing in a cake for a bunch of men, but as soon as they tasted it, any shit-talking that might have ensued flew out the window.

"Yeah, well don't count on—" My retort was silenced when the station's alarm sounded. All of us began moving at a frenzied pace as the operator's monotone voice spoke of a four-alarm fire over at the apartment buildings on one of the city's main streets. "Shit!" I cursed to myself, as I pulled up my suspenders, preparing to grab my helmet. I knew this blaze wouldn't be an easy one. Four alarms meant it was a doozy and the apartment building itself was at least ten stories.

"Let's go," Captain Waverly yelled as he got into the passenger seat of the rig.

I didn't need to hear anything else. I hit the gas, and the alarm from the truck sounded off, alerting those in earshot to get the hell out of the way. I heard the captain responding to the operator through his walkie-talkie. I was able to make out bits and pieces, while still keeping my focus on the road ahead of me. From what I could make out, only one truck had arrived so far, firefighters had entered and were able to pull out two people who passed out from smoke inhalation.

"Fucking move!" I yelled at the car in front of me hesitated or outright refused to pull over to let the rig pass.

"The fuck is wrong with people today?" Captain grumbled. "Run 'em over if you have to!" he yelled in my direction.

I was prepared to do just that if this one Honda didn't move from blocking my ability to turn onto the street where the apartment building stood. At the last second, they swerved left, freeing my ability to turn clearly. Turning onto the street, billows of smoke appeared. The captain and I got eerily quiet. I took that moment to assess the situation from what I could see—a group of people standing across the street, likely onlookers and residents of the building; one fire truck had its ladder up against the building.

We pulled up and jumped out of the rig, heading straight to the captain of the other rig to get an assessment. Once that was done, Captain Waverly began giving out orders.

"Harvard, Corey, and Don, you three take the second and third floors. Rookie, you stay on my ass. Got it?"

We didn't bother giving a response, we just picked up our gear and got moving. I was the third one in, behind the captain and rookie. When they turned left, I went right toward the door that read "Stairs" in black letters. I felt on the handle to see how hot it was. When it felt normal, I figured fire hadn't made it into the stairwell. Lowering my mask over my face, I pulled the door open to a stairwell that was almost black with smoke. I heard Corey and Don's footsteps behind me as we ran up the steps as fast as we could in all our gear.

"Cover your faces!" I yelled at a few of the apartment residents who were running down the steps, trying to get free of the thick smoke. We moved aside to let them pass, then headed up to the third floor first.

"Ah, shit!" I called when I touched the door handle that led to the third floor and could feel the heat of the metal even through my gloves.

"Is it hot?" Don yelled.

"Yeah," I returned.

"Too hot?" Corey asked.

Too hot meant that fire had burned through the third floor, and made it impossible or too dangerous for us to make our way through.

"Fuck!" I yelled. "Yeah, too hot. Second floor!" I ordered, and we turned in the direction of the second floor. Stopping again to feel the knob, I found it felt warm, but not too hot. I pushed through the door and saw flames at the far end of the hallway.

"Fire department!" Corey, Don, and I began calling out, banging on doors with the handles of the hatchets we held. I pushed my way through one door that was opened, calling out to see if anyone was still in here.

"Rescue Four copy!" I heard come through my walkie-talkie.

"Rescue Four. Harvard copy!" I yelled back still searching the apartment.

"Woman says her baby is still inside. I repeat, woman is frantic saying her baby was left inside."

"Shit! What apartment number?"

"Apartment 211."

I recalled that the apartment I'd just entered was 209. Knowing Corey and Don had gone in the opposite direction, I figured I was closest, so I made the call.

"Harvard going to check it out. Don and Corey, copy?"

"Copy. All clear down here," Don returned.

"Copy. I got a man down here!" Corey returned. "Bringing him out now."

Don returned that he was on his way to Corey to assist him in getting the man out. I headed out of the apartment I was in and moved down the hall to 211. I noticed how much closer the flames were.

"Corey and Don, you two get outta here!" I yelled into my walkie.

"Harvard, you bring your ass out here, too!"

"Copy, just as soon as I check 211!" I assured Don on the other end.

I shouldered my way through the locked door of the apartment and went straight to the first window I saw. I sighed in relief when I saw the fire truck ladder balanced against the apartment's side. I'd need that for my escape. I could feel the fire growing closer to the apartment. I left the window open and went to search the rest of the apartment for the baby. I pushed open doors, searching what I surmised was the master bedroom, but paused when I heard loud banging. I looked toward the roof and saw the white paint of the ceiling begin bubbling. The fire was melting through the beams and the second floor would soon be consumed.

"Shit!" I yelled. I searched the bed, under the bed, and when I was satisfied there was no baby in the bedroom, I moved farther down the hall. The next door I pushed open was to a nursery.

"Fire department!" I called out, knowing a baby wouldn't answer me, but maybe someone like a babysitter was inside, hiding with the infant. I ran over to the crib and pulled the blanket back to see an empty mattress. "*Fuck!*" I searched around the nursery, double checking the crib and under it. I even searched the closet, but nothing and no one was there. I wondered where else the baby could've been. I retraced my steps, this time searching the bathroom and the bathtub, knowing sometimes people get in or put their young children in the tub thinking that'll insulate them from the fire. Still nothing.

"Harvard, get the hell out of there. The second floor is about totally consumed!" Captain Waverly yelled through the walkie. At the same time, I heard the telltale signs of wood cracking from the front door. The flames were eating away at the door. Out the front entrance was no longer an option. Although my heartbeat quickened, I didn't panic, knowing I still had another out. I moved toward the window I went to when I first entered the apartment. I was going to take the ladder, except when I stuck my head out this time the ladder was gone.

"Shit!" I grumbled.

"Harvard to Rescue Four come in!" I yelled into the walkie.

I waited for a heartbeat before calling again. All I got in return was a bunch of static. I heard a loud BOOM sound and turned toward the front door. It was only a matter of seconds before the fire completely penetrated the door and would consume the entire apartment. Looking back to the ground and still not seeing a ladder, I had a decision to make. I could remain there and get burned alive, or I could take my chances and jump from this second story window. It wasn't extremely high, but with the extra hundred pounds of my gear weighing me down, the chances of serious injury or even death grew immensely. At that moment an image of Angela's smiling face as she danced behind the bar, staring at me, came to mind. *Fuck it,* I thought. If that was the last image I ever saw, I could go out peacefully.

I opened my eyes, said a Hail Mary, and stepped on the window sill, squeezing my body and gear through the window, and took a leap of faith. I held onto the image of a smiling Angela as I fell, right before everything went black.

****

"Wake the fuck up!"

I heard the anger in Don's voice, but behind it was a twinge of fear. I could feel him hovering over me. I peeled my eyelids open to see Don, Corey, Carter, and the captain's faces looking down at me in worry.

"Move back!" I heard an unfamiliar voice demand. "We can't help him if we can't get to him!"

I squinted. "Who's that?" I asked, staring at Don.

"Goddamn medic. How many fingers am I holding up?"

I looked down to see him holding up two fingers.

"This can't be the afterlife. 'Cause fuck all if the first thing I see is your ugly mug," I grumbled, feeling pain shooting through my back. My air tank was poking me directly in the back, my full body weight against it as I lay sprawled on the sidewalk … or the middle of the street. I wasn't too sure where I landed.

"He's good," Don chuckled, standing up straighter. "You can look him over, sweetheart."

I hear the paramedic suck her teeth. "I'm not your damn sweetheart." Her voice grew closer and then her face came into view. "Don't move. Do you hurt anywhere?" she questioned shining her pin light into my eyes.

I cursed, squeezing my eyes shut against the brightness of the light.

"Don't sit up!" she yelled, but I ignored her. I'd already taken the liberty of assessing my body. I could wiggle my hands and toes, moved my legs, and I still had my helmet and all my gear on. My back was sore as all hell, but that was to be expected, considering it was my tank that likely broke my fall.

"I'm good," I said, sitting up. "Wow." I held my hand out as the world spun. I blinked a few times.

"Did you inhale any smoke?" the medic asked as she helped me remove my jacket and gear.

"I don't think so."

"That's good. We'd like to place you on a gurney and take you to the hospital to check you out."

I waved her off before she could even finish talking. "I'm okay," I insisted. "I just needed a little help standing up. Are they still working on putting the fire out?" I had no idea how long I was out or if I even passed out really. I got my bearings and then stood with the assistance of the paramedic and Don.

"Nah, fire's still burning. We're moving a hose in now. All the guys have gotten out," Corey informed me.

I nodded in his direction. "All right, let's go."

"I still need to check you out!" the paramedic insisted.

"I'm fine," I yelled over my shoulder, following behind the rest of the guys as we ran back over to the rig.

"Cap, there was no baby in that apartment. I searched everywhere," I told the captain once I got back to the rig.

He frowned. "I'm sorry, Harvard. The baby wasn't in there. In her panic, the mother thought her baby was left behind, but she placed the baby in a neighbor's arms while she grabbed her three-year-old. Both kids are with her now. Safe and sound." The captain jutted his head toward a woman who stood in the front of the crowd, cradling a baby in her arms, a young child hugging her leg.

I risked my life for a baby that was already safe. I felt no anger, however. This was my job, and people often made such errors in their panic. I was just glad the baby was safe, and I thanked God I made it out of there. I tilted my head up and saw flames shooting out from the windows of the second-floor apartments. It was now totally consumed. I didn't dwell, though. We still needed to tackle this fire to prevent it from spreading to any of the surrounding buildings.

Chapter Fourteen

Angela

Butterflies fluttered in my abdomen when I heard the rhythmic knock on my door. Eric always knocked the same little beat whenever he came over. I quickly wiped my hands with a dishtowel, tossed it on the counter, and removed the apron I was wearing before heading toward the door.

I couldn't stop the spreading of my lips, even if I wanted to when I opened the door to see him leaning against the side of the door. His signature dark jeans and T-shirt clung to the muscles of his arms and torso. A slight smile creased his lips, causing a glimmer in his dark eyes. Those dark orbs lazily scanned up and down my body, taking in the bright pink sleeveless tee and ripped blue jean shorts I wore. His smile increased when his gaze reached my bare toes. When his eyes met mine again, they were on fire.

Before I could say anything, a long arm snaked around my waist, pulling me into him and capturing my mouth. The kiss was hard and hungry. I opened up for him, letting him have his way with my mouth. I heard the door slam shut at the same time my back hit the wall.

"You look beautiful," he said, once he finally came up for air.

"I'm just wearing a T-shirt and shorts."

"I know. Take 'em off," he said, his hands already pulling up my shirt, discarding it. Next, his hands went to unbutton my jean shorts and he began kissing a trail down my belly dropping to his knees. After lowering my shorts and panties, he pressed a kiss to my belly-button before he began tonguing it. Moisture seeped from my passage at the erotic move. My belly-button was a particularly erogenous zone for me; something only Eric had ever discovered. And since he had, he never neglected that hot spot whenever we were intimate.

His firm hands gripped the side of my thighs tightly, pulling me into him. His nose brushed against the neatly trimmed hairs that covered my sex. He adjusted, placing my left leg over his broad shoulder. I braced myself, one hand clamping around the hairs at the top of his head while the other reached for the arm he held against the wall. He covered me with his mouth and ate ravenously. Within minutes my entire body was trembling, only being held up by Eric's hands

"Oh God!" I moaned, back arching off the wall behind me.

He pulled me into his mouth even more. A low growl sounded at the back of his throat, telling me how far gone he was. When his lips wrapped around my hardened button and sucked, he inserted two fingers inside of me, curling them to reach my g-spot, my pelvic muscles spasmed uncontrollably.

"Oh shiiit!" I rasped, my orgasm hitting me like a mack truck. My grip on his hair tightened as my hips moved wildly, wringing out the last moments of my orgasm. Eric waited until my orgasm completely passed, to lower my leg to the floor and stand. I opened my eyes to see the intensity of his gaze and his top lip shining with evidence of my satisfaction. I cupped his chiseled jaw and leaned up, licking my juices from his lips. He pressed me back against the wall, once again his tongue and mouth seizing the moment to take over. Within seconds, I heard the distinct sound of a condom wrapper wrinkling. I pulled back, and he placed the now opened wrapper in between us, and I grinned. This had become part of our usual routine as well.

I plucked the condom from his hands and then placed the condom between my lips, so it was standing. Just before I sunk to my knees, I saw the look of surprise on Eric's face. Taking his erect penis in my hand, I lowered my head, moving to adjust my positioning, so my mouth was right over the tip. Slowly I used my mouth to roll the condom up the length of his shaft. When he hit the back of my throat, I released and pulled back, pausing to make sure the condom was securely sheathing him. I barely had time to finish my inspection when strong arms gripped me under my shoulders, pulling me back to my feet.

"You're gonna have to do that move again. Without the condom," he said against my lips. "But right now I need to be inside of you." He lowered himself, pulling my legs up around his waist and pushed himself fully inside of me.

"Ohhhh," I groaned, loving the delicious fullness I always felt when he first entered me. My hands went underneath his arms, to grip his back. I pressed my fingernails into the skin of his back through his T-shirt.

"Shit!" he grunted, grimacing.

I stiffened at the expression on his face. We've been in this position enough times thus far for me to recognize his looks of pleasure. This was not one of them. He seemed to be in pain, which he never had before when I pressed my nails into his back.

"What's wrong?" I asked through pants.

"Nothing," he responded quickly. Too quickly.

"Eric, are you o—"

My question was cut off by his mouth making contact with mine. He began moving his hips and soon enough any worry I was feeling fled into a distant memory. I was now consumed in a bubble of pleasure, supplied in only the way Eric could. He didn't start off slowly; he ground his hips into me with the ferocity of a starving man making his way to his first meal in days. My head fell back against the wall, as his continuous ministrations had me feeling weak. He pumped so intensely my head bounced against the wall. Leaning his head down into the space between my shoulder and head, he bit the sensitive flesh there. I squeezed my hands into his back again, and this only spurred him on. I moaned and blubbered some words, I was pretty sure weren't *actual* words, but it didn't matter at all. The tingling sensation started at my curled toes, worked its way up my calves and thighs and exploding once it reached my core, surging through my belly until it finally burst out of my mouth on a loud yell.

"Erriiiiic!" I yelled his name as if it was a sacred chant because right then it was.

I tightened my knees around his waist when he, incredibly, picked up his pace, pounding hard as he growled into the space of my neck, yelling out his own orgasm. I held onto him, doing my best to provide comfort through his intense orgasm.

We panted for a long while, trying to regain our sanity after that episode. When my feet finally landed back on the hardwood floor, I was grateful for Eric's heavy body still pressed against me. I was sure I would've collapsed in a heap on the floor, otherwise. We stood there, face-to-face for a long while, just staring at one another. Eric's eyes were conveying something.

I don't know how long we stood like that, but eventually, our silence was broken by his growling stomach. I giggled. "Worked up an appetite, huh?"

"Seems so," he answered, pressing a quick kiss to my lips before stepping back.

I watched, licking my lips as he removed the condom and stuffed himself back into his jeans.

"I'll throw this out." Turning, he headed toward the bathroom.

When he left the room, I felt as if I could take the first real breath since the moment he arrived. I bent over, stepping into my panties and shorts. I headed back into the kitchen and felt relieved when I remembered I turned the pots on top of the stove off. I made a quick meal of fried pork chops, cheddar mashed potatoes, and sautéed green beans after Eric and I decided we'd stay in that evening. His shift didn't end until six o'clock that evening, and when he called earlier, he sounded exhausted. I moved to the cupboards overhead, pulling down two plates, as I wondered what restored his energy between earlier and just now. He was like the Energizer Bunny out in the foyer. I still felt the tingling sensations thanks to the orgasms he gave me.

"Mmm," I moaned when I felt his strong arms envelop me from behind. Leaning back against his broad chest, I closed my eyes and inhaled deeply, loving his scent. He smelled like us—of what we just shared—and I couldn't get enough of the combination of our smells.

"I shouldn't be thinking about sex while I'm in the kitchen."

He kissed the top of my head. "Says who?"

I shrugged. "I don't know. Women of decorum."

He snorted. "Fuck them," he growled, lowering his head to my neck, kissing it. I tilted my head to grant him better access, on instinct. But when I felt his hands move to the button of my shorts, I shook out of his hold.

"No." I turned and pointed to him. "We have time for more of that later," I said, swatting at his hand reaching for my shorts yet again. "You need to eat first. Go sit."

He frowned, looking at me as if I was speaking a foreign language he didn't understand.

"I'm serious! Go!" I shooed him away, giggling when he muttered a few curse words under his breath. I grinned and hummed a little to myself all while fixing both our plates. I carried them out to the table. Setting one down in front of an empty chair, I held the other out in front of Eric... but then pulled it just out of his grasp when he reached for it. His face crinkled in confusion.

"Rescue Four arrives on the scene of a two-story dwelling located on a cul-de-sac in which a fire is burning on the first floor. A neighbor approaches the firefighters, telling them details about the fire. What should be the first question the officer of the rig asks him?"

"There are no cul-de-sacs in Williamsport," he grumbled, now eyeing the plate of food I still held.

"A. Where do you live and what is your address? B. Is there presently anyone inside the residence? C. Did you see any suspicious people around the house before the fire? Or D. How long have the owners lived in this house?" I continued, ignoring his statement.

"Seriously? You turned down screwing again because you insisted on feeding me, but now you're quizzing me instead of feeding me," he snarked.

"A, B, C, or D. Answer correctly and you get to eat. And we don't *screw.*"

"B. Is there currently anyone present inside the residence. And we just screwed."

I rolled my eyes, setting his plate down in front of him. "You're lucky you got it right." This had become part of our *thing* now, too. In helping him prepare for the lieutenant's exam, I would randomly ask him test questions I read out of his study guide or that I found online.

"Of course I got it right. As a firefighter, our top priority is ensuring the safety of others."

I nodded. "You're right about that. But we still don't screw. Ah!" I yelped when he pulled me onto his lap.

"Then what do we do?" he asked before shoveling a forkful of mashed potatoes into his mouth.

I stared, watching him chew for a few heartbeats. How could a movement so trivial hold my attention captive?

"We make love," I finally answered. "It's true!" I insisted when he snorted in derision.

"Okay, Angel. Just don't tell anyone else that."

My belly tingled at the nickname he'd given me. "Okay, macho man."

"Open," he said, pointing a forkful of fried pork chop at me.

"I have my own plate."

"I like it when you eat off mine. Open."

My jaw slackened and eventually opened, allowing his fork entrance.

"You need to eat," I insisted between chews.

"You do, too, and I'm not letting you move from my lap, so we'll eat together. I plan on finishing this plate and then feasting on you for the rest of the night." He reached up to kiss my neck.

I squeezed my thighs at the idea of spending the rest of the night with his head between them. I could already feel myself growing wet with anticipation.

"I shouldn't be this far gone over you already." I sighed, laying my head on his shoulder, chewing the mouthful of string beans he'd fed me.

"It was only inevitable, Angel."

"How so?" I asked, my head popping up.

"Ladies can't resist a fireman." He winked.

"Oh yeah?"

He grinned. "It's a well-known fact."

"Whatever!" I laughed, tickling his sides and back.

"Shit!" he grunted when I made contact with one particular spot on his back.

"What's wrong? Did I—" I moved, raising the dark T-shirt he wore, exposing his bare back. "Oh my God!" I screeched. On his beautiful, usually creamy-tanned back was a huge dark purple bruise. The thing ran almost up the entire side of his back. "What the hell happened to you?" I stood, moving around behind the chair, holding tightly to the shirt he tried yanking down.

"It's nothing." His tone lost all joking it held before.

"Eric, this isn't nothing. Are you okay? Did you break anything? Oh my God! I dug my nails into your back out in the foyer. I could've hurt you. Why didn't you tell me?!"

"Angel, calm down. It's just a little thing that happened at work."

"A little thing? Have you seen the size of this bruise? Did you break anything?" I used my fingers to scan the rest of his upper body, as he now stood before me.

"No, nothing's broken."

"What happened?"

"It was just work."

"Did you run into something? Or something run into you? Did you fall?"

"It was no big deal. Just part of the job."

"Part of the job? Tell me what happened?" I was growing angrier by the second. The thought of Eric being seriously injured at work made me feel unhinged all of a sudden. Of course, I realized danger was part of the job, but seeing it up close was scarier than I ever thought. My father and brother always did a good job of playing down the dangers of their jobs, and I let them, choosing to think about the good they did instead of the fact that they had a job that required them to put themselves in harm's way on a daily basis.

"I needed to jump out of a two-story window."

I gasped. "What?"

"The ladder had been pulled down, and I was searching for a baby inside."

"Oh my goodness!" I covered my face with my hands.

"Hey," he called, removing my hands from my face, "I'm fine."

"I know, but—"

"But nothing. We don't think about the what-ifs in my line of work, okay?" He didn't give me time to respond. My head fell back when he tilted my chin up, his lips devouring mine. I could taste the food he'd been eating on his lips, mixed with his flavor.

"Remember what I told you about my crew?" he asked, once he pulled back, my chin still in between his fingers.

My brain was foggy from his kiss. I tried to recall everything he said about the men he works with.

"They're assholes."

A deep chuckle moved past his lips. "Yes, and what else?"

The night we drove around and then parked out on the overlook where we listened to fire calls throughout the night came back to mind.

"They're the best of the best. Your insurance policy."

He nodded. "Exactly. You don't have to worry about me."

I knew they were just words. Knew he was saying it just to make me feel better. To feel less scared. But when he moved in again, his mouth covering mine, I had no more words, just the feeling of being swept up and carried by a wave. It took me a while to realize I was being carried. Eric had scooped me up in his arms and walked with me down the hallway. Finishing dinner took much longer that night.

****

Eric

"Oof! What are you doing?" I grumbled, sleep still in my eyes as I lay sprawled, stomach down in Angela's bed. She'd just climbed on top of me, straddling, but sitting lower on my back toward my butt, as to not place her weight on my bruised side.

"I'm giving you a rub down."

I laughed. "You didn't do that enough last night?"

"No!" she insisted. After we made love... wait did I say make love? After we screwed again, and then finished our dinner, my Angel insisted on giving me a back rub before applying ice to my bruises.

"Last night was cold to reduce swelling. This morning I'm applying heat to help loosen up muscles. Just lay still."

I felt a warm compress laid on my back and fuck all if it didn't feel like heaven. I caught the moan that tried to escape my lips just before it made its way out. Instead, I relaxed, laying my head back down against the pillow. Angela's soft hands reached up to my shoulders, rubbing and massaging the kinks out of them and my upper back. My body began to feel like jelly. This almost felt as good as being in between Angela's thighs as I slid all the way to the hilt inside of her. Almost. Nothing felt as good as that. Hell, not even fighting fires. And for the last seven years, *nothing* had felt better than fighting fires.

"What're your plans today?" I slurred.

"Spending the day with you... after I finish my wash day."

I opened one eye, looking over my shoulder. "What's a wash day?"

Her hands paused at my shoulders. "Have you ever dated a black woman before?"

"Yeah, a few. Why?"

"Have any of them had natural hair?"

"Natural hair? Isn't all hair natural?"

She laughed. "Clearly, you weren't too serious about any of them. You definitely would know more about our hair. Anyway, wash day is the day I set aside to pamper my hair. I usually reserve it for Sundays, but since I was otherwise occupied with you this past Sunday, I have to do it today." It was Wednesday, one of her regular days she had off. She took off the previous night to spend it with me, having recently hired a new bartender.

"What does it entail?" I asked, laying my head back down and she resumed her massage.

"I usually pre-poo with coconut oil—"

"Pre-what?"

A giggle burst from her lips. "Pre-shampoo. We call it a pre-poo because it's done before I shampoo my hair. I coat my strands with coconut oil to remove any shed hairs and detangle, then shampoo, do a deep condition, rinse it out, and then apply my leave-in and style." She finished the last part as if it were simple.

"Sounds complicated."

"It's not. You get used to it, and with my short cut it's much less time consuming than it used to be."

"I wanna help," I said, turning over to grab her waist and hold her in place as I shifted to lay on my back.

"Eric, your back!" she yelled.

"My back feels fine, especially after all your pampering. Let me help with your wash day."

She stared at me, hands at her waist. "This is what you want to spend your day doing? Helping me wash my hair?"

"You said it wouldn't take long, right? We can go see that damn chick flick you wanted to see when we're done."

A thirty-megawatt smile formed on her lips. "Really?" She leaned down, lips not far from mine. I took the opportunity to brush mine against them. Hell, I took every opportunity I could to feel her lips on mine and anywhere else I could get them.

"Yeah."

"Okay, let's go." She hopped off of me and out of bed. "You okay?" she asked, frowning when she saw me moving slowly to sit up.

My back did feel a little stiff, which was to be expected, but I knew it felt a shitload better than it would've felt without Angela's nursing it. The day before the captain insisted I take the day off. I hadn't wanted to but when I remembered it was a Wednesday, which meant I could spend the entire day with my Angel, my "no" suddenly became "okay."

"Never felt better," I responded, my hand at the small of her back urging her toward the bathroom.

"I didn't know you could use coconut oil on hair," I said, taking the jar with the liquid oil from her. "Do you pour it in your hair?" I asked. Although it was well into September, the temperatures had remained in the high eighties, allowing the oil that solidified during the colder months to remain in its liquid form.

She laughed. "No, I do this," she began explaining and demonstrating at the same time. I watched as she took large sections of her hair and coated them with oil, removed any shed hair, and then put the section in twists. When she got to the back part of her hair that was too short for twists, she simply coated those strands with the oil.

"The coconut oil helps to prevent the shampoo from stripping too much moisture from my hair. Which is important since I added the color."

I looked over and felt one of the twists she'd done, feeling the softness of her hair.

"Let me," I said, reaching for the bottle of shampoo in her hand.

She blinked. "You want to shampoo my hair?"

"Yeah. It's not hard. Get in the shower," I directed, turning on the water. When I looked back to see her still standing there, an unsure expression on her face looking unsure, I reached for the T-shirt she wore, which was the one I'd worn the night before, pulling it over her head. My mouth watered when I saw she had nothing on underneath. "Get in." My voice dropped an octave.

This time she did as requested.

I pushed the boxer briefs I wore to the floor, removing them, and stepped in behind her. "Is the water too warm?"

She shook her head.

I nodded slightly, taking her head and tilting it back so that it fell underneath the spray of the water. I made sure to drench every strand. Next, I turned the bottle of shampoo over in my hand, dropped the bottle when I had the sufficient amount, and then began massaging the cleansing agent into her hair. I started off doing small circles at the back of her head, moving my hands up and over her scalp. I lowered my eyes to her face to see her eyes closed, mouth parted.

"Is this good?" I questioned.

Her hands reached up to my wrists, holding them lightly. "Mmm," she moaned. "Perfect. Don't stop. Don't *ever* stop," she repeated in a whisper.

My cock jumped between us, pressing against her belly. I quickly rinsed the shampoo out of her hair, knowing the inevitable was about to occur. I turned our bodies so that her back was against the wall, as I continued massaging her scalp with my fingertips. The spray of the shower head was now hitting my back as I leaned in, shielding her from it. I couldn't stop even if I wanted to. I stole a kiss from her parted lips, then another and another. Her hands ran down my arms and up over my biceps until they reached the back of my head, pulling me into her. Using my knee I pushed her legs apart, reaching down with one arm to pull one of her legs up around my hip. I slid inside of her easily, and instantly an electric zing ran down my spine over my buttocks, causing me to thrust into her even deeper. My hand in her hair tightened, pulling her head back, exposing her neck to my awaiting mouth. I kissed, sucked, and nibbled on just about every part of exposed flesh as I could reach while thrusting in and out of her.

"E-Eric!" she panted.

I grew harder at the sound of my name spilling from her. I lost track of all time and space, getting completely caught up in her. My hips pumped and moved vigorously, needing more of this feeling. The muscles of her sex tightened and I growled when a feeling like no other came over me.

"Fuck!" I cursed into her neck, reveling in all the sensations that were pulling at me. Her muscles spasmed around me again, and I knew she was coming. I held on tighter, pushing her to her climax. I leaned back to watch her come—eyes squeezed shut, bottom lip sucked in between her teeth, face contorted, the vein in her neck bulging. *Absolutely gorgeous.*

I felt the swelling of my cock and knew I was about to explode as well.

"E-Eric," she panted. "W-we didn't use protection."

I tried to make sense of what she was saying, but all I wanted was to feel my release let go inside of her.

"You h-have to pull out," she continued, now pushing at my chest with her hands.

Through my daze, I realized why this time felt different. There was no barrier between us.

Shit! I didn't want this feeling to end. I thought about staying right where I was, allowing my sperm to blast off in her womb.

"Fuck!" I cursed as I made my decision and pulled completely out of her, my come spilling on her upper thighs and stomach, and the floor of the bathtub.

I pressed my hand against the tiles of the bathtub, leaning into Angela, both of us, catching our breath. It took me a minute to process just how far gone I was and how close I was to ejaculating inside of her without any protection. Something I've *never* done before.

"Thank you," she whispered, kissing my chin.

My hand went to the back of her neck, cupping it. I pulled back slightly, to let her see my eyes. "I won't come inside of you until we're married."

Her eyes bulged at my declaration.

"Until?" she repeated.

I nodded. Then put my hands back into her hair. "You do the conditioner next, right?"

She stared at me for a moment before nodding. I knew I just dropped a bomb on her and she was figuring out what I meant. If I was serious. Of course I was serious. We may only be a few months in, but a man knows when he knows. And I knew.

Chapter Fifteen

Angela

"Hey! Open up!"

My head swung in the direction of the front door to *Charlie's*. I blew out a breath when I saw it was just Sean at the door. We still had an hour until the bar opened for the day, which meant it was just me.

"Hey, thanks for coming," I said, once I unlocked and opened the door for my brother. "Where's my nephew?"

"I'm not enough?" he asked.

"No. Where's my guy?"

"He's with his mama. Damn shame. I can't even get a hello from my own sister since his little ass came in the picture."

I laughed, swatting his chest. "I did say hey and thanked you for stopping by to fix the faucet." The faucet behind the bar had been acting funny, and when I mentioned it to Sean, he offered to stop by to take a look at it. He was the consummate handyman.

"Yeah, whatever. Speaking of your guys, why didn't you ask your little friend to come take a look?"

I gave him a dry expression. "Don't refer to Eric as my little friend. Especially, since he's about the same height as you."

"Yeah, but he's scrawny."

I laughed at the ridiculousness of his statement. "He's hardly scrawny. You've seen firsthand that he's very well chiseled."

My brother snorted, lips twisted in disgust. "Don't fucking remind me."

I laughed, remembering how Sean had walked in on us the day before...

"Angela you— Oh shit! The hell are you doing here and with no shirt on?" Sean yelled, as he walked into my house, using the house key I given him.

"Sean!" I screeched, moving around Eric and entering the living room. "What are you doing here?"

My brother frowned, giving me an incredulous look. "What am I doing here? This is my parents' house. The house I grew up in. The more appropriate question is what is he doing here, and with no shirt!"

"You probably should calm down."

My eyes bulged when I heard the challenge in Eric's voice as he stepped around me, getting in between Sean and I. I couldn't let this happen.

"Yo, who the hell—"

"Hey, hey, hey!" I yelled, getting in between the two giants. "Let's everyone take a breather." I inhaled, as a example, and then exhaled. "Okay, Sean, you already know Eric. He and I are... dating."

"Dating?" Sean acted as if it was a foreign word to him.

"Yes, dating, as in seeing each other, a couple," Eric spoke up.

"Yes, Sean, we're dating. And this isn't your house. It's mine, and I've told you to call before you come over."

My brother sucked his teeth, giving me a side-eye, before directing his attention back to Eric.

"You're dating my little sister? This better not be some game, or for gossip around the station." He pointed at Eric.

"If it were, you would've heard about it by now... not that it's any of your damn business."

"My sister is my business. And I know how you bunch at Rescue Four blow through women."

"Not any more than you all at Rescue Two," Eric retorted.

Sean looked stumped there.

"Whatever, man. You just make sure you do right by my sister."

"I don't have to be told that, but thanks for the reminder."

"Yeah, whatever," Sean grumbled, taking one last look at me and then heading out the door he just entered.

"That's what you get for barging into my house without calling first. Serves you right," I told Sean, leaning over the bar.

"Whatever, Angela. I just hope you know what you're doing." He planted the small tool bag he brought with him on the counter.

"And why wouldn't I?" I asked defensively.

"Because I know how women fall all over firefighters. I am one, remember? We talk a few sweet words, tell 'em a story or two about the job, and they're putty."

"Gee, thanks for the vote of confidence."

He pursed his lips. "I'm serious, Angela."

"I'm serious, too. I'm not a young twenty-something falling for the hot guy with the dangerous job. I was raised by a firefighter and the big brother I always looked up to is one, remember?"

Sean, peered at me dead on, his lips twitching at the compliment. He sighed.

"I mean, the two men I've loved my whole life are firefighters and set the bar pretty damn high on how I should be treated. It only makes sense I'd fall for a firefighter who treats me pretty damn special as well."

I looked up to see a raised eyebrow staring back at me. "Fall for?"

I hadn't even realized my slip of the tongue there. "Yeah," I sighed.

"And you think he's as serious about you as you are him?"

I thought back to the previous day, Eric's wet body pressed against mine in the shower. The words he spoke about not releasing inside of me until we get married. Not *if* but *when.*

The acuteness of his gaze as he looked me right in the eye. As if it was a foregone conclusion.

"Yeah, I think so," I responded; my voice sounded airy to my ears.

Sean paused, watching me for a few moments before finally nodding.

"Why didn't you have lover boy come fix this faucet since he has you all starry-eyed and shit?"

"He offered, but he had to work, and I needed it looked at before his shift ended. Thank you very much!" I added, popping one of the maraschino cherries from the bar into my mouth.

He feigned hurt. "So I was your second option?"

"Yes. Don't pretend like your feelings are hurt, I offered to make you and my nephew my double fudge brownies as a token of my appreciation."

"And I'm holding you to that, too." He pointed at me as he sank to the floor to take a look underneath the faucet.

I waved my hand in the air dismissively. "I know. I know."

****

Eric

"Studying hard?"

I peeked over my shoulder to see Carter rounding my cot. I had a stack of notecards in my hand, all with facts, figures, and information that would be pertinent to the lieutenant's exam. I carried them with me everywhere these days. Whenever there was a free moment at the station, I pulled them out. I was loathed to admit out loud, but part of the reason I was so drawn to the cards wasn't solely because of the exam. It was also the adorable, cursive handwriting that Angela had written on the cards. Interspersed between the actual information-filled cards were notecards that read things like "You've got this in the bag!" or "You've already aced the test!" or "I'm so proud of you for passing!" Who does that type of shit? Better yet, what type of a sap got a thrill out of it?

Me.

That's who.

It was pure joy knowing I had that type of support. I mean, sure the guys at the station were supportive, but nothing compared to hearing Angela tell me what a good job I was doing. I think I could've lived on her compliments alone.

"Yeah, the test is in little less than a month," I responded to Carter.

He nodded, sitting across from me on his cot. "And what happens after the test?"

"Well, *if* I pass, then I'll have to interview with some department heads. They'll check my resume, test scores, commendations, and all of that, then make a decision."

"And if you get promoted there's a chance you'll be out of Rescue Four, right?"

I almost flinched at that reminder. The department didn't like to promote within the same station since it was believed that the new lieutenant would have a less likely chance of being respected. From their standpoint, it was hard for a group of firefighters to now look at someone who'd been their peer for so long, now as someone they had to report to.

"There's a possibility, but since Rescue Four needs lieutenants, I'm hoping they'll promote within."

"Since Gary..." Carter's gaze dropped to the floor. A solemn feeling hovered in the air. Gary was Rescue Four's other lieutenant who died while doing the job we all love so much. Carter was injured while trying to save him. He died in Carter's arms.

"He would've wanted the job filled. And I know he'd be honored to have you take his place," Carter finally spoke.

I kept my gaze lowered, as a weight settled in my chest. We didn't do a lot of sappy emotions here, so when we did, it hit you in your chest.

"Now, let's see what you got for these questions." Carter broke up the moment, snatching the stack of notecards from my hands.

Leaping up, I reached to snatch the notecards from his hands. Carter pulled back. "I'm just trying to help, man. Relax." He looked at me as if I was ridiculous. "All right, let's see, okay...You've just reported for your shift at the station, and while stowing your gear, you hear a noise in the bathroom. You go to check it out and see Firefighter B slumped over in a stall, the stench of alc—" He broke off, realizing the remaining part of the question.

"Just give me." I reached for the cards, and he moved again.

"No. No, it's fine. You should know the answer to this question anyway. You smell the stench of alcohol, what do you do. A ..." He rattled off the answer options before stopping to look at me, expectantly. "You've already lived it, and you made the right call. What do you do?"

"Carter—"

"Harvard, answer the question. What do you do?"

"Report it to an officer."

He flipped the card for the answer. "Correct. See, that wasn't so bad. Okay, next question."

I blew out a breath, arms folded across my chest as he flipped to the next card.

"Well, what's this here? *I'm so proud of you,*" he read from the card in a mock girly voice. "Awww, isn't that the cutest thing," he sing-songed. "With the little hearts around it for emphasis," he continued taunting me and turned the card, holding it up for me to see.

That's when I lunged for him to grab the stack. "Shut the fuck up!" I yelled over his roaring laughter.

"Does she cut the crust off your sandwiches, too?" he gibed.

"I'll fucking kill you," I growled as we wrestled.

"Better men than you have tried." His laughter sounded like taunting cackles in my ear.

A deep clearing of the throat followed by, "Gentlemen," broke up our ruckus.

From the floor, both of our eyes first went to the shiny black boots directly in front of us, up the legs, torso, and eventually the stern face of Captain Waverly.

"Entertaining yourselves in between calls?"

I peered over at Carter, shoving his shoulder as we both stood up. I snatched the stack of notecards from him when he was unaware.

"Sorry, Cap."

"I was just trying to help Harvard study." Mirth still filled Carter's voice.

"I see. Might be helpful to do that with a little less wrestling."

"Noted," Carter nodded his head and responded.

"I need to speak with you." Captain's eyes were planted on Carter.

"Sure thing, Cap."

Captain turned and walked away in the direction of his office. Carter started behind him, giving me a look over his shoulder.

"I hope you're getting fired," I tossed at him.

A grin broke out on Carter's face.

"No such luck, Harvard," Captain yelled over his shoulder, causing Carter's laugh to intensify.

I chuckled, shaking my head as I watched the pair disappear behind the Captain's door. At the same time, my cell phone rang. I picked it up from my cot without looking and answered, "Hello."

"Hi, son."

My eyes snapped shut in regret. I should've checked before I answered.

"Hey, Ma."

I've barely spoken to my mother since the night of my father's birthday party. When we did speak, she tried to ask if I was still seeing Angela. Hearing the disapproval in her voice, I chose to maintain my distance for the time being.

"Are you working?"

"Yup."

"Okay, I don't want to keep you, but I did want to ask if we could meet for lunch or dinner. I'd like to talk. We haven't spoken, *really* spoken, in so long."

I snorted. "I can't do lunch or dinner. I'm working an overnight shift."

"What about tomorrow?"

I closed my eyes, chest rising as I inhaled. "We can do breakfast around nine-fifteen tomorrow morning."

"You won't be too tired after your shift?"

"I'll be fine."

"Okay, let's meet at that little breakfast place not too far from campus that you love."

"I'll be there."

"Okay, son. I love you."

"Me too, Ma." I disconnected the call wondering what to expect at breakfast.

****

I walked into the breakfast place that was just a block away from the university where my mother had been a faculty member for more than twenty years. When I looked around, I saw my mother waving in my direction, already seated at one of the booths. I sauntered over to her table, feeling the eleven calls we went on the previous night. My goal was to get this over as soon as possible and head home for some sleep.

"Hey, Mom," I greeted, pressing a kiss to her cheek before sitting.

She frowned. "You look tired."

"We had a busy night." I ran a hand down my face.

"I figured you would be tired. I ordered a cup of coffee for you. Black." She pushed a mug of piping hot coffee across the shiny surface of the wooden table towards me.

Relief flooded my veins as soon as the smell of the coffee hit my nostrils. This jolt of caffeine would help hold me over for the next hour or two until I could get home to my bed.

"Thanks for this." I took a sip. "So, what'd you want to talk about?"

"Let's order breakfast first, shall we." She waved her hand for the waitress.

I held my tongue just wanting to get this over and done with. I was tired as hell, and frankly, I was leery of what my mother had to say. She ordered an omelet with toast and fruit, while I got a breakfast sandwich on an everything bagel.

"Okay, breakfast has been ordered."

"What about juice? We haven't ordered any—"

"Ma, please." I did my best to control my voice.

"Okay, okay. It's just that I feel like I see you so rarely these days. I'm afraid you're going to rush away."

"And whose fault is that?" I clasped my hands, placing them on the table and sitting forward.

Her eyes narrowed. "I'm still your mother."

I nodded. "Which is why I'm here. You are my mother, and I love you very much. But that doesn't mean your behavior toward Angela didn't disappoint me or that I'd let it stand."

My mother sat back in the booth, using one hand to push her short hair behind her left ear. "You care for this woman."

"Very much."

"Why?"

I tilted my head. "You want me to explain why I care for her?"

"Yes."

I sighed and thought about it for a moment. Not about why I cared so deeply for Angela—that answer was as easy to come up with as breathing—I pondered whether or not I even wanted to answer my mother. I didn't feel like I needed to explain myself or my feelings to her. But then I remember how important it was to give a little when it came to relationships with others, even parents... hell, especially parents.

"I adore the way she can light up a room. How she works to make others around her feel included and acknowledged. I love how supportive she is and that she isn't shy about telling me how well I'm doing while studying for the lieutenant's exam."

"You're studying for the exam? For a promotion?"

I nodded.

My mother clasped her own hands on the table, her gaze averted. "I didn't know that."

"That makes you upset," I observed.

She peered up at me, blinking, trying to hide the sadness in her eyes. "No. Yes. Maybe. I don't know."

I frowned. "You're confusing me, Ma."

We grew quiet when the waitress brought out our plates. My mother's face remained somber, as she unfolded a napkin, placed it in her lap, and picked up her knife and fork in preparation to begin eating, which we did in silence.

"I just feel like I don't know you anymore. You're my only son, and we've grown so distant over the last seven years. Ever since you became a firefighter."

I peered up at her from my half-eaten sandwich, wiped my mouth, and swallowed the last bite I took. "That's not the job's fault, Ma."

She held up her hands. "I know."

"When I joined, you and Dad made it clear how much you despised the idea. I don't know if you realize, but going through the academy was the toughest thing I ever did. It would've been nice having my parents support me through that." I clamped my mouth shut, not wanting anymore to spill out. I held that in for the last seven years. Since the academy, I've been through a hell of a lot more, but still kept it from my parents because I knew if I dared speak up on the darker side of my job, they'd be down my throat about my quitting and going back to work in finance.

"You're right. But you have to understand our point of view. We put you in the best schools we could get you in, spent money on all the best tutors and lessons to get you into Harvard so that you could have the opportunities that not many others could even dream of."

"I appreciate all of that, Mom. I do. But what about what *I* wanted? I tried the life you and Dad placed me in. I did the finance thing, and I was miserable every day. I knew early on my calling was to help others, to be a fireman. No, it doesn't require the Harvard education, but it is a worthy career."

"I know that," she defended.

"Then why couldn't you just support me?" My voice rose higher than I intended. I exhaled, shaking my head and staring off out of the window. "It doesn't even matter," I stated, my gaze pinned on a passersby. "All I want to know is what any of this has to do with Angela? Why are you so reluctant to get to know her?"

"She's just different," my mother insisted. "I always pictured you with some introverted girl, who'd make the perfect stay-at-home mom or working a regular nine-to-five. Not someone with purple hair who owns a bar."

"Again, your dream not mine."

She held up her hand. "You're right. It's taking me time to come around to the idea that you are your own man. And honestly, when I saw you with her the night of your father's birthday, you two seemed to complement each other. It made me a little jealous."

"Jealous?"

"Yes." She nodded, taking a sip of her coffee. "You've never been that close to me. I felt left out, especially when I saw how your father melted at her charms as well."

I grinned. "Angela has that effect on people."

"I saw. I went down to that bar she owns."

My head snapped back in shock. "When?"

"Two weeks ago with some colleagues. She didn't see me. We walked in, and she was dancing behind the bar, making drinks, and making sure everyone was having a good time. When she came from around the bar to greet guests at the tables, I ducked and headed to the bathroom," my mother admitted sheepishly.

I chuckled. "Were you on a recognizance mission?"

She shrugged. "I just wanted to see her for myself. See who she was when she wasn't putting on a front for her boyfriend's parents."

"And?"

She let out a little moan and sighed. "She seemed just as genuine."

"Though you obviously loathe to admit it."

"It's not that. I just feel like I've lost so much time with you, and now this wonderful woman has come into your life and…" She paused and shrugged. "It seems like I'll get even less of you."

"Ma—"

"I know, I'm being silly." She waved her hand around. "I just, your life terrifies me," she admitted and ducked her head, dabbing at her eyes with her napkin.

"My life? You mean my job?"

"Your job is your life. At least it was until this Angela came along. And I feel left out of that, too, and it all just terrifies me." She sighed heavily.

I was still confused as to what she meant by all this.

"It's hard to explain, son. You'll understand when you have your own children. You raise them and have this image of who they'll be, and then they grow up to be their own people, and you just want to go back to the time when you were their whole world."

"I don't know how to respond to that." I felt for my mother, so I reached across the table to grab her hand.

"You don't have to respond. I just need to do better at learning to accept you for who you are and not who I want you to be."

"That'd probably save us a whole lot of trouble."

She let out a small laugh. "Probably."

Covering my hand with hers, she squeezed. "I love you, son. And I'm so sorry for not being there like you needed us during your training."

I nodded, touched by her apology. "Thanks for that."

"With that said, I'd like to have you and Angela over. For a do-over. No extra guests this time. You, me, your father, and Angela."

I raised an eyebrow.

"Your father and I would really like to have a second chance."

I blew out a breath. "I'll talk to Angela about it, and we'll see when our schedules are free."

My mother smiled a genuine smile.

We finished up our breakfasts, talking a little more just catching up with one another. I missed my mother—both my parents in the last few weeks, but even longer than that. I've never really expressed how hurt I was while training during the academy. I remember wanting to quit more than once and feeling like I wasn't cut out for this career. But it was the will instilled in me by my parents that made me forge ahead. All the stories I heard growing up of what my grandparents went through just to come here and fend for themselves spurred me on. *If they could endure that, I sure as hell could endure this,* I spent many nights repeating over and over to myself.

I insisted on taking care of the bill once we finished. After giving my mother a kiss on the cheek and promises that I'd do my best to set up that date, I headed home. I planned to get some sleep before I needed to return to work that night, but not before stopping over at *Charlie's* to see my favorite girl.

Chapter Sixteen

Angela

"You're really going to do it? You're going to walk into the lion's den again?"

I frowned at how dramatic she made it sound. I hit the speaker button so that I could talk while I continued to apply my makeup at the vanity in my bedroom. "Yes, Janine. I'm going to go to dinner with Eric over to his parents' home. And stop calling it the lion's den."

"But what if she invites his ex over again?"

"Eric's not thinking about her, and I doubt his mother would do that again. He was so pissed the first time."

"If you say so." She sucked her teeth.

I laughed at her sarcasm. "I've already been assured she wouldn't do that."

"From Eric, but what about his—"

"Not from Eric. From his mother. She got my number from Eric and personally called to apologize for our last encounter and invite us to dinner. No surprises this time."

"At least she had the class to invite you personally."

"Right? I think that was a good sign. So tell me what's going on with you." Picking up my black eyeliner, I stuck my head closer to the mirror, pulling on my cheek to make my water line easier to access, and began applying the liner. I heard Janine sigh through the line.

"Same ol', same ol'. Matt is still acting a fool. I think I'm over it. I'm so over his shit and this city in general."

I snorted, switching eyes. "I've heard that before."

"I think I'm serious this time. Matt obviously isn't in the mood for marriage anytime soon. Boston is full of yuppie professionals who are more into playing games than building a family. Maybe it's just me."

"Well, if you're for real, you know my cousin still rents out her place and is looking for a tenant while she travels. You'd have plenty of opportunities to find a job in interior design here in Williamsport."

There was a pause on the other end of the phone. I pulled out my powder brush, dabbed it in the brown powder that matched my skin perfectly, and tapped it a couple of times on the edge to remove the excess before I applied it.

"Hello?" I called, swirling the powder around my chin, cheeks, nose, and forehead—my typically shiny areas.

"I'm thinking." Janine's voice was pensive. "Can I get back to you? How long before your cousin rents out the place?"

"I don't know. Her current tenants are moving out at the end of this month, and I think she has someone staying for a month after that, but she wants someone long-term."

"Hmm, I need to think about this."

I could picture my friend biting her thumbnail, contemplatively. She rarely made a decision without thinking about it in a thousand different ways.

"Okay, I have to go, but I'll give you a ring this weekend."

"'K, bye."

Just as we hung up, that familiar rhythmic knock on the door sounded. I cursed, wishing he was just five minutes late.

"Coming!" I yelled, rushing to the door still in my tan camisole and high-waist jeans.

"Hi, I'm running a little behind. Oh, sorry," I said, pressing a kiss to his lips. "I was talking with Janine and got a little sidetracked."

"How is she?" Eric asked, stepping in and shutting the door behind him. I took a second to admire the black pants he wore instead of jeans and a blue Polo shirt. We've talked before about Janine and the many good times we had in college and afterward.

"She's still hung up on her guy. But I think she's considering moving out of Boston."

"Change can be good."

"Yeah. Okay, let me finish getting dressed. I'll be right out."

"Sure, but first ..." He grabbed me around the waist, pulling me to him. He first nibbled at my bottom lip, using my gasp to give his tongue entrance. My arms ended up around his neck. We kissed for what felt like forever, and still not long enough.

"Good thing you hadn't put on your lipstick just yet."

I grinned. "I don't know, I think you'd look pretty good with my *Ruby Woo* red lipstick smeared all over your lips."

"Yeah, I don't think so." He released me, taking a step back to allow me to pass by to finish getting dressed.

I decided on a sheer, sleeveless top and my long, light grey cardigan that stopped just above the floor in the four-inch heels I chose to wear. It was getting close to early October, and the fall weather was breaking here in Williamsport. I applied my favorite nude lipstick and grabbed the overnight bag I packed earlier since I was staying at Eric's place tonight.

"All set?" he asked when I rounded the corner.

"Ready, Freddie!"

He stopped, hand on the doorknob, looking at me crazy.

"What? It's a saying. Let's go, we don't want to be too late. Your mother already hates me," I joked.

Eric didn't like my joke much if the frown that marred his face was anything to go by.

"I'm kidding."

"Yeah," he tutted, opening the door.

Forty-five minutes later, we were pulling up to the home of his parents. Though I was hesitant, I knew whatever the issue was Mrs. Kim had with me it wouldn't be resolved by my refusing ever to see the woman again. Eric assured me that it wasn't my fault, or rather that his mother's issue wasn't personal, but something all her own. He said they had a good talk over breakfast a few weeks back. I certainly wasn't about to be the wedge standing between Eric having a good relationship with his family, so it was an easy choice to make when his mother called. But that didn't mean I didn't have my doubts.

"Come in." Eric's mother waved us in, once we rang the bell. Her demeanor was more affable than last time.

"How're you, Ma?" Eric asked, leaning down to kiss her cheek.

"I'm well. Hi, Angela, how are you?"

"I'm well, Mrs. Kim. Thank you for inviting us again."

"You're welcome. And what do you have there?" She tipped her head to the plate in my hands.

"I didn't want to step on your toes again, but Eric said you like these ginger cookies, so I made some."

She hesitated, but then said, "Thank you."

Her eyes moved to Eric and then back to me. "Will you follow me and we can set them in the kitchen?"

I briefly peered over at Eric, noting the surprise and then doubtful expression, before I followed, placing a hand on his wrist when he tried to follow.

"Eric, your father's in the dining room. He's expecting you," Mrs. Kim called.

He hesitated, but I urged him with a nudge of the shoulder, and after a pause, he finally moved in the opposite direction toward the living room.

"You can set those right on the counter." Mrs. Kim pointed, and I did as requested. "I wanted to talk to you alone, before dinner," she said, stating what I already guessed.

I remained quiet, waiting for her to make her peace.

"I know Eric told you that he and I spoke."

"Yes, he did."

"It was a good conversation," she sighed, wiping her hands with a dishtowel. "Probably long overdue. Eric's father and I weren't there like we should've been when he went through the Academy. I'm sure he's told you about his schooling and former job."

I nodded.

"Yes, well, Eric obviously had other plans than what we set out for him. And we're still coming to terms with that. You just got caught up in the middle of all of that."

"I see," I stated, still not really understanding.

"I don't think you do," she retorted. "I think once you have children you'll understand. You do want to have children, right?"

"Yes. Three," I answered, quickly, then slapped my hand over my mouth.

Mrs. Kim laughed.

"Don't tell Eric I said that. We haven't discussed children," I implored.

"Your secret's safe with me," she whispered, laughing.

"Mrs. Kim, I don't know what it's like having a son who's a firefighter, but I do know what it's like having a father, brother, and now the man I love as firefighters. It's scary thinking about the fact that every time they go to work, they put themselves in harm's way. I've seen the bruises he walks away with, and it makes my heart stop."

Mrs. Kim gasped slightly.

"I'm sorry. I didn't—"

She waved my apology off. "No, it's okay. Well, it's not *okay.* His job terrifies me. My husband and I intended for him to grow up and taking over as CFO of Townsend Industries once his father retired. And if not there, somewhere else."

I remained silent, nodding.

"But he had other plans." His mother lips pursed, her eyes appearing regretful, making me even sadder.

"Mrs. Kim, I know you and I didn't get off to the greatest start, and I wouldn't presume to know more about your son than you do, but ... Eric was born to be a firefighter. It's just in him. I see it. The way his eyes light up when he talks about his job. The way he reaches for his radio scanner in the car, even when he's not on shift. The joy he expresses when talking about his colleagues. Even in how intensely he's been studying for the lieutenant's exam. He's a natural. At least from what I see. And it'd be a shame to try to persuade the person I love from not doing what he's called to do. While his job scares the hell out of me, it also makes him who he is. So I can accept the fear because I wouldn't want to change him."

I twisted my fingers in front of me, feeling like once again I over-spoke. Here I was telling a mother about her son, in her kitchen. I was trying to make a good impression, but I couldn't hold back what was in my heart.

The wrinkle around her eyes increased as she narrowed her gaze at me, folding her arms across her chest. "I think you just might know him better than I do."

I exhaled, totally not expecting that. I shook my head. "No, I don't—"

"Yes," her head bobbed up and down, "you do. That's what happens when you fall in love with someone. You get to know them inside and out. For the men in his family that seems to happen in a relatively short period." She let out a sound that strangely mirrored a laugh.

I cracked a smile. "Eric said you and his father married two weeks after meeting each other."

Her cheeks turned a rose color as she blushed. "It was more like thirteen days. But that's a story for another time." She waved her hands around. "Would you like to help me set up the table?"

"Just point me in the direction of the silverware and plates," I offered.

Ten minutes later the table was covered with the food his mom prepared, and Mr. Kim and Eric sat at the table with us. This night was markedly different than the first time around. Both Mr. and Mrs. Kim asked questions of Eric and I. Not in an interrogative way, but conversationally. I felt more at ease and welcomed. When Eric squeezed my hand under the table, I squeezed his right back feeling as if we successfully passed this little hurdle in our budding relationship.

****

Eric

"That wasn't so bad, was it?" I questioned, as we stepped out of the elevator to my floor. Angela's hand was in mine while her overnight bag was slung over my left shoulder.

"I guess not," she sing-songed, stepping out in front of me, hands still connected as she twirled herself around. I grinned at how carefree she seemed. A marked difference between the somber mood she was in after we left my parents' house the last time around.

"I see that look you're giving me. You're thinking about the last time we had dinner at your parents, or rather, how that night ended."

We'd just arrived at the door to my condo. I turned her by the shoulders, pressing her back against the wall, and leaned in. "Guilty as charged."

She sighed against my lips, and I moved my head lower, kissing down the line of her jaw, reaching her neck.

"Don't think I'm just going to let you have your way with me anytime you want," she slurred.

I chuckled into her ear before biting it. I laughed when I felt her tremble. "You sure about that?" I licked her neck.

A sigh accompanied a small moan.

"Y-yes, I'm sure. You have to study. Your test is coming up in less than two weeks."

"I plan on studying. All. Night. Long." I completed each word of that last sentence with a kiss.

"Eric?"

My body stiffened at the sound of the female voice coming from farther down the hall. I slowly raised my head from Angela's neck to see Brandi striding toward us, dressed in a short black dress, showcasing her long legs. Anyone else would see this was obviously a private moment and have made their way past without drawing attention to themselves, but not Brandi. I cursed myself for not taking this party inside, behind closed doors. The sneering look Brandi was giving Angela said this wasn't going to be a friendly encounter.

"Brandi," I stated. Pulling my keys from my back pocket, I began inserting my key into the door.

"And you are?" She spoke directly to Angela.

I tightened my grip around Angela's waist when she started to pivot in Brandi's direction. "I'm Angela." On the surface her introduction sounded personable; I've memorized every inflection of her voice. However, the small hitch when she said her name told of the challenge she held.

"Oh, Amanda. Nice to—"

"Angela," she cut off Brandi's catty reply, and I was over this little showdown.

"That's enough, Brandi. You have a good night." I finished unlocking and then pushed my door open, using my hand on Angela's waist to push her toward the doorway.

"He'll dump you soon enough once he's done with you. Just like he did me," Brandi spat.

"Look, Bianca, it's time you let it go," Angela retorted, breaking free of my hold. "Whatever you *think* you two had is over and done."

"It's Brandi!" she yelled.

Angela shrugged. "Bianca, Brandi, same difference."

"What the hell makes *you* so special?"

"For one, I'd never pair that dress with those heels," Angela mocked, her eyes peering down at Brandi's feet.

"You bi—" Brandi's angry retort, hand high in the air like she was about to hit Angela, was halted by my hand and body pushed in between the two women.

My grip was firm enough that Brandi's nudges couldn't pull it away but not tight enough to the point of pain.

"Don't ever try that bullshit again," I growled. "Don't fucking darken my doorstep with your presence again." With narrowed eyes, I slowly loosened my grip on her wrist and watched as she backed up a few steps, then headed in the direction of her door. Once she disappeared behind her door, I pushed my own open, following Angela inside.

As soon as the door shut, I was pushed back against it.

"You keep that hussy away from me. You actually dated her?"

"Define dated?"

Her eyes narrowed, and she pushed away from me when I went to pull her to me by the waist.

"Cheap ass dress," she mumbled while swatting my hands. "You should've let her try and hit me. I would've whooped her—" Her rant was cut off by my mouth on hers. I spun us so she was pressed against the door, and I let my hands run up and down the sides of her body. I pressed my full weight against her.

"Are we done talking about her?" I asked once I pulled back.

"Talking about who?" she sighed.

"Good answer." I kissed my way up her neck until I made it to her mouth, where I sucked on her tongue and lips.

"You haven't even given me a tour of your place," she purred, head tilted upwards for better access, eyes closed.

"In the morning," I murmured into the column of her neck. I held her by the waist and walked her backwards to my bedroom. This was Angela's first time at my place in the months we've been dating. I generally went over to and spent the nights at her place just because hers felt more like home than my condo.

I felt her hands go to the buckle of my belt, fiddling with it until it came loose.

"I want you in my mouth first."

That was enough to make any man just about come in his pants.

She pressed one kiss to my lips before heading down south, easing my pants down as she went, having undone the button and zipper already. Her soft hand made its way into my boxer briefs, cupping my cock before pulling me out. When she puckered her lips and pressed a kiss to the tip a chill ran through my entire body. She began swirling her tongue around the head, and I felt myself growing harder with each passing second. I groaned, helplessly, needing her to end this torment. Moving my hand to her hair, I urged her on. She giggled before opening and fully sheathing me with her hot mouth.

Nirvana.

Heaven on Earth.

Paradise.

All of those descriptions felt too shallow to describe the feeling of her lips gliding up and down my shaft. Her tongue ran along the veins, creating tingling sensations throughout my entire body. My hips began pistoning involuntarily, seeking more pleasure. My Angel took it like a pro. I reached down, cupping the sides of her face, and began pumping harder when her hands went around, gripping my backside. Much too soon, my body tightened up, and semen shot from my cock. To my surprise, Angela didn't budge. Instead, she took it all, swallowing my load. I almost came a second time when she pulled back and licked her lips.

"You have way too many clothes on." She stood up, pulling my shirt overhead.

"I'm not the only one who's overdressed." I stepped completely out of my pants and shoes, falling back on the bed when Angela pushed me onto it. She quickly straddled me. I frowned.

"You're still wearing too many clothes." I sat up to rid her of the camisole and bra she wore but was stopped by her hand on my chest.

"I need to tell you something."

"Now?" I asked impatiently, trying again to reach for her clothing.

"Yes, now," she insisted. Her hands pressed against my shoulders, pushing me onto my back again. "It's serious."

I observed her. The space between her eyes was wrinkled, brows slightly furrowed, lips pouty. She was heavily contemplating her next words.

"I love you." She blew out a breath, looking relieved at hearing her own words. "I'm in love with you."

"Oh."

"*Oh*? That's it? That's your response?"

I chuckled, hands going to her ass. "I've been waiting for you to say it."

She blinked. "Excuse me?"

"I've been waiting to hear you say it," I reiterated.

"Me?" She sprang up but remained straddling me because my grip on her wouldn't let her move. "What about you?"

I screwed my face up. "What about me?"

"You could've said it if you were waiting on me. I mean, if you feel the sa—"

"I did."

"What? When?"

"In the shower when I told I wouldn't come in you until we were married."

Her eyes looked as if they'd pop out of her skull. "*That* was you telling me you love me?"

I frowned. "Of course. What else would it mean?"

She covered her face with her hands, shaking her head. "You *seriously* need to work on your communication skills, Mr. Kim."

Grinning, I tugged her hands from her face and brought them to my mouth, kissing her knuckles. "I can think of something else we need to work on." I adjusted, flipping her onto her back and moving on top of her, so now our position was reversed. I leaned in, placing a kiss on her forehead, tip of her nose, and finally lips. "I love you, too, Angel."

Her face opened up, and I swear I would've said those three words much sooner if I could get her to make this face over and over.

"But make sure you're only saying it because you *want* to. Not because you think I—" Her response was cut off by my tongue in her mouth.

"You're talking too much," was the last thing I said before taking her mouth again and removing the rest of her clothing.

Chapter Seventeen

Eric

I pulled out my phone from my back pocket, checking to see if I had any messages. Frowning when I saw I had none, I stuffed it back into my jeans.

Maybe she's busy, I told myself, then I told myself I was ridiculous for harping on this. I was gearing up to walk into my lieutenant's exam—the same one I've been studying for, for three months now with the help of my own personal Angel. And here it was the morning of, and I haven't gotten a call or text message wishing me luck. Sure, we spoke the night before, and she was her usual encouraging self, but something felt off during our conversation.

"Okay, we're getting ready to begin. You may enter the room, sitting at the assigned desk numbers you were given..." The female proctor of the exams began giving out instructions. I pushed my thoughts of Angela aside and mentally prepared to focus for the next two hours. The exam was given at the Fire Department's Headquarters in downtown Williamsport. Making my way down the hall toward the room, I took glances at the faces of former fire department chiefs who've served over the decades.

You're going to be captain one day, Eric. Maybe even chief. Captain Waverly's words all those months ago rang in my ears.

That reminded me of the conversation I had with Angela two days ago about the exam.

"I'm so proud of you already," she said.

"I haven't passed the test yet," I retorted.

She shrugged, leaning over the bar. "The test is just a formality. You've already passed the test every day at your fire station. It's obvious the way your crew looks at you, respects you. You already are their lieutenant."

We were in public, but that didn't stop me from taking her face between my hands, pulling her to me, and possessing her lips. I conveyed the impact her words had on me through that kiss. Forgetting where we were, I didn't let up until I heard the applause and chants from the guys. When I finally pulled back, I grinned at the dazed expression on her face, her kiss-swollen lips. Her eyes dipped then glanced over my shoulder to where the guys were still whooping. I tossed them a glare over my shoulder, along with a middle finger.

I turned back to Angela, staring into those tawny eyes. "With inspiration like that, I have no choice but to pass the test and interview."

She waved a dainty hand. "Interview, sminterview. While your communication skills could use some work in the personal life department, you've got the professional communication skills down." The laughter she let out when I grabbed her by the arms, pulling her closer to me, had my cock stirring in my jeans.

"I'm going to marry you."

"I love you, too."

I pressed another quick kiss to her lips, knowing she needed to get back to tending to the bar but hating to let her go. I planned on hanging around until she closed and then taking her home to show her the exact effect her words had on me.

Pulling myself out of that memory, I sat down at the computer station I was assigned and punched in the log-in information that was emailed to be the day before.

"All right, you have one-hundred and twenty minutes to complete the multiple choice and essay sections of the exam. Remember, you cannot go back and check over a section once you have completed it, so I advise you to check, and double check before you hit submit. You will find out your score on the multiple choice section as soon as you complete the exam. Your essay scores will be emailed to you within fourteen business days, at which time you will also find out if you've been invited for an interview. Are there any questions?"

I grew irritated when a couple of hands went up for questions. I had none and was just ready to get this shit over with. As soon as the proctor was finished answering questions, she took a seat at her desk and let us do our thing. I began answering questions, remembering not to second guess my answers on a few of them, reminding myself that in a real-life situation there's no time for second-guessing and your first instinct is usually the correct one. Second guessing led to time wasted. If your decisions were wrong, there would be plenty of time afterward—if you made it out—to analyze where you fucked up. In the moment was not the time for that analyzation.

Feeling confident, I breezed through the multiple choice section in about forty-five minutes. Next, I started in on the first of three essays. I knew this was the section that tripped most people up, but I've written essays since I was in elementary school all the way through college. Communicating my thoughts and analysis in written form didn't intimidate me thanks to my formal education. I finished the three essays with about fifteen minutes to spare, according to the timer on my computer screen. Reading over my essays, I made a few revisions until I was finally satisfied, and then hit "submit." An immediate weight lifted off my shoulders. The pop-up on the screen instructed that I wait while it scored the multiple choice section of my exam. When the final number came up, I blew out a heavy breath and finally stood, stretching the kinks that'd developed in my muscles over the last two hours.

I headed over to the proctor to give her my name and ID to let her know I finished and then headed straight to the only person I wanted to see.

****

"Harvard, what're you doing here? I thought you had your exam this morning?" Captain Waverly questioned, glancing at his wristwatch.

"I did. I finished not too long ago. I came by to pick up the uniform I left the other day to take it home for a cleaning," I explained.

Captain gave me a funny look. "Well?"

I lifted my eyebrows as if to say 'well what' while I stuffed my uniform pants and shirt in my duffle bag.

"How'd it go?"

"It went well," I answered, distracted.

He gave a short snort. "You really are the conversationalist," he chuckled.

I returned his laugh. "I'm waiting to tell someone about my exam first before I let anyone else know."

He gave me a nod. "That's understandable. Well, happy ghost and goblins day!"

I paused, standing in front of the captain, giving him a look.

"So focused on the exam you forgot today's Halloween? We'll be pretty busy tonight. Lucky you have off. Or not so lucky. What type of firefighter wants to be off on the busy nights?" he mused to himself.

"October thirty-first," I mumbled.

"That's usually the day Halloween falls on."

I blinked. "Hey, Cap, sorry, I gotta go." I didn't even give him a backward glance. I slammed my locker closed and hitched my duffle bag over my shoulder, rushing down the stairs and out the back entrance of the station to avoid running into anyone. I wasn't in the mood to be held up by talk or questions of the exam.

I felt like a complete and total heel as I drove. Having checked my messages after the exam and only having one from my mother and father wishing me luck on the test, I became slightly agitated. Seeing my parents make more of an effort to support my career felt good, but I've grown not to need it. The one voice I did want to hear wasn't in my voicemail. I drove to Angela's home but got no answer when I knocked on the door. Next, I stopped by the bar but was even more surprised when she wasn't there either. Stephanie, one of her employees, stopped by at that exact moment to prepare for this evening, and informed me that Angela had taken the night off. I tried calling more than once, but my calls went straight to voicemail. It took the captain reminding me that it was Halloween to realize what I forgot.

I pounded on the horn as drivers in front of me seemed to be taking their sweet ass time. With each passing second, my impatience grew. I've been so focused on my test that I completely shut out thoughts or the lives of those around me. I wouldn't let that happen again. Not when it came to her.

I stopped at a local flower shop and picked out a small colorful bouquet, with a huge sunflower in the middle. I remember Angela told me her mother loved sunflowers. Taking the bouquet from the cashier, I made it back to my car and was once again on the road that led to the Williamsport Cemetery in record time. Ten minutes later, I parked in the lot off the cemetery and climbed out of my car. I had to ask one of the groundskeepers where the plots for Angela and Theodore Moore—Angela's parents—were. I thanked him once he pointed me in the right direction.

The Williamsport Cemetery was divided into three sections because it was so huge, and Angela's parents were buried about a quarter of a mile from where I parked. When I came up over a small hill, that's when I saw her. From behind it looked as if she was sitting, cross-legged. As I grew nearer, I could see her shoulders shaking, in the telltale sign that she was crying, but doing her best to hold it together. I picked up the pace to make it to her, stopping just behind her, not wanting to intrude on her private time with her parents but also wanting to be there for her; to be her comfort just as she was mine all those late nights of studying.

Before I could announce myself, her head popped up, and she turned, looking over her shoulder. My heart slammed into my chest when I saw how red and puffy her eyes were from crying. Instinctively, I widened my arms, opening them to her, and she leapt up into them, shudders wracking her body as she cried into my chest. I squeezed her to me, holding her through her tears and pain. I only loosened my grip when her shuddering reduced to a slight tremble, and she pulled back.

"How did you know?" she asked through watery eyes.

I swiped her soft cheek with my thumb, wiping away tears. "October thirty-first. You told me." The day her parents died on the trip they took to celebrate thirty years of marriage.

"You remembered." Her lips trembled as she gave me a small smile. "Even with the test this morning."

"I'd forgotten, but when the captain reminded me of the date, it came back to me."

She dipped her head, wrapping her arms around my shoulders. "Thank you for coming."

I pressed a kiss to her forehead. "Of course." I honestly didn't know if it was the right decision or not. I thought maybe she might've wanted to be alone in her grief. But the idea of her grieving all alone didn't sit well with me. I would've left if she wanted me to, or at least, gone back to my car to give her some privacy. But not showing up at all was totally out of the question.

"Sean usually works on this day. Says it makes him feel closer to Dad. I guess that makes sense." Her shoulders lifted and dropped. "I come to their grave and talk to them and usually go home to bake and then eat my feelings." Her voice hitched on the last word. She looked back at the grave, her arms still surrounding me. "Want to meet them?"

I gave her a nod when her eyes returned to me. Removing the arm holding the flowers from her waist, I held the bouquet in front of her. "I brought these for them."

A small gasp escaped her lips. "A sunflower." Surprise filled her tone. "Mama would've loved this." She squeezed me around the neck, kissing my lips before taking my hand and walking us closer to the two graves.

Twin grey headstones stood side-by-side, both of them inscribed with the names of each of Angela's parents. Underneath her father's name read "Psalm 66:12."

"God will bring you through the fire," I stated.

Angela turned to me, forehead wrinkled. I jutted my head at her father's headstone. "Psalm sixty-six, verse twelve. Guys around the department translate it as *God will bring us through the fire.*" I wasn't a religious guy, but some things you pick up being in my line of work.

Angela leaned into me. "He used to repeat that to my mom whenever she got worried. He'd say, *'just remember, Psalm sixty-six, twelve.'* Sean insisted we include it on his headstone."

I placed the flowers down in between the two graves and stood back, wrapping my arm around Angela's shoulders. She turned, nuzzling her face into my side, inhaling deeply. A minute later, her head popped up, her eyes peering at me.

"How'd the test go?"

I blinked, having forgotten all about the exam I took just that morning. A grin spread over my lips.

"Ninety-five."

She gasped, jumping into my arms. "I knew it!"

The passing requirement for the multiple choice section was a score of seventy-five.

"Hear that? I snagged a genius!" she blurted out, turning back to her parents' headstones.

"My daddy always said *don't bring no dummies home, Angie,*" she laughed a little.

I laughed, too, at the fake deep voice she put on imitating her father.

"Glad I could fill that requirement for you." I pressed a kiss to the tip of her nose just because, before wiping away remaining moisture from her tears under her eyes. Turning away from her, I crouched low in front of her parents.

"Mr. and Mrs. Moore, I want you both to know I love your daughter very much. She's going to be my wife one day soon. One day we'll bring your grandchildren here to meet you. I promise to keep her safe in the meantime." I took a moment, letting my words settle. They felt so right leaving my mouth, there was no question as to whether or not I meant them. I felt Angela's hand on my shoulder. I grasped it with my opposite hand and brought it to my lips, standing. Another sheen of wetness coated her eyes, but this time there was a mixture of happiness with the sadness.

I moved her in front of me, wrapping my arms around her slender waist, and resting my chin on her shoulder. She pressed her head into my chest, and our breathing grew in unison. She squeezed my hands and then turned in my arms. We stood that way for I don't know how long, a peace settling over me.

Chapter Eighteen

Eric

"You heard about the rookie, right?" Don clapped me on the shoulder as he entered the kitchen.

"Yup," I responded, taking a sip of the coffee I held in my hand.

"So you're back to drinking the regular stuff like the rest of us, huh?" he asked, pouring a cup from the coffee pot on the counter.

I tipped my mug up to him. "For now."

"Oh well, another one bites the dust," he tutted, taking a sip and sitting down at the table.

I waved my head from side-to-side a little. "The job isn't for everybody."

"Yeah, kinda figured he didn't have it in him."

I made a noise that indicated I agreed. The rookie who was slacking over the last few months finally called it quits. The captain alerted me of the news as soon as I arrived for my shift, calling me up to his office. He also gave me some news about my prospects for becoming a lieutenant. It's been a month and a half since my exam. I got my essay scores back two weeks after the exam, officially telling me that I passed both parts of the exam. Three weeks later I interviewed at the department headquarters with Captain Waverly, two other captains, and the fire chief himself even sat in on the interview for about thirty minutes. It's been a waiting game in the weeks since then.

"Where's Carter and Corey?" The captain's booming voice pierced the air of the kitchen, cutting off my thoughts.

"Out back, Cap."

"Go call 'em for me, Don."

A few of the other guys sauntered into the kitchen, obviously called by the captain as well. Don returned a minute later, Corey and Carter on his back.

"I brought you all in here because I have some important announcements to make. I'm sure you've heard by now, there's been a shakeup here at the station. Michael Zaveri, also known around here are Rookie Number Two, has turned in his resignation. Effective immediately."

So that was his name.

Not only had his rookie status hampered our ability to get to know him, but the guy was just quiet, and not quiet in the same way I was. He was almost eerie in how standoffish he was. I shrugged my eyebrows, tossing it out as nothing more than his not being cut out for the job. Probably knew it early on, too, but stuck with it to save face. A lot of people weren't cut out for this job, and the first year fighting fires always exposed the real firefighters from the phonies, if the Academy didn't get them first.

"We heard, Captain," Don interjected, sounding as if it was no big deal.

"I'm sure you all have." Captain looked around at all of us in there. "There're some other shake-ups that are taking place. Rescue Four's been without a captain and the sufficient number of lieutenants for some time now. As your captain for the last five months, I can say it has been an honor and a privilege, and I look forward to many more years at Rescue Four. But a captain can't do it alone. We need others to step up and take charge when we're unable to. I'm well aware of the tragedy that befell one of our previous lieutenants." He paused, and the air got thick around us; each one of us remembering our fallen lieutenant. The sound of the bagpipes that played at his funeral stuck out most in my memory. "And out of respect, the department waited to fill the position. In addition to just being their usual slow selves." We all chuckled at the fire department's notoriously slow turnaround times. "But that wait is over," he continued. "The department has assigned two new lieutenants to Rescue Four. Some of you already know our Eric Kim here took the lieutenant's exam. Passed it with flying colors and sailed through the interview process. And though it's still unofficial while we wait for the paperwork, Harvard is one of our newest lieutenants."

I was nearly knocked over when Carter and Don's strong hands clapped me on the back in congratulations. Corey pushed both of them out of the way, yanking my hand for a handshake, and briefly wrapping his free arm around me. "No one deserves this more than you," he said in my ear before pulling back.

I became surrounded by the guys as they congratulated me and told me how they always looked to me as their lieutenant anyway.

"But it's nice to get the pay bump to accompany the responsibility," Don joked, making us all laugh.

They took a few more minutes joking about how this called for a new hazing process. That idea was nixed when I quickly reminded them all that I knew all the nooks and crannies of this station *as well as* where all their own personal dirt was buried. No one spoke of trying me after that. New lieutenant or not, I wasn't new to this job, this station, or these men.

"Hey, Cap, you said Harvard was one of two new lieutenants. Who's the second?" Carter asked once it quieted down a little.

"'Bout time you paused kissing Harvard's ass to ask about your other lieutenant." He waited while the roar of laughter died down. The captain was gaining the respect of the men, and he's even loosened up a bit around us. "Your new lieutenant ..." He trailed off and he took a glance back over his shoulder, as a large form appeared in the doorway of the kitchen.

"Aw hell no!" Corey called out.

"This is bullshit!" Don yelled at the same time.

Their cries were accompanied by a few other grumblings from the other guys in the room.

"What's this, a family affair?" Don asked me.

I lifted my brows at him, just as surprised at this turn of events as anyone else.

"You're dating his sister, and now you both are our lieutenants," Don continued.

"Watch your damn mouth about my sister." Sean mean mugged Don as he fully entered the kitchen, dropping his duffel bag in front of him. "Hello, fellas," he greeted, a shit-eating grin plastered on his face.

"Rescue Four, your second new lieutenant is Lieutenant Sean Moore, formerly of Rescue Two."

Sean's reception was much less enthusiastic than the one I was given just a few minutes prior. A few of the guys who knew Sean from previous calls gave him a head nod, but the rest of us just stared at him. To his credit, he stared us down right back, not blinking or averting his gaze. Every new guy got their hazing, and this was just the beginning for Sean, but he didn't seem too worried about it, and neither was I. Over the last few months Sean and I developed a friendly rapport. He was protective of his sister at first, naturally, but something changed after the anniversary of his parents' death. I suspect Angela told him about my going to her at the cemetery, but he never mentioned it. Either way, I wasn't surprised that he got the lieutenant job.

He waited longer than I did, having taken the test the previous year. Also, coming from another rescue station, I figured he'd have an easier time adjusting.

I looked over at Sean as Don approached him. "Just know, you're not playing in the minor leagues anymore. This ain't Rescue Two," Don growled, bumping his shoulder and departing the kitchen. Instead of taking offense, Sean laughed. More of the guys followed Don out until it was just the captain, Sean, and I.

"Good luck," Captain Waverly chuckled, patting a firm hand on Sean's shoulder, before leaving as well. He was leaving it up to us to figure it out. At any station, the captain is like the parent of squabbling teenagers. And like any already stressed out parent of teens should know, unless there's bloodshed, you let the siblings figure it out amongst themselves. It makes their bond that much stronger. The captain would let us haze Sean as needed and either he'd step up or step out. As long as things didn't go too far, Captain would leave us to our devices.

"Welcome to Rescue Four," I finally said, approaching Sean. "Hope you brought your helmet."

"I brought that and so much more," he retorted.

I nodded. "Good. You'll need it." I started to walk out at the same time the alarm sounded. Sean would get his first baptism by fire with Rescue Four early. We both hustled to retrieve our gear and hopped in the rig, the thrill I always got when jumping in the driver's seat of the rig, overcoming me, as we pulled off.

God, I love this shit.

****

Eric

God, I love her, I thought, a hint of a smile gracing my face. To most people in the crowd would likely guess the smile had more to do with where I was standing than the woman who was looking on from the audience. They'd be wrong. Sure, I was proud as hell to be dressed in my navy blue dress uniform, standing on stage while the Chief of the Fire Department made a speech. Soon he would begin the pinning ceremony, giving myself, Sean, and a number of other guys our official lieutenant pins, followed by those receiving their captain pins. But as I stood under the hot lights of the stage, listening to a speech that was rather uninteresting, my gaze kept going to the tawny eyes that reminded me of an angel. She sat in the audience, eyes planted on me, and full of pride. Goosebumps skittered up my skin, when her lips parted, her smile bursting on her lips.

It wasn't until I saw her clapping that I blinked, noticing the rest of the audience began applauding as well. I turned back to the chief and realized he was beginning the pinning process.

About time. My eagerness was beginning to get to me; the ring box I held in my pocket began feeling heavier by the moment. I twisted my hands into fists at my side, silently urging him to hurry up. I looked to my right and caught Sean's eye. He gave me a hint of a smile before turning out into the audience, his lips spreading wider when he put eyes on his son, who sat next to Angela. He already knew my plans for after the ceremony, as I went to him to inform him of my intentions. I wasn't one to ask permission, but as Angela's closest family member and someone I now worked with, I thought it'd be good to let him know where I stood.

I glanced toward my left and finally saw that the chief had reached the guy next to me. I was next.

"On behalf of the Williamsport Fire Department and the City of Williamsport, congratulations on successfully meeting the requirements for the role of lieutenant. Rescue Four is lucky to have such strong leadership." He lowered his voice on that last part. He removed the badge sitting on the left side of my chest and replaced it with the official lieutenant badge.

I felt my Adam's apple bob up and down when I swallowed, my vision blurring just for a second. Instead of letting my emotions overrule me—which I'd never live down—I looked out into the audience to see my Angela shedding tears for me. My entire body filled with warmth, my chest swelling with everything I felt. I willed myself to wait patiently until the ceremony was over to go to her. It was difficult, but somehow I made it.

"Congratulations! I'm so proud of you!" Angela giggled and yelped at the same time her arms went around my neck.

I nuzzled my face into the crook of her neck, inhaling to fill up my lungs with her scent.

"How does it feel, Lieutenant Kim?" she pulled back, asking.

I stared down at the woman in my arms, felt the pats on my back from the guys and people around me, and said, "Feels pretty damn good. But it's going to get better before the day's over," I responded cryptically. Angela gave me a confused look, but even as her mouth opened preparing to ask what I meant, I placed my hands on her face, pulling her to me, cutting her question off. The usual buzzing that often sounded off in my ears whenever we kissed started, and I savored it, diving into her and not caring who was around.

"Get a room. There are children here!" I vaguely heard, but only when Angela pulled away, laughing did the kiss finally end.

"Sorry, Sean and little guy," she said to her brother and nephew.

"Aunt Angie, we want cake!" Little Jeremiah yelped, excitedly.

"Okay, okay. It's time to head out anyway."

We were headed over to *Charlie's* to celebrate with the rest of Rescue Four and more family and friends. While I insisted

Angela didn't need to cook for all of us, she was just insistent that she wanted to.

"I'm sorry your parents didn't make it to the ceremony," she stated, grasping my hand that rested on the center console in my car. I squeezed her hand back, bringing it to my lips while keeping my eyes on the road.

"Everyone that I needed there, was." I invited my parents, of course. They both told me they'd try to make it. While we had made strides in the last few months, my parents both still had a difficult time accepting my career. I figured they'd come around eventually.

"Look what the motherfucking cat dragged in. Donnie, it looks like we got ourselves a lieutenant!" Corey called out as soon as we entered *Charlie's.*

"Not just one. Two fucking lieutenants," Don returned, noticing Sean entered behind Angela and I. The guys around the bar went up in a roar of laughter and congratulations, pushing Sean and me toward the center of the bar. I unbuttoned the jacket of my uniform. I was growing hot in the stifling uniform, especially with so many people patting me on the back and pulling me in for an embrace. Regretfully, I lost Angela in the sea of people who gathered around for Sean and I. His old colleagues from Rescue Two showed up, and save for the normal jibing, Rescue Four got along with them. We all talked trash, but in the end, we all held an immense amount of respect for one another.

I turned and waved to one member of another station, who called my name from across the room. I began heading in the direction my name had been called, while also searching for Angela since she wasn't behind the bar when my pathway was cut off by a petite figure. I lowered my gaze, and the side of my lips turned up upon seeing the smiling face of my mother. My father stood next to her, looking just a jovial.

"Sorry we're late, son," my mother began, almost bashfully, which was so unlike her. "We tried to make it to the ceremony, but I got caught up at work and then had to finish making the ginger cookies." She held up a large tin she had in her hand.

"At least you made it." I leaned down and pressed a kiss to her warm cheek before pulling the tin from her, allowing her to wrap her arms around my neck for a quick squeeze. Next, it was my father's turn.

"We're so proud of you, adeul."

Adeul. "Son" in Korean. The last time he said that exact phrase to me was the day I graduated college. I blinked a couple of times, clearing my throat.

"Thank you. It means a lot that you're here. I'm going to put these on the food table, and then introduce you to the guys."

My mother smiled. "We'd like that."

I nodded and headed off in the direction of the food table, which is where I found the woman I've been looking for. She was rearranging the dishes on the table, as more food was being brought out.

"I can't believe you cooked all this," I said over her shoulder, pulling her into my arms from behind, once I placed the tin down.

"It's not a lot. I ordered the sandwiches, kabobs, and pigs in a blanket. I just made the chocolate chip cookies, yellow cake with chocolate frosting, and the cheesecake tarts … oh, and the chocolate lava cake that'll be brought out later." She clapped as she spun around in my arms.

"That's it?" I asked sarcastically. The woman loved cooking and entertaining. I couldn't believe she did all of this. And the fact that we just ended the holiday season where it seemed like she spent every day making some dessert or dish for her employees, neighbors, or for me to bring to the station.

She slapped me on the shoulder. "Don't make fun. I show my love with food."

I placed a kiss on the tip of her nose. "I'm not making fun. I've got another way you can show your love." My head dipped.

"Oh yeah?"

"Let me show you," I answered just before our mouths touch. I had to summon the strength to reel myself in when every cell in my body ignited from that kiss. I wanted nothing more than to take her upstairs to the apartment above the bar, strip her naked, and hear her yell out my name. *That* was the only way I wanted this day to end. Instead, I pulled back, silently promising myself that would take place later.

"I love you, Angel." I said it so many times over the last few months that it just rolled off of my tongue, but I meant it more and more each day.

"I love you, too, Lieutenant Kim."

My heart actually skipped a beat when she used my new title. Though I wanted to wait a little longer to do this, I trusted my instincts and decided that moment was the right time to do what I've been waiting to do all day.

I took a step back, one hand falling from her waist to reach into my right pocket.

"How much do you love me?" I asked.

A bark of laughter exploded from my mouth when she said, "Enough to shut down my bar on one of the busiest days of the week to accommodate your friends and family for your celebration party. If it were *just* for Sean, he would've had to wait until a Monday night. But don't tell him I said that," she whispered the last part.

"Your secret's safe with me."

"I know it is," a sincere note hit her voice as she stared up at me.

"What if I told you I loved you enough to spend the rest of my life with you and make you the mother of my children?"

"You tell me that at least once a day."

"True." I nodded. "But what if this time I told you with a ring?" I asked at the same time I sank down to one knee, opening the small black box, exposing the Valencia one karat diamond ring.

Angela's jaw dropped, and her eyelids rose, surprise and shock written all over her beautiful face. I put this moment off long enough, not wanting to propose on Christmas or New Year's or anything cliché like that. Instead, I wanted to do it on a day I knew I'd remember forever, and what better day than when I got promoted?

"Angela Marie Moore, my Angel, will you marry me?" Simple and sweet. I didn't use a bunch of flowery words to convey what I felt. Didn't need to. Action always appealed to me more than words. The black tears from her mascara streaming down Angela's face told me she knew exactly how I felt. The room around us seemed to go silent, but I wasn't focused on anyone but the beauty in front of me.

"Y-yess," she cried, bending down low to wrap her arms around me.

I stood, so she didn't have to bend too low. She pulled me in so tight, I struggled to pull back to be able to put the ring on her finger. Another round of applause sounded around the room when Angela held up her hand, now with the ring on it, waving it around for the crowd to see.

"That's how you do it!"

"Look at that ring!"

"Congrats, Harvard!"

Amongst the shouts and cheers, I recognized Don, Corey, and Carter's voices. Captain Waverly had made his way over to us, first pulling Angela in for a brief hug and word of congratulations before squeezing me by the shoulder to show his affection. Next came my parents, my father welcoming Angela into the family, followed by my mother. Despite the rather rocky way they started off, my mother and Angela had developed a decent relationship over the last few months. Even with all the different people around tugging at us, I kept a firm grip on Angela's hand, refusing to surrender her to anyone. I figured we'd have to keep up this public appearance for at least another two hours before I could get her behind closed doors, and do things that would have half the people in this room blushing. I sighed, as I discreetly adjusted myself in my pants, my cock swelling a little at just the thoughts of what I'd planned for that evening.

"What was that sigh about?" Angela whispered in my ear.

"There's too many minutes between now and when I get to have you naked underneath me." My Angel grinned and tipped her head. I decided to press on, whispering in her ear all the ways I planned on having her that night.

"Hey, cut that shit out," Sean's gruff voice interrupted the shortly-lived alone moment we were having.

"You really should get your own woman," I told him, pulling Angela's back into my chest.

"I'll think about that," he answered sarcastically. "Look, I just wanted to say congratulations to you two and welcome to the family, Harvard."

I raised my hand, taking the hand that he proffered. We gave each other one shoulder hug before Angela moved into his embrace, wrapping her arms around his neck.

"Thanks, Sean! I love you sooo much!"

Jeremiah wedged his little body in between the two of them, first hugging Angela, before coming over to me. He and I had gained a relationship over the last few months as well. Being around him had made me excited to have my own kids one day.

Chapter Nineteen

Eric

Two Months Later

"I *cannot* believe your mother is so insistent on those white rose bouquets as the centerpieces. I mean, they were beautiful, but come on white roses? I much prefer the purple and white lilies. After all, that matches the color scheme of the wedding perfectly, but she is so insistent."

I paused with the toothbrush still in my mouth and peered over my shoulder at my soon-to-be wife. It was early morning, and I was up getting ready for my day shift, while my woman continued talking about wedding plans. The previous day she and my mother went out with the wedding planner—my mother insisted on paying for one, looking at locations and decor and all that shit. I was more than relieved to leave them to it. Just as long as I knew where to show up, what to wear, and what time, I'd be fine.

"Oh, and we have to decide between the carrot, vanilla bean, or the red velvet cakes for the reception. I loved the vanilla bean, but the carrot cake was pretty good, too. What did you think?"

I turned back around but raised my eyes to look at her in the mirror, behind me. Bending down, I spat out the toothpaste and rinsed my mouth out before answering.

"Whatever you think is best, Angel." I place a kiss on her nose, noting the frown she wore. Moving from the bathroom, I made my way across the hall to the bedroom, grabbing my work T-shirt and placing it on before proceeding down the hall to the kitchen, Angela hot on my heels.

"That's what you always say, babe," she whined. "I know you wanna be hands off with most of the wedding stuff, but I want you to at least have a say in what we eat. Especially, since the wedding cake is a big deal and we'll be eating it a year later on our anniversary."

The glass of freshly squeezed orange juice that she kept in the fridge stopped halfway to my mouth.

I screwed my face up. "Why would we eat year-old cake?"

She rolled her eyes, lifting her face toward the ceiling. She looked so adorable, I was tempted to take a step forward and peel off the white camisole and boyshort panties she wore.

"It's a tradition. The couple freezes the top layer of the wedding cake in the freezer for a year and eats it on their first anniversary. It's for good luck. Don't give me that face!" she continued, when I stared, bewildered, having never heard of such a thing.

"*Anyway,*" she droned, "that's why it's important you have a say in the wedding cake."

I finished my glass of orange juice, cursing myself for drinking it right after I'd brushed my teeth since now the taste was off. I woke up late...or rather, got out of bed late due to early morning activities with my fiancée. Now, I was rushing to get to work on time.

"Angel, I don't care what type of cake we eat." I pulled her into me with one arm and stopped her reply with my mouth on hers. I took her chin up between my thumb and forefinger. "As long as you're there looking beautiful and we both say I do, I'm good. I gotta go. Love you," I hurried, kissing her once more and grabbing my duffle, breezing out the door to my car across the street.

I let out a snort once I was on the road thinking of all the details Angela and I talked about while discussing this wedding. More like, she "discussed" while I listened—partially so. I knew my mother wanted to be as hands-on as possible and Angela was hesitant, but eventually agreed since she wouldn't be able to share this occasion with her own mother, a fact that saddened her deeply. And while they bickered on place settings and other dumb shit I couldn't care less about, they hadn't had any major fights, so I was fine with the arrangement as it stood.

Climbing out of my car, I looked up at the station's marquee and the feeling that puffed my chest out that always overcame me was there once again. I felt on top of the world. Not only was I moving up the ranks in my career, but the woman I loved even more than fighting fires would soon wear my wedding band on her hand. Hell, she was even working with my mother to plan our wedding. As far as I was concerned, there was nothing and no one that could bring me down.

"Morning, Lieutenant."

I turned to see the guy we referred to as rookie number one, smiling. "Hey, Jack," I greeted. He's since moved past the no-name stage of his hazing.

He looked up, too. "Does it ever get old?" I heard the wonder, excitement, and awe in his voice.

"No," I simply answered. Because it never did.

We turned and headed inside, welcomed by Corey, Carter, Don, and Sean who were all laughing and joking in the kitchen.

"Roll call!" I called out, clipboard in hand. Although I've been doing roll call for some time, now that I was officially a lieutenant, I took even more pride in the simplest of things.

"Hey, you and Angela looking at houses this weekend?" Sean asked, once roll call was over, and we began the usual routine of cleaning out our equipment. Angela and I agreed to buy our own home to start our lives together. I put my condo on the market a month ago, and it sold within two weeks. Since then, I moved into Angela's place. She was still torn on whether or not she wanted to sell her current home or rent it out. I pushed for her to rent it knowing she'd be too sad to sell the house her parents built for their family. We could keep it in the family and pass it to our children or Jeremiah, Sean's son.

"Yeah. Our realtor has a couple of houses in mind that are close to both the station and the bar."

Sean nodded. "Sounds go—" His mouth clamped shut, eyes rolling toward the ceiling when the station's alarm started sounding off.

In typical Rescue Four fashion, a flurry of activity began with guys grabbing their gear and throwing it on, sliding down the pole, and lockers slamming shut. I had my gear on in less than two minutes and was running toward the driver's seat of the rig. Relief flooded my body when I felt the keys in the ignition.

"Ten-forty-nine in progress at a two-story warehouse," the voice of the female announcer came through our radios.

"Ten-forty-nine," Captain Waverly snorted. "Small," he commented. That was the code for a relatively small fire. Probably only two trucks would show up to this one, ours and another station. Nonetheless, I stepped on the gas, pushing us closer to the fire. We didn't know how many people were inside or if anyone was trapped, injured, or worse.

When we arrived, we learned from the truck that was already there that the fire had mostly been contained to the second floor. It was Rescue Four's duty to go in and check to make sure no one was inside. Captain Waverly stayed outside, allowing me to take the lead, followed by Corey, Carter, Don, and Jack. Sean and a few other guys remained at the station.

Each of us scattered once we entered the building. The smoke was thick in the air, causing us to keep our masks on to keep from inhaling it.

"All clear over here!" I recognized Carter's voice.

Then came Don and Corey's all clears, at which point I continued farther down the hall. It was longer than I suspected upon first entering the building, as it wound around the side of the building.

"Harvard to Rescue F—" Before I could call back to the guys that I was all clear, a loud crackling sound cut me off. My head shot upwards, and just before I was struck, I made out the second-floor roof of the warehouse collapsing directly on top of me.

****

Angela

"Hey, you okay?" Stephanie asked while I wiped down a spill at the bar.

I blinked, taking a second to realize she was addressing me. "Yeah, sure. Why?"

"Because that customer's been trying to get your attention for some time now." She nodded her head in the direction of a man waving, obviously wanting to order a drink.

"Shit." I hurried over to the man, apologizing and taking his order. Once I passed him the lager he ordered, I went back to wiping up the counter.

"You're sure you're all right?" Steph asked again.

I gave a half shrug. The truth was, I wasn't. Over the last hour, a sense of dread had settled in the pit of my stomach, and I couldn't shake it. It weighed my mood down like a twenty-pound boulder. Though I tried not to think about it, the only other time in my life I felt like this was when my parents went away for their anniversary. Within a few hours of that feeling, I got the call telling me they died. But I wasn't about to share that with Stephanie.

"I'm fine, it's just that Eric's mom has been so insistent on these bouquets as place settings for the wedding, and I don't like them that much," I lied.

Thankfully, Stephanie was none the wiser. "Oh, see that's why I'm eloping when I get married."

"Eloping?" I asked, laughing a little.

"Yeah, wham, bam, thank you ma'am type of thing. We'll go to a little chapel in Vegas or maybe Reno and do it there."

"That's so cheesy, Steph."

My phone, which I placed on the counter behind the bar, buzzed and I picked it up seeing that I'd received a text message. I opened it to see it was from Eric's mother.

How about these?

The question was accompanied by a picture of an all-white bouquet of lilies. I rolled my eyes.

"See what I mean?" I held up the message for Stephanie to read.

She made a clicking sound with her tongue. "I'm telling you, Vegas or Reno."

"That's not sounding like a bad idea all of a sudden," I mumbled while I typed a response. Placing the phone down, I worked to get out of my funk. I did my best not to think the worst. Two of the most important men in my life worked as firefighters, and I prayed to the Man above that this feeling in my gut wasn't telling me the worst has happened to one of them. I'd be devastated if something happened to Sean. I simply doubted I'd even make it if something happened to Eric. I shook my head of those thoughts. It was probably just the nervousness and tension of all the wedding talk or something. I went on to serve more customers, ignoring my feelings. One of my favorite songs came on the jukebox and customers started clapping, urging us to dance. I almost convinced myself I was feeling better. That is until Sean came barging through the door.

I looked up just as he entered. Seeing his ghosted eyes, I knew.

I just knew.

My heart rose into my throat, and it became impossible to swallow.

My hands began trembling so badly that I dropped the bottle I was holding. I didn't even notice the shards of glass on the floor around my feet. I was planted in place. I wanted to get to Sean—ask him what happened—but I couldn't move. I thought I made out his form striding toward me, but everything felt like it was happening in slow motion. My heartbeat tripled, and a buzzing sound took over in my ears. I panned down to his lips, and it was then I realized they were moving. He was saying something.

"Angela." My brother's voice alone almost broke me. It was so heavy. So full of sorrow.

"I-is he...is h-he dead?" I managed to croak out, tears already streaming down my face.

"You need to come with me." He used the voice he used when he needed to be firm yet gentle with Jeremiah. The same one I heard him use when telling Jeremiah our parents died.

I don't know how I got from behind the bar to my brother. I think Stephanie told me she'd take care of everything, and pushed me to get moving. Then again, maybe Sean came around the bar to tug me to get me to move. I don't know. The next thing I remembered was Sean helping me into his car, placing my purse in my lap, him proceeding to get into the driver's side, and pulling off.

I had a million and one questions shooting around in my mind, but I couldn't talk. Didn't *want* to talk. Talking would make it real, and I didn't know what was worse, the made-up scenario in my mind or reality. I opted to clamp my mouth shut and just watch the lights of the city pass by as we drove to the hospital. I twisted the engagement ring I've worn since the day Eric asked me to be his wife, around and around, hoping it'd provide me some comfort.

"He's in Room 221," Sean said in my ear, taking my elbow and leading us to the elevators. I was so grateful for his strength right then.

When the elevator doors opened my heart nearly stopped for a second time. Lined down the hallway were firefighters on either side. Some were dressed in their fire-resistant gear. Some wore their regular uniform, the same uniform black trousers and navy blue T-shirt with black boots that Eric rushed out of the house wearing just that morning. At least I thought it was that morning. How could it have only been that morning and yet felt so long ago?

They all turned in my direction. Some wore looks of pity, some outright sorrow, and tears, while others barely held eye contact with me. I was most jarred by the red-rimmed eyes of Don's. He was usually the first person to speak, make a joke or try to lighten the mood. He turned his head to the linoleum floor and didn't look back up as we passed.

"Angela." Captain Waverly came up to me.

"H-how is he?" I asked, my voice cracking. I honestly didn't know if I even wanted the answer to that question. The expressions on the men's faces I just saw told me it wasn't good.

"The doctor is saying it's touch and go but won't give us any more details than that. They were waiting for…"

"Next of kin," I finished for him.

Just then the doctor came out of the room.

"Doctor, Eric's next of kin is here," Captain Waverly spoke up, pointing at me.

"You are?" the older man asked.

"Angela Moore, his fiancée."

The doctor tilted his head almost in familiarity. "He's been asking for you."

"He's awake?" There was hope in my voice.

"Yes, but I must warn you his situation is grave. He has three fractured ribs, one of which punctured his lung. We believe he has some internal bleeding, but we're not sure where it's coming from. His vitals weren't stable enough when he first came in to perform surgery. We're trying to wait for his vitals to raise to perform surgery. For right now, it's a waiting game."

"Oh God!" I covered my mouth with my hand. My stomach lurched, and I felt like the room was spinning.

"Angela," Sean called, turning me to him, "you need to be strong for Eric right now. Okay? He wants to see you."

I nodded vigorously, dabbing at the tears that wouldn't stop falling. "O-okay. Um, his parents. Someone needs to tell t—"

"They're being brought to the hospital as we speak," Sean confirmed.

I nodded and blew out a shaky breath. I could do this. I could be strong for the man who was always so strong for me. I inhaled and stepped toward the door. Blowing the air from my lungs, I moved to push the door open. The room was eerily quiet save for the beeps of the monitors. I pushed past the curtain and had to cover my mouth to prevent the gasp that wanted to escape.

Eric was laying in the bed, the white sheet only covering up to his waist. He was shirtless, although wide bandages were wrapped around his chest and upper stomach areas. The skin that was showing above the bandages was bruised. His face. His beautiful face was swollen on one side, marred by black and purple bruises. His breathing was so labored. I stopped, being as quiet as a mouse as I watched the slow rise and fall of his chest. With each inhale his face—the half that wasn't bruised—contorted a little, as if it pained him just to breathe.

I crept around to the side of his bed, still not making a sound. His eyes were closed, and I assumed he fell back asleep. As frightened as I was, I needed to touch him. I needed to feel him to know that he was still here. Fighting for his life. I leaned a little on his pillow and began lightly stroking his silky hair. I figured that would be the least painful place I could touch him. Just that morning I ran my fingers through those same strands for entirely different reasons.

"A-Angel," his voice was between a croak and a whisper, causing me to jump.

"Hi, baby."

"I'm sorry, Angel," he said, then paused, face contorting.

"Sorry for what?"

"Scaring you like this."

"Don't you dare."

"No, I mean it, Angel. I got sloppy at the warehouse. Should've checked the roof as I was inspecting the hallway for people." He paused, coughing and then grimacing.

"Shshshsh. Don't do that. You were doing your job, baby." I tried to shush him as every word seemed as if it pained him, but he kept talking.

"Remember that night I took you to that overlook? Where we spent the whole night listening to calls over the radio, and you asked me to describe what each of the codes meant? The night you dry humped me in my backseat?"

In spite of myself, I let out a giggle.

"That was the night I knew. I knew you were it for me, Angel."

"That was our fourth date." I smiled down at him through watery eyes.

"I told you we fall quick and hard in my family. I might not have acquired my dad's passion for finance and business, but when it comes to claiming the women we love, I'm his son."

I let out a small laugh and pressed a kiss to the top of his head, my lips barely grazing his skin. I was too afraid to cause him any more pain.

"That's not right. I need a real kiss. Right here?" He slowly lifted his hand and pointed to his lips.

Not wanting him to strain because it looked like he was actually trying to lift his head to reach my lips, I lowered to him, brushing my lips over his. I tasted the salt from my tears.

"Don't do that. Angels aren't supposed to cry."

I squeezed my eyes tight, willing the tears away. *You need to be strong for him.* My brother's words echoed in my mind.

"A week after that date is when I started shopping for that ring on your finger."

I inhaled sharply, stunned. Lifting my left hand, I stared at the beautiful diamond ring.

"Are you serious?" I asked above a whisper.

"As a heart attack. Took me about a month to decide on that one, but I'm glad I did. That ring was made for you."

I think he smiled, but it came out as more of a grimace due to his swollen face.

"I remember thinking, 'if she's willing to sit out with me all night listening to calls, she's going to make one hell of a firefighter's wife.' That was the night I decided, but I was patient, letting you come around to the idea." He had to stop when he began coughing, his face crumpling in pain every time.

"Baby, stop talking. You need to rest," I implored, wanting to keep him as calm and in as little pain as possible.

"Wait," he breathed deeply, and my heart ached from how much it looked like it hurt him. My big, strong firefighter was struggling just to get air into his lungs.

"I need to say something else."

My normally quiet man was full of words right then, it seemed.

"The cake ..."

I looked at him quizzically but remained quiet, waiting for him to continue.

"I've been thinking about our wedding cake. I know this morning I told you it didn't matter, but I've changed my mind. I loved the vanilla bean cake with the white icing, too. That's the one that has my vote."

A damn wedding cake was the absolute last thing on my mind at the moment, but if that's the one he chose so be it.

"Okay, baby. We'll go with the vanilla bean cake."

"We'll have it at the wedding and our one year anniversary," he reminded me.

Another sheet of tears coated my eyes, and I swallowed the lump forming in my throat. "Y-yup. Whatever you say, baby."

"Good. Okay," he said with so much conviction as if it was a promise. "Oh wait, one more thing," he added.

"Baby, you need your rest."

"I know, but this is important … I love you, Angel. I don't remember if I told you this morning, so I'm telling you now. I love you."

"I love you, too," I told him, leaning down and burying my nose into his hair. I inhaled against the familiar scent, and then the world closed in on me. The monitors above me started going haywire. I pulled back and saw that not only were Eric's eyes now closed, but his head was also slumped down in a way that it wasn't when I first walked in.

"Oh God!" I cried.

Doctors and nurses began rushing in, alerted to his condition by the monitors.

"Pulse is thready!"

"Blood pressure is low!"

I stood there until I was pushed aside.

"Ma'am, you can't be in here," a stern female voice sounded off in my ear.

"W-wait, I'm his fiancée. What's happening?" I knew I was in the way, knew the hospital staff needed as much space as possible to do their jobs, but I just couldn't leave him.

"Ma'am, let us do our jobs," the woman said again, pushing me outside of the room.

I started to go back in when a hand on my wrist stopped me.

"Angie, they have to help him now."

I didn't even acknowledge my brother's words. I couldn't. But thanks to his firm grip, I remained where I was. Seconds later, the hospital room door flew open and Eric's bed was brought out, doctors, nurses, and hospital staff surrounding it, yelling so many different things I couldn't make anything out. I could tell by the tone of their voices, however, that it was serious. Dire. My knees buckled when my eyes fell to an unconscious Eric in the bed. His skin had taken on an ashen color.

Again, Sean was there to hold me up. When they disappeared down the hall with Eric, I fell into Sean's chest, tears flowing freely. The memory of what Eric told me in the room just minutes ago came flooding back. The memories of our third date and when he knew he fell in love with me. The shopping for my engagement ring. All things that it seemed he wanted me to know.

"Please no!" I cried heavily as the realization sunk in. He was telling me everything he wanted me to know before he died.

Chapter Twenty-One

Angela

"That's a good picture of him."

I turned to my right, Eric's mother staring ahead at the picture of her proud son dressed in his dress uniform receiving his lieutenant's pin. I could make out the red rims of her eyes. I blinked a few times, halting my tears from falling. I was just as emotional that day. As I turned back to the image in front of us, I swallowed, looking at Eric the day he officially became a lieutenant. He told me it was one of the happiest days of his life. Not just because of the advancement in his career but also because it was the day I agreed to be his wife.

I'd carry those words with me forever.

"I'm so thankful you were there for him that day. At the ceremony. It's written all over his face how much it meant to him that you were there." Mrs. Kim gestured to the picture next to the one she'd been looking at. That photo was from the same day and was of Eric and me, his arm draped around my waist. I was gazing up at him, my hand resting at the center of his chest, as he looked down at me. I remembered the intensity of his gaze during that picture. His dark eyes conveyed a promise I couldn't make out at the time. As I stood observing that picture, it was then for the first time that I noticed the slight bulge at the left side of his pants, by his pocket. He was carrying the ring, which he would later propose to me with. My head dropped, and I looked at my left ring finger.

It was still there now.

I've worn it every day since the day he first put it on.

Except now, the diamond ring was accompanied by a beautiful white gold wedding band.

"There you are."

My eyes fluttered shut as my husband's words flooded over me at the same time his strong arms wrapped around the bodice of the vintage white, lace wedding dress I wore, pulling me into him from behind.

"Thanks for watching over my wife while I was occupied, Mom," Eric told his mother. He was ambushed by the men of Rescue Four during our wedding reception—which, of course, was held at *Charlie's.*

"My pleasure, son." His mom patted him on the arm, then reached up on tiptoes to plant a kiss on his cheek before leaving us. "I need to go find your father. Make sure he's not eating too much."

I turned in Eric's arms, bracing my arms around him as he stared down at me. For a while, he didn't say anything, but he didn't need to. He let his eyes do the talking for him. They held so much love that I needed to blink a couple of times to keep myself from falling into the abyss of his dark gaze.

"I'm surprised they let you get away." I jutted my head to the bunch of guys behind us. His squad.

He glanced back and then turned his gaze upon me again. "I told 'em if I missed another minute with my wife I was putting them all cleanup and shit duty for a month."

I lowered my head, giggling into his chest. Rescue Four recently got a dog at the station. Everyone hated cleaning up after it, or what they referred to as *shit duty*, so that was left to the new rookies.

"You're terrible," I laughed.

"And I'm all yours."

"I wouldn't have it any other way."

That set him off. His body tightened, and his eyes—which were already dark—grew even darker. He leaned down until his lips hovered just above mine. "I need you." His voice was low, but hard. He captured my lips, and my body naturally melted into his. I felt the swelling in his tuxedo pants pressing against my lower abdomen.

"Come here," he ordered, pulling back and then taking me by the arm to follow him.

I frowned, looking around at all our guests. "Where're we going?"

"Upstairs."

I gasped. "Eric!" He didn't stop or even look back at me.

We were staying in the upstairs apartment while we waited to move into the new home we purchased together. I opted to rent out my parents' home, and the new tenant wanted to move in right away.

"Eric, we have guests downstairs!" I insisted as he slammed the door shut, locking it and pressing me against the door, pressing a kiss to my neck.

"So?" His retort was muffled because his face was buried in my neck, his hands going to the back of my dress, undoing buttons.

"Eric, it's extremely tacky to leave our wedding reception to have sex!" I hissed and then moaned, slightly raising my head to grant him better access.

"Angel, it's been three months since I've been inside of you. We're married now, and I'm all healed up. Take off the damn dress!" he growled, pulling the edges of my dress away from each other, lowering it to my hips. His hand went to my strapless white lace bra, pulling it down, both breasts popping out. Seconds later, his tongue wrapped around a distended nipple.

I pressed the back of my head against the door, moaning at the most intimate touch I've experienced with him in months. After Eric was first injured and rushed into surgery, the doctors, thankfully, were able to find the source of his internal bleeding and stop it. His liver was seriously injured when the roof collapsed on him. He was in the hospital for three weeks after that, coming home to another month and a half of rest and then physical therapy. I refused to be intimate with him even after about two months when the doctor gave us the all clear. I was terrified of hurting him again, as he was still at only about eighty-percent. But he was still insistent on us continuing with the wedding planning, so his mother and I forged ahead. Then came the buying of our new house and our moving into the apartment above *Charlie's*. With all of that going on, I continued to refuse his advances. But right then, with his mouth sucking on my right breast, while one hand massaged the other, and his other hand continued to push down my wedding dress, I knew the wait was over.

My hands went to the buttons of his tuxedo, and he brought his lips back to mine. We feasted on each other's mouths, our hands working to disrobe one another. When the final button of his dress shirt came undone, I pushed the sides over his shoulders and down his arms, exposing his broad chest and chiseled abdomen. His stomach now held a new scar, from the surgery that stopped the internal bleeding and saved his life. I ducked down and ran my tongue along the scar and pressed tiny kisses along its jagged edges. Then, kissing my way up his abdomen and chest, I played with his nipples the same way he just did mine. I smiled against his skin, feeling his body go rigid with pleasure.

"Enough," he growled. He pulled away, and I felt the remnants of my dress being pushed down my legs before he swept me up in his arms and carried me to our bedroom. Eric tossed me on the mattress of the queen-sized bed, and I giggled at the serious expression on his face. My laugh didn't last long when his insistent hands tore my lace panties from my body.

"Eric! I wanted to keep those!" I reprimanded, but he was too busy using his big body to maneuver my legs apart.

"Too bad." He wasn't even a bit repentant, and soon enough, I didn't care either when I felt his hot mouth on my lower lips, while I sat up on my elbows, my head flopped back, eyes rolling to the back of my head. I couldn't believe I went three months without feeling this. Eric made love to me with his mouth, moaning against my growing wetness. My toes curled, and I dug my heels into the mattress when he wrapped his arms around my upper thighs, pulling me into him.

"Eric!" I panted his name over and over. In response, he continued stroking my clitoris with his tongue, and then sinking one and then two large digits into my core. A fluttering around his fingers began, and soon enough I came apart under his relentless urging. Squeezing my eyes so tight that stars formed, I let out a yell of pleasure unlike one I've ever let out before. My husband was making me his in every way possible.

Even before I could open my eyes, I felt him move up my body, planting his mouth over mine, letting me taste myself on his lips. I curled my arms around his broad shoulders, but then gasped when I felt the wide head of his cock penetrating me. I had no idea how he got his pants off so quickly, nor did I care. My fingernails dug into the hard planes of his upper back, and he drove into me so forcefully that my lower back arched off the bed entirely.

"Oh shit!" I yelled as he continued stroking my walls with his thickness.

"Fuck if I ever go three months without this again," he growled just before biting my earlobe and then lowering his head into the space between my head and neck.

"I love you, baby," I panted while silently thanking God for keeping my man alive. I prayed that he always made it home to me, and for the strength to endure the life of being the wife of one of the best firefighters in the Williamsport Fire Department.

"Come with me, Angel," my husband insisted.

I'd give him whatever he wanted, especially when he angled himself to continue stroking me and have the top of his cock brushing against my swollen bud with every down stroke, the way he was doing.

"Yes!" I answered.

He sat back on his haunches and pounded into me, hands underneath the round globes of my asses, gripping tightly. Moments later I felt him swell inside of me and I squeezed my pelvic muscles, encouraging his release as he encouraged mine.

A heartbeat later we were both yelling out as our releases hit us. For the first time, I felt Eric completely release inside of me, and my greedy canal milked him for everything he had.

My eyes finally fluttered open, and my handsome, strong man looked spent. I braced myself when he collapsed down toward the bed, but instead of falling on me, he wrapped his arms around my waist, and fell over to his side, rolling us so now I was on top of his heaving body. Leaning down, I pressed a kiss to the center of his sweaty chest.

"Now that round one is out of the way ..." He trailed off, his attention on my breasts as he licked his lips.

"Babe, we still have guests downstairs," I tried again. We got one good round out of the way, surely, we could finish this later.

Instead of seeing things my way, he frowned. "Fuck them. We need to get started on making my five babies."

My eyes widened, and I burst out laughing. "You are ridiculous." This was the one thing we couldn't agree on. I wanted three children, while my husband insisted on five. *Five* kids!

"And you're going to give them to me," he grunted, circling my nipple with his pointer finger. I began to feel his shaft growing stiff again.

"So greedy," I purred.

"For my very own Angel."

My heart fluttered, as it did every time he used that nickname. I was powerless to rebuff any attempts after that. Our guests would just have to make due until we made it back down.

Eric's dark gaze rose to meet mine and moisture flowed from my core; my hips began moving of their own accord. His hands were at my waist, encouraging me.

Five isn't really that many, was the last coherent thought I had before bliss completely took over and I proceeded to make love to my husband.

The End

Looking for updates on future releases? I can be found around the web at the following locations:

FaceBook private group: Tiffany's Passions Between the Pages

Website: TiffanyPattersonWrites.com

FaceBook Page: Author Tiffany Patterson